Bound by Sorcery
(The Half-Goddess Chronicles)
Book 1

by Antara Mann
Copyright © Antara Mann (2017). All rights reserved.
http://www.antaraman.com

Edited by Elayne Morgan: serenityeditingservices.com

No part of this book may be reproduced in any form without permission in writing from the author. Reviewers may quote brief passages in reviews.

This is a work of fiction. Any resemblance to actual events or persons, living or dead, is entirely coincidental.

Sing-up for my newsletter and get two free fantasy stories!

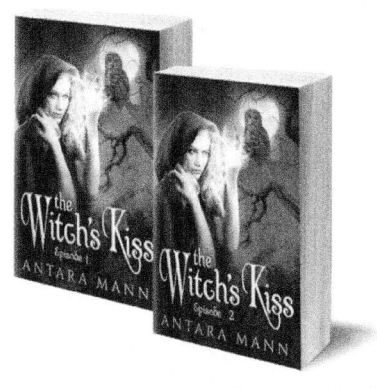

If you want to be notified when my next novel is released and get free stories and occasional other goodies, please sign up at my mailing list at:
> http://www.antaraman.com/bbs

Your email address will never be shared and you can unsubscribe at any time.

Prologue

Daniel Stone stood by the window of his luxurious office on the eighteenth floor, staring at the panoramic view: Manhattan immersed in light — the Empire State Building, the Chrysler Building, Central Park in the distance, a multitude of other buildings all sparkling in the cool fall night. He glanced at the moon. A few nights ago had been the new moon, and it was now only a tiny crescent — the perfect time for new beginnings. He smiled, then glanced impatiently at his wristwatch. At any moment his master and teacher would arrive for the final step in Daniel's training. Daniel envisioned himself becoming all he had ever dreamed he could be — powerful and glorious. His dull, trivial existence would be a thing of the past. The almighty sorcerer Daniel Stone — that's how future generations would remember him.

A sudden crack caught his attention and he turned. A tall slender man, dressed in black, stood shrouded in shadows.

"On time as always," Daniel said respectfully. The stranger approached Daniel and stood with him at the window, taking in the view of the nighttime city.

"Watching the night, I see," the newcomer said, still staring through the window glass. "The biggest mystery is hidden in the night. As Goethe wrote, 'Night is the other half of life, and the better half.'" The man turned to Daniel, putting his hand on his shoulder.

Daniel said hastily, "Master, I'm ready. I've done everything you requested of me. I'm ready to receive the knowledge you promised." His eyes glittered with excitement.

The man nodded. "Of course. You have worked very hard and you shall have your reward. Before we proceed, however, let us drink to your progress in the occult mysteries. You have brought wine, I trust?"

"As you requested, master." Daniel turned to his desk, where a bottle of wine stood waiting next to two glasses. Taking the bottle, he poured an equal amount into each of the two glasses, then handed one to the master.

"To your initiation night," the man said as they clinked their glasses. "Isn't it amazing what a year can do to a man? When I first met you, you were just an ordinary banker working hard for your seven-figure income, but look at you now. I'm speechless. You have far exceeded my hopes for you."

At these words from his master, Daniel felt an unexpected rush of pleasure. "I... I'm flattered, master. I can't tell you how much your approval means to me."

"I know, Daniel, I know." He set down his wineglass and patted Daniel on the shoulder, then, in one swift motion, drew a silver knife from his thigh sheath and sank it into Daniel's chest. The movement was so fast and so skillfully performed that Daniel had no time to react. He fell to the floor, mortally wounded, a trickle of blood dripping from his mouth.

"Your glory will begin soon — right after your death." The dark man gave a sinister laugh, then bent and twisted the knife into Daniel's heart.

The last thing Daniel saw before he died was his master's wicked grin. "The order is greatly indebted to your sacrifice, my friend. You will be always remembered. You will live forever."

Chapter 1

"Our business is dying, Alexandra." Naomi's voice startled me out of a colorful reverie of big business profits and supernatural power.

The clock on the wall in front of the register in our small bookstore showed a few minutes past nine a.m., and I had been woolgathering. I turned to her, surprised she had used my full name. She must really want to get my attention. "What do you mean?"

Naomi and I had been best friends since our days at the Magica Academy, where we both completed our magic training, I as an elemental mage and Naomi as a hedge witch. After graduation we went into business running an occult bookshop, The Steaming Cauldron.

Although the name invoked associations with witchy love potions and the like, those weren't our primary focus. In addition to the potions and various herbal remedies and concoctions — Naomi's specialty, as a hedge witch — we offered occult items and literature, as well as tarot readings and divination. For our wealthier customers, we offered special magical artifacts. I had obtained some of them by chance, and others on various adventures. But few customers could afford them; most of the artifacts were priced in the four-to-five-figure range.

Our shop's name was Naomi's idea, a simple but effective marketing trick. Just as Naomi predicted, a lot of teenage girls visited our shop because of the name. We were young to be running our own business — I was twenty-four, Naomi a year younger — but we had done all right.

For a while.

"The shop's not doing well, Alex," Naomi sighed as she leaned back in her chair. "It's already the beginning of October and we've made less than half of what we made last year. Unless a miracle happens, we're going to be in the red this month."

Her remarks revived my own dormant anxiety. Another magic store, Magica World, had moved in. We lost business to them, and a client mentioned their low prices yesterday when she picked up her incense. Who would have thought we would have competition for our shop in a small town like Ivy Hills, Connecticut? Our situation was doubly worrying, since Naomi and I lived above the Steaming Cauldron, Naomi on the second floor and I on the third. It wasn't only our business in trouble; our home was on the line, too.

"Alex, we need to find a way to bring in more money. I've been thinking about this for a few days. Why don't you apply for a position as a mercenary at Chaos Corporation? With your talents and magical abilities, they'd probably pay you crazy money, or at least enough that we could support ourselves — paying the shop's bills, buying food, and covering the shortfalls. I can stay here and take care of the shop."

I nodded gloomily, now fully alert. "You know I've considered that since even before we opened the bookstore. It's tempting — chasing vampires, fighting demons, dealing with all sorts of magical troublemakers. But it'd be dangerous for me to be among so many other supernaturals," I said.

Chaos Corporation was the top organization for handling criminal supernaturals. Such organizations were of utmost importance in maintaining the trust between the human and supernatural governments, which was the only way to keep the majority of humans unaware of our existence.

Naomi was right that at Chaos Corporation my talents would be highly valued and I would be paid well. Although my father died when I was an infant, my guardian, Awen, told me that I came from a long line of elemental mages on that side. But my own magic was unique and didn't fit into the elemental mage package: I had healing powers when the moon was full or nearly full, and sometimes — rarely — I could read an object's past.

My mother had been a fleeting presence in my life, and I'd only seen her a few times before she finally disappeared for good when I was seventeen. I never got to know her; I didn't even know what kind of supernatural she was. Awen — who, in addition to serving as my guardian, was also my mentor and close friend, had raised and trained me until I went to the Magica Academy, and he was the only one who had ever really known her.

Awen warned me not to reveal my talents to outsiders or strangers, only to trusted friends, lest I risk attracting monsters and ill-wishers. Naomi knew about my talents, of course — we lived and worked together, after all — but she seemed oblivious to my mixed feelings about joining Chaos Corporation. If I worked for Chaos Corporation, though, my peculiar magic would definitely draw other mercenaries' attention. Besides, I wanted to stay in my hometown, in case my mother ever returned. I knew it was foolish, but I still cherished that hope in the back of my mind.

"If you don't think it'd be safe, then okay," Naomi sighed, seeing my worried face. "But if we don't find another source of money, we won't make it. We have to find some way to survive."

The Chinese amulet over the front door jangled, notifying us of the arrival of new customers — a young couple and, judging by their accents when they greeted us, from Boston. They walked around our cozy shop, looking at the displays.

"Oh, you do divination?" the girl exclaimed, seeing the sign that hung over the cash register. She looked at us with a mixture of curiosity, skepticism, and uneasiness. I wasn't surprised — that was a typical human reaction.

"Yes, ma'am." Naomi gave her a silky smile. Tarot reading was her specialty. She offered three different services — a simple card reading, a reading of both the cards and the customer's aura, and the deluxe reading, where she lit incense and communicated with the person's inner spirit or guardian angel.

Driven by curiosity, the girl chose the most expensive reading. I saw Naomi purse her lips when she started the divination. Naomi connected with the girl's guardian, a unicorn, and she sketched out the girl's weaknesses, strengths, and possible dangers she should look out for.

The couple bought a few figurines — witches riding broomsticks and stirring potions in cauldrons, our shop's trademarks — and after they left I turned to my friend. "I saw you pursing your lips. You always do that when you're seeing something bad."

Naomi waved her hand dismissively. "Just a small misfortune — they're going to have a little accident on the way home. Nothing like last month. Remember? When I gave a divination and saw the customer murder someone?" She sighed and clasped her hands. "Anyway, that's over a hundred dollars' profit." She smiled.

"See? The situation isn't as bleak as you described," I said, and Naomi gave me a disbelieving look. To be honest, I knew she was right: we couldn't survive on what we were making.

"If you don't want to bail us out, I could move to New Haven. I know a few hedge witches there who run a bigger magic shop — much more profitable," Naomi said, then headed into the storeroom, leaving me to ponder her words. Was that a threat?

When she came back out, she said, "What about Brendan? He might use your services to investigate some supernatural criminal case. You know the Magic Council pays quite well."

I snorted skeptically. "Please. Brendan Sax hasn't checked up on me even once since they moved him to NYC." I bit my lip and doodled something absentmindedly on the back of our expense book to distract myself. Since Brendan had been summoned to New York City — the city with the most supernatural activity, according to the Council — he hadn't phoned me once, not even to ask how I was. So much for ex-lovers! Or, as he had called our relationship, "friends with benefits."

"No, he hasn't. But you can still call him."

I gave Naomi a look.

"Oh, come on! There still must be *some* need for your help." She didn't give up easily.

"Yeah, so long as it involves sweating under the sheets," I said derisively.

She was about to fling a book at me when the amulet over the door jangled again. Aside from announcing the arrival of customers, the pottery fragment with its Triple Spiral of Life design also chased away evil spirits and brought good luck to our store.

Maybe it would have been a better idea to get something that attracted money.

"Hello, girls!" Mrs. Stokely, a regular customer since we opened the shop, came bustling in, followed by her snow-white poodle. A plump, middle-aged woman with a pleasant chubby face and a peculiar sense of fashion, she was always very talkative. She amused us — and sometimes annoyed us — by telling us all the local gossip and complaining about her husband. Ever since the other occult shop opened, she'd visited it regularly and kept us informed about its products. Her reports confirmed what we already suspected: it had become very popular.

"What a dreadful week, girls! Rob, come here." She tugged on the leash of her poodle, who sniffed at an African statuette of a warrior three times his size. I'd acquired it about a year ago but, because of the steep price, we hadn't sold it. The upside was that it gave an exotic, upscale feel to our humble shop.

"I barely made it through last week." Mrs. Stokely continued. "George has locked himself in his man-cave — probably so he can smoke his nasty cigars — they stink up the whole place — and hasn't spoken to me for three days. Men! And my colleague at the medical center has kicked up a stink about some nonsense, why I hadn't given her some papers — she kept me on the phone for half an hour last night blabbering about it, just as I was heading to bed. Can you imagine? Rob, come *here*." She pulled at Rob's leash; he now sniffed around the table at which Naomi did her divination. "I think someone has put a curse on me," she announced dramatically, then added, "What do you think, girls?"

Naomi and I exchanged looks, and I cleared my throat. "Well, I suppose it's possible..."

"I knew it!" She clapped her hands, dropping the poodle's leash. Rob dashed around joyfully for a few moments before Mrs. Stokely's iron hand snatched the leash back up. Adjusting her old-fashioned hat, she asked, "Do you have anything to attract positive energy?"

I smiled at her. "Yes, ma'am, we have just the thing for you — superb quality, handmade by Naomi." I opened a drawer under the cash register and pulled out a neatly folded bag full of green grasses. "A magic potion to attract positive emotions and respect from others. Works like a charm — pun intended." I winked at her.

Mrs. Stokely beamed. "Sounds perfect! How much is it?"

"It's a hundred and twenty dollars — steep, but worth it. I guarantee that once you try it you won't experience any more of the tension you've suffered in the last week nor fight with your husband or colleagues."

She pursed her lips, squinting her eyes. She clearly thought the price high. Finally, though, she smiled and said, "Okay, girls, I'll take it. All your potions are foolproof. They may be more expensive than Magica World's, but they're better — and I think they're worth it."

Naomi and I glanced at each other at the mention of our competitor's prices, then I packed Mrs. Stokely's potion and we sent her and her poodle off with our best wishes. When the door closed behind them, followed by the rattle of the Chinese trinket, Naomi turned to me.

"Did you catch that?"

I nodded as I turned to the computer to check our company email. "Yes. That's the second time she's mentioned their prices being cheaper."

Naomi spread her hands helplessly. "I don't get it. How are they doing it? We buy from the cheapest supplier in New Haven. Where is Magica World getting their merchandise from?"

"No idea," I said. We'd received a few emails from various suppliers, but nothing else.

"It's strange," Naomi mused, leaning on the cash register. "We have to learn who this guy's supplier is if we want to survive. If we buy from the same place we can afford to be more competitive."

"He's probably buying at the same price we are. I don't think there are any cheaper alternatives. I bet he's selling at a loss to attract customers and hoping to recover his investment over the long run."

I didn't say, *After he drives us out of business.*

I frowned at the invoice for South American statuettes — three hundred dollars. We needed to stop purchasing such expensive stock; almost nobody bought it, anyway.

With a sinking heart I did the calculations, realizing that after we accounted for our expenses for the month, we were likely to be several thousand dollars in the red.

The month isn't over yet, said the voice in my head, giving me a start. My heart began to pound.

The voice had started only a few days ago, and I hadn't figured out what to think of it. Was I losing my mind? I didn't dare tell anyone, not even Naomi. It spoke up mostly during moments of stress, though not always.

At the thought, it chimed in again. *If this isn't a stressful situation, I don't know what is.*

"You know, we should ask him," Naomi said, pulling me from my inner dialogue. I raised my head from the laptop.

"What?" I had no idea what she was talking about.

"Seriously. We're colleagues, after all. I think his name was Drake or Derek — something with a 'D' anyway."

Ah — our competitor. We'd been to his shop; it was somewhat larger than ours, but he didn't offer tarot reading or divination. Those services remained our best-sellers, along with our herbal potions for health, love, and prosperity. Over the years, a few customers had come to us seeking potions or spells to harm or eliminate an enemy. Sometimes we managed to convince them to try protection spells instead, but we never sold or encouraged any type of dark magic. Not ever.

Our competitor's shop, on the other hand, had a darker aura. I couldn't say for sure that the owner sold dark magic, but the energy over there differed from our shop's cozy atmosphere. Maybe it was because we were two women, but a difference definitely existed.

Our morning passed quietly, with only a few other clients before noon: a shy teenage girl and another pair of tourists. Tourists were one of the main advantages to living in a small seaside town.

I had just ordered a packet of incense and candles online when the shop door opened and an attractive man in his early thirties strode briskly in. I immediately recognized him — the owner of Magica World.

"Hello, ladies." He looked around our small shop before his gaze switched to me, then settled on Naomi.

Naomi was a free spirit — she loved to party, and she often had a new boyfriend every other week. Her motto was "Love 'em and leave 'em." She was accustomed to attention and flirting from men and had never been shy, but she blushed under this man's shamelessly lecherous gaze.

Perhaps the fact that he was our competitor bothered her.

"Hello. What can we help you with?" I intervened. He gave me a smug look, still mentally undressing my best friend.

"I'm Desmond Cohen, the owner of Magica World," he said.

"Nice to meet you, Desmond. I'm Alexandra Shaw, and this is my business partner Naomi Mitchell."

He shook our hands and said, "It's nice to have colleagues in the occult and magic business." A smile flickered across his face. "Especially when they're beautiful ladies like you. I'd love to get to know you better, so I want to invite you to a lecture a friend of mine is holding tonight at my shop." He approached the cash register and handed each of us a flyer. "I'd be delighted if you could come. The topic will be 'Worship Practices of Egyptian Gods and Goddesses.'"

"How long will it last?" I asked.

But Naomi had pulled herself together and said, "Yes, we'd love to come. When does it start?"

He smiled, showing his white teeth. He was easy on the eyes, with a toned body, dark brown hair, blue eyes, and cute dimples, but something about him — something I couldn't put my finger on — repelled me.

"Eight o'clock is the official start time, but Garrett will probably begin the presentation around eight-thirty."

"Wonderful. Our shop closes at eight, so we'll have time to freshen up first." Naomi employed one of her trademark seductive smiles, maintaining eye contact with him.

"Great. I'll look forward to seeing you there." He smiled at us and left, but not before giving my friend another lewd look. This time, however, she wasn't embarrassed — on the contrary, she was checking him out too, especially his ass.

"Wow! What was that, Noe?" I asked.

She gave me a mischievous look. "We need to be friendly with the competition. Explore our options."

"Friendly, huh? By your body language I'd say you're thinking about something more than 'friendly relations.'"

Naomi raised her eyebrows and nudged me. "Desmond's pretty hot. You can't deny it."

I won't even try, the voice in my head chimed in. *But be suspicious of him.*

I started, then looked at the flyer he'd handed me. White text against a black background said, "Night of the Egyptian Gods at Magica World. Hosted by Desmond Cohen with special guest Garrett O'Brien. 8 PM. Free admission. Snacks provided."

"This guy is trying pretty hard to attract the amateur supernatural crowd — and I guess it's working. He's even managed to arouse your interest," I said, glancing at Naomi. "You two will make a great couple. You can name your children after Ra or Osiris. Ozzy for short."

Naomi flung her flyer at me and I chuckled. But underneath the teasing, I was glad we'd have the opportunity to get a closer view of Desmond's operation.

***

We headed to Desmond's place that evening after closing up our store and changing our clothes. Naomi insisted we wait until after nine to show that we were uninterested, and a fairly large crowd was already there when we arrived. All kinds of people — mostly younger — were talking, nibbling on chocolate cookies and snacks, and sipping iced tea, coffee, or water.

When Desmond saw us, he came over to shake our hands. "I'm so glad you're here. I asked Garrett to delay the lecture until you guys arrived," he said with a smile, pointing out a tall, thin man dressed all in black with piercings in his ears, nose, and upper lip.

After the two men exchanged a few words, Garrett moved toward the center of the shop where chairs had been arranged in a circle, and most of the guests began taking their seats. Naomi and I joined the crowd.

The man introduced himself as Garrett O'Brien, an occultist specializing in ancient Egyptian religion and mythology. A lecture about the ancient Egyptian cult of the goddess Isis followed: about her magical abilities and the legend of her union with Osiris.

The speech might have been interesting, but Garrett spoke quickly and somewhat unclearly. After a short while, I gave up on listening. Some of the visitors took notes while others held muted conversations around the edges of the room. I signaled to Naomi, and we went to the other end of the shop, toward the shelves with books and other merchandise. Some of Desmond's products were the same as ours, but looking at the prices, we had to concede that most of the items here were indeed cheaper.

"I wonder how he's doing it," Naomi said.

"Perhaps you can ask Desmond in private after the lecture," I suggested. Naomi nudged me. She was examining a statuette of the god Osiris when two women — one with pink streaks in her hair, the other with blue hair and a long black trench coat — came over. They looked a few years older than us, and I could feel the weak hum of their powers.

"Hello! I don't think we've met. Are you from around here?" the blue-haired lady asked. Now that we stood face to face, I noticed she had an eye of Horus tattooed just below the hollow of her throat.

"Yes. We run the other occult bookshop in town, the Steaming Cauldron. It's just a few intersections from here. You're welcome to stop by any time." Naomi smiled at her.

"Cool," the pink-haired girl said. She wore several rings on each hand, and a triquetra pendant hung around her neck. "Are you guys going to attend the Temple of Isis meeting on Thursday? Have you been there? Is it any good?"

I glanced at Naomi, who said, "Pardon? The what?"

The pink-haired girl smiled. "From what Desmond and Garrett told us, it's an occult club —"

"Something like a coven," interrupted the blue-haired woman. "So you run an occult bookstore — are you witches?"

I chuckled and looked at Naomi. She nodded, watching the two young women. "Yes, I'm a hedge witch. I'm Naomi Mitchell."

The blue-haired lady stretched out her hand. "Nice to meet you, Naomi. I'm Amelia Gordon. I'm a green witch, and this is my friend, Colleen Reed; she's a hearth witch."

They both turned their gaze to me. "Um, I'm Alex," I said, "and I'm just human. I don't have any superpowers even though my parents did." I laughed awkwardly.

They looked at me with eyes full of pity. If their own magic were powerful enough, they would have felt my magic as I felt theirs, but I preferred to pose as a human whenever possible, to be on the safe side. I couldn't risk random people becoming aware of my abilities.

Good choice. And I'd be suspicious of that coven, too, if I were you.

I didn't answer. I was afraid if I got in a conversation with myself, someone might notice my distraction and figure out I was talking to myself.

After we exchanged a few pleasantries, the two young witches headed off to talk to Desmond, and Naomi and I were alone again.

"Do you have to be so paranoid? Why can't you just admit you're a mage?" Naomi whispered as I sipped my wine.

"You know it's dangerous to reveal your magical abilities to strangers, especially at gatherings like this. There could be all kinds of freaks around," I whispered back.

"Whoa! Easy there, girl. Does that mean you and I are freaks too?" She grinned at me as I took a chocolate cookie from the table. In the center of the room, the crowd burst into a smattering of polite applause, signaling that Garrett had finished his lecture.

"Mmm, these are delicious," I said over the hubbub. "Try one."

"You can't deny Desmond's making an effort," Naomi said as she tasted a cookie.

"Speak of the devil, here he comes."

Naomi followed my gaze over to Desmond. His eyes fixed on my friend and the corners of his lips curled in a subtle smile.

"Did you like the lecture, ladies?" he asked when he was close enough.

"Yes, we really enjoyed it. Great food, by the way," I said with my mouth half-full. He barely glanced at me, not wanting to take his eyes off Naomi.

"You've certainly attracted some interesting and diverse people," Naomi said.

"Yeah. We've got participants from New York, Salem, even San Francisco. The supernatural community is very active over there." He'd dressed with casual elegance: a black blazer with a dark blue shirt and tailored dark pants. The dark colors made his cool blue eyes stand out. Although I felt uncomfortable in his presence, I had to concede his attractiveness.

I told you, the voice said in my head.

Shut up, I snapped at it.

"We heard about the club you're running," Naomi said.

"Oh, yes, the Temple of Isis. Would you two be interested?" He smiled at us.

I might have imagined a slightly mocking tone which disappeared as quickly as it had come. Maybe my mind was playing tricks on me.

"Need you ask? Alex and I are interested in all sorts of supernatural and religious practices."

"In that case, you're more than welcome. Our next meeting is on Thursday." He stepped closer to Naomi and put his hand on her shoulder, saying quietly, "I have some rare artifacts which I believe may interest you."

She laughed, and he led her across the shop. I winked at her as she left.

Most visitors stood around the refreshments table, talking. Some surrounded the lecturer, asking him questions. The shelves and the objects on them reminded me of our own shop. Naomi was right: If we couldn't boost our profits by at least a few grand a month, we had to think about alternatives. Since the Chaos Corporation would pay well enough for my skills that we could keep our business running, I needed to consider it.

But it worried me. I would need to undergo tests to assess my magic so they could assign me tasks based on my skills and abilities. What would the tests reveal? I didn't know what kind of supernatural my mother had been, and she had disappeared from my life. What if she was a demon? No, that was ridiculous.

I spotted Naomi across the room, reading a book, and Desmond with an arm slipped casually around her waist. I smiled and took one last sip of wine, then left the bookshop.

The fresh fall air cleared my head, slightly dazed from the fragrant wine and the magic in the shop. I loved autumn in our little coastal town. The cool, refreshing sea breeze and the colorful palette of the lush foliage invigorated me.

Wandering through the alleys and streets of Ivy Hills, my thoughts again drifted to my mother:

Where was she? Was she alive? Did she remember me at all? I felt the rush of hot tears — in all those years, I hadn't been able to overcome the sadness that arose when I thought about her absence.

At that moment I felt terribly lonely — I needed someone special in my life. I recalled my last date with Brendan, and my stomach churned.

I might not have any answers about my mother, but one thing seemed certain: My love life was doomed.

I decided to head over to the home of my mentor and old friend, Awen. He had been a father figure as well as a mother figure to me throughout my childhood. He trained me and taught me so much before I enrolled in Magica Academy. My mother, during one of our rare, brief meetings, told me that whenever I needed help, I should turn to Awen.

Her advice was sound. He was a centuries-old druid. He had lived in the Vedic, Egyptian, Babylonian, Greek, and Roman civilizations, to name a few, and knew all the ancient Celtic rites and rituals. In fact, I suspected he had invented most if not all of them. He could transform into two animals, a coyote and a hawk. I had always found this impressive; even when a teenager I knew a lot of shifters, but usually they could transform into only one animal.

But Awen was more than just my teacher and guardian; he was a good friend. He had even loaned Naomi and me the money to start our bookshop — money we made sure to pay back within the very first year.

It was a little after eleven in the evening when reached Awen's two-story Victorian house at the edge of our small town, but I knew he would still be awake.

I knocked to announce myself and let myself in the front door. As I closed it, Awen's steady steps sounded on the creaking floorboards.

"Is everything all right, Alex?" he asked, a worried expression on his face.

"Yes, yes. I was just at a lecture with Naomi. She stayed at the event, and I wanted to talk to you." I headed for the spacious living room where I'd spent so much of my childhood. Books filled Awen's living room — mythologies and the rites and rituals of all sorts of religions and spiritual traditions. As a teenager I had tried to read them all — a Herculean task, even for someone as desperate for knowledge about her magical heritage as I was.

I took off my leather jacket and sat on the couch. Awen's living room was warm and pleasant, with a fire in the fireplace even though it was early October. My mentor kept his house colder than most people: he preferred the lower temperatures, which reminded him of Britain. He lit the fireplace as soon as the first chilly days of fall came around, but the living room was the only warm room in the house. I noticed a cup of tea on the table and an open book next to it — a typical evening for Awen.

He cleared his throat, breaking the silence. "Well, what did you want to talk to me about? Is everything okay with the Steaming Cauldron?" He winked at me. From the beginning, Awen teased us about the sexual innuendo in the shop's name. I wondered what my attitude to romance and sex would become if I lived as long as Awen had. Would I be laid back, like him, or would I be skeptical about love?

Hell, I'd become skeptical already.

"That's why I'm here, actually. Have you heard about the new occult shop, Magica World?"

He nodded.

"Well, it's eating into our profits. Naomi and I have been wondering what to do, and considering my special magic abilities, she…" I cleared my throat. "She suggested I apply to Chaos Corporation." I cast a look of anticipation at Awen.

He rubbed his chin, then came to sit next to me on the couch. "You should do whatever you think is best, but I strongly advise you, for your own sake, not to work for them."

I stared at him, thoughts forming in my head. Truth be told, he wasn't very pleased when I started working as an independent supernatural consultant. He hadn't said anything, but I'd felt his silent disapproval, and in the back of my mind I always wondered if it was related to my lost mother and her lineage.

Awen sighed and gave me a hug. He'd never said so but I suspected that, in addition to his other gifts, he could read minds. "Alex, you're an adult. You know the importance of being cautious. It's not like you're going to a party and announcing your powers to try to impress a boy from the Academy. Chaos Corporation's pre-hiring tests are complex and your more unusual abilities will instantly show up, especially when the moon is waxing gibbous or full."

He hesitated for a moment. "Speaking of your abilities, have you noticed any change lately?"

I stared at him. "No, everything's normal."

Awen nodded thoughtfully. I'd always felt he knew what my mother was, and therefore what I was besides an elemental mage. My father could control all the elements but was especially talented with fire and air — skills I had inherited from him. But even a Magica Academy freshman knew that the ability to self-heal isn't part of the elemental mage package.

I leaned slightly toward Awen and looked him in the eyes. "Awen, I am twenty-four years old, and still don't know my full heritage. Don't you think it's time I knew what kind of blood flows in my veins? I'm certain you know. Please, Awen, I'm begging you."

I needed to know the answer to decide whether I could survive in the supernatural sandbox of Chaos Corporation. And whether it was my pleading voice, the sincerity in my eyes, the late hour, or all those things put together, it almost worked. He had just opened his mouth to reply when my mobile dinged.

I swore aloud — of all the times, why now? I almost ignored it but saw it was Naomi. I'd better make sure she was all right.

"Hey, is it an emergency, or can I call you back? Okay, great, I'll talk to you when I get home. Bye."

I hung up and came over to stand next to Awen, who had gotten up and moved to the fireplace, staring at the burning logs and yellow-orange flames. It was nice and cozy, watching the fire.

"So you were about to tell me something about my abilities," I said, but I could tell the moment had passed. *Thank you, Noe, for spoiling the chance I've been chasing for years!* I'd been trying to extract this information from Awen ever since my mother disappeared from my life, but he'd always evaded my questions.

Awen turned to look at me. "Whatever you decide, Alex, know that you'll do great." He hesitated. "I want to give you something. Will you wait here for a second?"

"Of course," I replied, surprised.

I stared at the fire and listened as Awen climbed the stairs to the upper floor, and then, a few minutes later, as he came back down.

He handed me a package, well wrapped in leather. "Here you go, Alex. I think you'll need this, whether you stay here in Ivy Hills or go to one of the big cities as a magic mercenary."

I unfolded the package. Inside was a knife with a long silver blade. Looking closely, I saw what looked like runes inscribed on its blade.

"Thanks, Awen," I said, smiling. "You're amazing, as always."

"This is not just an enchanted knife — it's a highly dangerous one. Use it only when you need to kill your enemy."

I felt my eyebrows shoot up and looked at the knife again. "It's so beautiful." I slid my fingers over its surface, touching the symbols on the blade and feeling their magic pricking on my skin. "What are these markings? They look like runes, but none I've seen before."

"They're druidic symbols — not something you learned about at Magica Academy," he said with a chuckle. "'Victory and Liberty.' That's what the inscription on the blade says, in an ancient Celtic language." Awen smiled. "This knife belonged to your mother, Alex."

His words reminded me that, a moment ago, I'd thought he might reveal to me the knowledge I'd yearned after for so long. My heart sank into my boots and I turned to him, invoking the name of the Celtic goddess he worshipped above all others. "In Brighid 's name, Awen, I beg you with all my heart — please tell me what I am."

But he only smiled, gave me an affectionate hug, and said, "Soon you will learn, my child, soon. Whatever is meant to happen will happen in due time — not earlier, and not later. Trust me."

I cursed my bad luck and he smiled, as if reading my mind, then headed for the stairs. Visiting him had eased a little of my tension, but I still couldn't decide.

Halfway up the stairs Awen stopped and turned to me. "One last thought: do you occasionally hear a voice in your head?"

His sudden question took me by surprise. "Do I look that insane, Awen?" I asked in a lightly mocking tone to hide my worry. The truth was that the voice scared me a little. Had Awen been able to read that worry in my mind?

He stared at me for a moment, then said, "I'm serious, Alex. If you begin to hear a voice inside your head, please listen to it."

"Okay, you got me: I do hear a voice inside my head." I cracked an apologetic smile, trying to make light of it. Then I changed my mind. If I couldn't tell Awen, who could I tell? "The truth is, I've been scared to confess it."

"It's all right, darling: this voice is a good thing. Trust it."

A good thing? I wasn't crazy? It felt as though a tremendous weight had been lifted from my shoulders.

He nodded curtly then climbed the last of the stairs and disappeared from my sight, retreating down the hall and leaving me to ponder. What did he mean about the voice in my head, and what could this knife tell me about my mother? Was she a warrior? I looked once again at the symbols inscribed on the blade. Victory and Liberty. I liked that.

Sure you do, said an unmistakable voice in my head.

Chapter 2

I woke early the next morning from my recurring nightmare about my mother. In the dream I walked along a dark corridor as flaming torches on the walls cast a dim light. Suddenly, I saw her in the distance and called her name. "Andred!" She turned to me, smiled, and looked upward — and I awoke with a scream.

What did it mean? I had, of course, shared my dream with Awen. According to him, it had no particular prophetic significance or meaning. As he put it, "The dream only shows your deep melancholy and desire to glimpse your mother again." Naomi couldn't tell me anything more substantial.

After I came back home from Awen's last night, I first put the precious silver knife that Awen gave me into a separate drawer, then Naomi and I chatted for a while. I asked her how it went with Desmond and whether anything interesting happened between them. Naomi assured me he wasn't her type and pointed out the vibe we'd both felt in him: something about his aura, some hint of dark magic. Perhaps the conversation about Desmond's nature had given me the nightmare.

I got out of bed, showered, put on my workout clothes and began my morning yoga routine. If anything could help ease my sadness about my mother, it was yoga. But even that wasn't enough, today.

After I finished my yoga exercises, I changed into my business clothes. I'd decided that we needed the money enough that I'd try for a job at Chaos Corporation, despite Awen's disapproval, so I went for a more professional look than usual: white shirt, black skirt falling to just above the knee, and stockings. After applying some discreet makeup, I looked at myself in the mirror with approval. My dark brown hair reached the shirt collar, the fitted shirt highlighted my breasts, and my earrings were the same sea-blue color as my eyes. I looked fabulous.

Too bad I was single. "Brendan, you're a loser," I said out loud.

Maybe the problem was me. I shouldn't have fallen in love so quickly with an arrogant werewolf, let alone one working for the Magic Council, the governing body of all supernatural beings in the United States. Still, there had been perks to my short-lived relationship with Brendan. Not only was he incredibly sexy, with a good sense of humor, but the job he offered me at the Council as an independent supernatural consultant had paid quite well.

I met Brendan through a mutual friend, a classmate from the Magica Academy, at a party.

We'd been walking together one evening when a vampire attacked me and Brendan got a glimpse of my skills firsthand. He had known I was a mage but didn't know about my fighting skills. Awen had helped me greatly as I learned to fight but I seemed to have been born with some innate fighting skills.

Brendan was intrigued by my fighting abilities and magical talents, and he asked me to work for the Council not long after. We worked together till he was transferred to NYC. And that's the last I heard from him.

I liked working for the Council, though. The paychecks were good and the work was anything but boring. Yet I had to admit that in the course of my work with them, I encountered a lot of monsters and vile supernaturals. That was part of the job, I guess, but I seemed to attract all sorts of magical freaks. Even Brendan had once joked about — ugh! I had to get him out of my head! He wasn't worth thinking about.

Irritated, I went to the kitchen and poured myself a cup of hot coffee. If I'd done fine as an independent supernatural consultant, I reasoned, I would also do well as a magic mercenary in Chaos Corporation. Feeling more confident, I went downstairs into the shop.

Naomi had some other errands to run today, so I was on duty in the shop. I turned off the alarm, opened the blinds, turned on our laptop, set up the cash register, and my workday officially began.

I went online to get Chaos Corporation's number. When I dialed it using the coded spell they had for supernaturals, a melodious female voice answered the phone. I asked if they were recruiting mercenaries, and she immediately asked if I had magic — a compulsory question in the protocol judging by her voice — and what type, and whether I'd had suitable magical training. After I told her briefly about my education and abilities, she replied, "Chaos Corporation always needs well-trained mages. Please send us your resumé and your school transcripts, and we will contact you for an interview."

I wrote down the email address she gave me, but it seemed I wouldn't be visiting Chaos Corporation today after all. A quarter of an hour later, I was about to send my CV when my mobile rang, startling me. It wasn't even nine a.m.; who could be calling me? I hoped nothing had happened to Naomi. When I looked at the display and saw Brendan's name, anger and excitement overwhelmed me at the same time. What did the bastard want?

Let it ring.

I sent the email to Chaos Corporation. When it finally went to voicemail, I breathed a sigh of relief and began to unpack the latest shipment, but rather than leave a message, he called back immediately. I tried to stay focused on my task, completely ignoring his calls. After several calls he finally gave up, and I relaxed: I wasn't yet ready to talk to him.

I'd just started to wipe down the shelves when I heard his pleading voice in my mind. *"Alex, where are you? Please answer me."* I swore silently. I'd forgotten that, as a shifter, Brendan possessed the ability to communicate telepathically with other supernaturals.

"You're not welcome, Brendan. I'm surprised you're even calling me right now. What happened to make you remember my existence?"

"God, Alex, do you have to act like a teen? I'm sorry I haven't called you, but I've been pretty busy."

"That's not good enough, Brendan," I snapped. *"Now, if you don't mind, I have some business to attend to. I'm pretty busy myself."*

Just then the amulet over the shop door jangled and a girl came in. She looked around shyly and asked for a love potion. I smiled and showed her the shelves containing the potion bottles.

"Please, Alex. I need you. The Magic Council needs you, too," Brendan's voice continued in my mind.

"This conversation is over," I said. I left the girl looking over the potions and went back to the register.

"Alex, there's been a horrible murder with supernatural features. We need your help."

I hesitated for a moment.

Brendan continued, *"A senior banker was killed at his NYC office. The sign of a long-extinct order was carved into his chest. The Council is worried that tensions in the supernatural community may escalate if the culprit isn't caught quickly. And who knows what that might lead to..."* His voice trailed off. *"We all need your help."*

The news caught me completely off-guard, especially him saying that they all needed my help. Brendan could speak to me telepathically, but couldn't hear me unless I consciously projected my thoughts, so I didn't have to worry about him 'overhearing' things I didn't want him to. I contemplated his words while I rang up the girl's purchase and bagged it, while he continued trying to convince me.

"The Council is offering double the usual rate. Please, Alex!" Finally he asked, *"Are things really that busy in your shop?"*

"Yes, as a matter of fact, they are," I replied aloud. Since the girl had left, I could talk out loud, now. "I just sold a love potion to a teenage girl. Don't you realize how important my job is?"

He chuckled inside my mind, but then his tone became serious again. *"Listen, I need your help. If you can't do it, let me know now so I can find someone else."*

I frowned, bustling around behind the cash register while I tried to think. We needed the money, and the Council certainly paid well — and for this investigation the wage would be doubled. Instead of starting work with Chaos Corporation, moving to one of their centers in the big cities, and having to work with complete strangers, I could work with someone I already knew — Brendan.

And when we solved the case, then I'd never speak to him again.

I sighed. True, he was an arrogant asshole and I was pissed off at him, but the money mattered more than my wounded ego. I doubted Chaos Corporation could offer better pay than the Council was promising.

"Alex?" Brendan's voice sounded again in my head.

What was the worst that could happen if I investigated this murder? Especially since, in the process, I could take the opportunity to knock Brendan down a peg or two for having abandoned me — not that I'd take the case *just* because of that.

I took a deep breath. "Okay, I accept," I said. I hoped I wouldn't regret it.

"Excellent! Come to the first floor of the Universal Credit Bank building, number one West Wall Street. It's near the Holy Trinity Church." Although I couldn't see his face, I knew he was grinning. There was a hesitation, then he added, *"Alex... thank you."*

"Not so fast, Brendan. I intend to give you hell."

***

I couldn't use my own magic to teleport because the full moon was still seven days off; a teleportation would exhaust me. Besides, the distance from Ivy Hills to Manhattan was significant, and I might land somewhere else, like Pittsburgh or Newport. My teleportation abilities only peaked as the full moon drew near; at other times, they were rather sloppy. Today, the day of the first quarter, was outside my limit; I certainly wouldn't gamble on them right now.

Besides, even if I'd been reasonably capable of doing it, I couldn't leave the shop unattended. I had to call Naomi and ask her to come back. Fortunately, as a hedge witch she had special boundary talents, including making transportation charms, which she kept locked away safely in her apartment, so I'd be able to leave as soon as soon as she arrived with one.

While I waited, I changed into a white top, black cotton pants, comfortable boots, and of course my leather jacket, and gathered my most valuable possessions: my weapons. I had a bronze chakram which Awen had given me for a long-ago birthday, enchanted so that it always returned to me after being thrown, and a few bronze crescent knives, also enchanted.

When Naomi finally came, I told her about my new assignment.

"Double pay? But that's great, Alex! Who'd have thought?"

Finally, I was ready. I teleported to the address Brendan had given me and looked around to orient myself. The Holy Trinity Church was to my left, and the tall glass building of UCB Bank was nearby. The flags of the USA, the UK, Germany, France, Canada, and a few other countries were waving at the entrance. This building was obviously home to businesses worth billions of dollars. Inside the lobby, I headed for the reception desk, but Brendan, waiting for me, was already walking over. His hair was carelessly ruffled, and several days' worth of stubble graced his face. His magic rolled over me, powerful and alert; he was ready to attack should the need arise.

Supernaturals' magic often, for lack of a better word, 'tastes' like its owner. In Brendan's case, it felt like a strong malt whiskey in the back of my throat, combined with a stiff mountain breeze — his bond with nature and being a werewolf — and it had charmed me the first time we met. Why did he have to be so sexy? His tall muscular body didn't help.

"Hello, Alex." He handed me a folder with data about the victim as we headed for the elevator. "The victim is Daniel Stone, a CEO of UCB. The murder took place on the eighteenth floor, in Stone's office." I saw his gun beneath his jacket.

"What do *you* know?" I asked. As a shifter, Brendan was able to sense things others couldn't, and he might have gathered some information already.

"Not much: The victim was killed last night around midnight, or just before. We're still waiting for the coroner's report; we should have the preliminary by the end of the day. Looks like he was stabbed in the heart. There are photos in the folder for you to review, and once we get upstairs you'll get to see the murderer's artwork face-to-face." He smiled grimly.

I had half a mind to annoy and tease Brendan, but now, seeing his worried face and feeling his anxiety as he filled me in on the details, I faltered: it'd be stupid of me. I decided I'd put on my bitch hat only if he provoked me. The elevator arrived with a quiet beep, and we got in.

"What we know so far," Brendan said as the doors closed, "is that the victim was the CEO of Universal Credit Bank. Forty-seven years old, divorced. He's been with UCB for fifteen years, and he made CEO five years ago. The problem is the symbol carved into his chest. It's stirred up tensions between the Courts of Heaven and Hell, which makes this a very important case. A small but extremely influential part of the supernatural community is watching it closely."

I hadn't yet decided how to behave with Brendan, so I said nothing. Hell, if the money weren't so good, I wouldn't be getting involved in this even if World War III were breaking out, in the supernatural *or* human world.

Brendan ran a weary hand across his head, and I couldn't help imagine running my fingers through his hair.

Shit, Alex. I knew this would happen. Keep your cool, girl, the voice inside me said.

Only yesterday Awen had told me to listen to it, and I had to admit he may have been right. The voice's advice was solid. I had to maintain my distance from Brendan, and definitely shouldn't have sex with him again. Not for all the world. *Ever.*

"Hey, are you all right?" Brendan asked — concerned, perhaps, by the look on my face.

I was fine — just trying to look pissed off at Brendan while resisting his sex appeal. I said curtly, "I'm still angry at you for not calling me even once during the last eight months. Let's keep this a working relationship only — nothing else." The smirk on his face infuriated me. "What's so funny?" I growled.

But the elevator doors opened and Brendan sobered. "Let's leave this conversation until later, okay?" He strode toward the end of the corridor and I followed him.

The corridor swarmed with uniformed policemen. One approached to block my way, but Brendan waved him off, signaling that I was with him. Brendan passed under the yellow "Crime scene, do not cross" tape draped across the victim's office door, and I followed him in.

I found myself in a spacious office with huge windows and a nice view of Lower Manhattan and most of the skyscrapers. But my enjoyment of the panoramic view was spoiled by the dead body sprawled on the floor, just a few feet from the leather chair next to the huge mahogany desk. I focused on the scene in front of me, breathing deeply and activating my photographic memory. The body was that of a man in his mid-forties. His nostrils were crusted with dried blood, his shirt was torn, and a circle was carved into the flesh of his chest. Inside the circle was a hexagram, with another symbol inside that — maybe a sword? I knelt down next to the victim, making note of the two wine glasses placed casually on the mahogany desk, and closed my eyes. Sniffing the air, I felt the definite presence of magic, dark and dangerous. This was the work of a supernatural, without a doubt.

It seemed likely the victim had known the culprit. Judging by the two wine glasses, the victim had probably shared a drink with the killer prior to the murder. What surprises fate held in store for us — one moment, a friend; the next, a deadly enemy and your executioner. I shivered.

When I opened my eyes, I saw an unfamiliar face watching me intently from a few yards away. I stood up instantly.

"You must be Alexandra Shaw," the man said. "Brendan mentioned you'd be joining us on the investigation. I'm Carlos Delvalle." He stretched out his hand and I immediately felt his magic: Powerful and dominating, it felt like strong waves crashing against the shoreline. He was definitely a shifter, too; and, judging by his ginger hair and stubble, I'd bet he was a tiger shifter. A few years older than me, he had a slim athletic body and attractive green eyes that were warm and inviting and made me feel at home. I instantly liked him.

"Brendan spoke highly of you," he said, looking me in the eye.

Okay, maybe I could delay being a bitch to Brendan. "Very nice to meet you. Have you two been working together long?" I asked.

"It's our first case together," Brendan interjected.

Carlos smiled at me. "I was called this morning from Sao Paulo to come help Brendan with the investigation. So what are your first impressions, Miss Shaw?" he asked politely.

Wow. The Magic Council must really be worried if they were calling in investigators from all over the world, Brazil in particular. Brazil was famous for its well-trained investigators.

"Please, call me Alex." I smiled back at him. "Well, it's definitely the work of dark magic." I looked around the office again, noticing the palm plant next to the window and the painting on the wall opposite the desk. It was a dark picture, and I shivered looking at it.

There's dark energy and magic in this place, just like the killer's, the voice inside told me.

"The banker obviously knew his killer," I said. I shifted my gaze to the wine glasses. One was nearly empty, while the other was more than half-full.

Brendan nodded. "The security footage from last night shows that no one entered Stone's office — at least not from the hallway — which confirms that the murder was committed by a supernatural. Probably a warlock or even a sorcerer — not a shifter, in any event. I would have sniffed it if the culprit were one of us."

I cast a slightly worried look at the policemen bustling around us.

"Don't worry," Carlos said reassuringly. "We cast a spell so they can't hear what we're talking about." He went to the couch across the room, where a laptop rested. He pressed a few buttons and waited.

"We're assuming that's the victim's computer," Brendan informed me.

I nodded. "Do you think this murder could be the work of a demon?"

Carlos looked at me thoughtfully. "It's possible," he said slowly. "My grandmother used to say, 'Never greet a stranger in the night, for he may be a demon.'"

"Yeah, or a werewolf." I glanced toward Brendan, who grumbled in irritation. "A nice quote, though."

Brendan said, "Demon or not, we have to assume Stone knew his killer, and the killer clearly used magic. That's peculiar, because the victim is a human with no criminal record. It seems unlikely he'd have gotten involved in the supernatural world," Brendan mused aloud.

"And what do you make of the symbol on his chest?" I asked, indicating the bloody circle.

"Now we're getting to the good stuff," Brendan said sardonically. "That, Alex, is a symbol related to an ancient order of demon-hunters, and if they are involved, then I'm afraid we're going to have trouble between the gods and demons."

I raised my eyebrows. That was a pretty apocalyptic scenario, and Brendan wasn't usually a dramatic type of guy. "Can you fill me in on the meaning of the symbol?" I studied it more closely. I had never seen any runes similar to it.

Brendan began, "Sure. It's a — "

It's a supernatural military symbol, the voice in my head chimed in.

"Fuck," I said aloud.

Carlos started. "I beg your pardon?"

"Um, nothing. I'm thinking out loud. Please go on, Brendan."

"As I was saying, it's the symbol of a group whose purpose was slaying demons. They were disbanded in the beginning of the twentieth century, and no one's heard of them since. It was assumed the order died out."

"The Holy Order of Shadows is the name," Carlos said. "The Court of Hell is concerned that there may be a descendant cult on the loose, or perhaps just some maniac who learned about the group. They're afraid someone is starting to kill their minions — excuse me, I mean their *agents*."

"It may be true," Brendan said quietly.

I leafed through the sheets in the NYPD folder Brendan had given me, which had information on the murder. The Magic Council worked with the US government on supernatural cases; the US authorities gave us carte blanche and kept us fully informed, and didn't meddle in our affairs. Supernaturals handled the supernatural, humans took care of human affairs. That was the mantra: theirs and ours. To human eyes Brendan worked as an NYPD sergeant, but in reality he was the Magic Council's agent.

I looked over the entire NYPD report, but found nothing other than what Brendan had summed up for me. Daniel Stone didn't have so much as a parking fine in his background, but here he lay on the posh marble floor with a bizarre symbol carved into his chest. Whoever he had gotten involved with, he had bitten off more than he could chew.

"Tell me more about that group, the Holy Order of Shadows," I said, closing the folder.

"It was founded in the Middle Ages," Brendan said, "and its soldiers were trained mainly in Tibet and India. Right after the First World War, an agreement was reached between the Courts of Heaven and Hell that no one from either Court would kill members of the other, and the Order was abolished. In fact, one of the conditions for the peace treaty was the suspension of the Order — another reason this has us worried about relations between the two Courts." Brendan nervously rubbed his forehead. This case was clearly stressing him out.

"The Court of Hell must be pretty gullible," I mused, "to think someone would bother killing an ordinary person, some boring banker, just to take revenge on demons. Can we link the victim to any dark magic? Can we be certain he even knew about the supernatural world? Seems more likely to me that he was killed in a dark-magic ritual — by some twisted supernatural, a sorcerer maybe."

Standing behind the desk, Carlos picked up something wrapped up in a plastic baggie and handed it to me. "Judging by this relic I found among the victim's personal items, I think he was indeed interested in the dark arts."

It was a statuette, with horns resembling a demon's, and an inverted pentagram engraved around the base. When I looked closely at the underside of the base, I saw a tiny 'D' scratched into the enamel but found no other markings. Probably for "Daniel."

"Stone was well off, so he certainly had enough leisure time and money to pursue that sort of hobby, glorifying demons or the dark side in some occult society," I said, examining the statuette. It seemed rather ordinary. "But this doesn't prove anything. The inverted pentagram is a popular symbol with some people these days."

One of the police officers pulled Brendan aside, and they exchanged a few words. At the officer's signal, a team of paramedics came in, and Brendan moved to stand next to me while they prepared to put the corpse into a body bag and carry it out.

"You're right," he said. "We need to learn more about Stone, about his character. A single statuette doesn't prove anything." Brendan walked slowly around the spacious office, his eyes gleaming in their distinctive werewolf way. Whenever he had to concentrate or was under pressure, Brendan drew on his werewolf power. This manifested most often in a change in the color of his eyes, which now shone yellow-green. "Let's review the events from the victim's last twenty-four hours. We know that Stone was in his office, on the phone with a client, at eight forty-two p.m. Based on the guards' statements and the camera footage, no one entered his office after six forty-five in the evening, and no one came into the bank after six, when it officially closes."

"Who discovered the body?" I asked.

"Stone's personal secretary, Mary Connor. She found him this morning at eight-fifteen. The first police officers on the scene called me at eight-thirty, and I arrived within half an hour."

I looked at my watch; it showed just past eleven. "The Council's pushing you pretty quickly," I said.

Brendan grimaced. "Because of the symbol. And rumor has it that Kai, the leader of the demons, flew into a rage when he learned about the murder."

"Seems like much ado about nothing. I really don't think someone's out there targeting demons or using people for some grand demonic plans or whatever."

"Tell that to the Council," Carlos said.

"Yeah. Kai would really appreciate it," Brendan added, mischievous sparks flashing in his eyes. "In the meanwhile, let's talk to the secretary."

We took the elevator down a few floors. Mary Connor's office was right next to Stone's, but given the police presence, they had temporarily moved her to the fifteenth floor. Brendan flashed his police badge at the busy woman behind the receptionist's desk.

She started slightly. "Hello, Sergeant... Sax," she said, reading Brendan's badge. She looked questioningly at me and Carlos.

"These are my colleagues," he said, "Alexandra Shaw and Carlos Delvalle."

"I'll let Mr. Larson know you're here." She picked up the desk phone, but Brendan forestalled her.

"Actually, we'd like to talk to Mr. Stone's secretary, Mary Connor, if that's convenient."

Brendan smiled at the secretary. She looked like she was in her early thirties — an attractive brunette with big dark eyes and a pleasantly husky voice. I'd always wondered how they chose secretaries in big companies like UCB: for their skills and experience, or based on looks, too? Judging by this secretary's appearance, I guessed physique played as important a role in the hiring process as brains did.

The woman pressed a button on the landline and, after she exchanged a few words, got up and walked into a room behind her desk, which I presumed was her boss's office. She wore a short black skirt, which showed off her long legs, and a black jacket. She looked both stylish and sexy. I glanced at my partners, but didn't sense any emotion in them; they didn't even give her a second look. A few moments later she returned and invited us into the deputy CEO's office to question Mary Connor.

The deputy CEO's office was identical to Daniel Stone's; the only differences were a few more potted palms here and more cheer and color in the framed pictures. On the wall facing the desk was a large picture of a beautiful young girl standing in the rain, with the sun making its way through the clouds. The atmosphere here was much more relaxed than in Daniel Stone's office. Of course, it helped not having a body sprawled on the marble floor.

Behind the large desk sat a man in his fifties. A young woman in a chair next to him, clutching a notebook in her hands, read off something to the man, who keyed it into the laptop on the desk before him.

"Mr. Larson, Mr. Sax from the NYPD, and his colleagues, Ms. Shaw and Mr. Delvalle." After introducing us, the secretary left the room, closing the door behind her. Brendan and Mr. Larson shook hands and, after exchanging a few words, Brandon asked to speak with Miss Connor in private. Larson agreed, saying they could finish updating Daniel's work later, and opened a door next to his office revealing a small conference room.

While Miss Connor, Carlos, and I took our seats, Brendan pulled Mr. Larson aside, asking him not to leave his office; we'd need to interview him after we were done with Miss Connor. Larson nodded and went out, closing the door behind him. Brendan sat in a chair next to the secretary.

"I'm sure this is a blow to you, Miss Connor," Brendan began, applying all his charm. "It must have come as a terrible shock."

The secretary trembled slightly. "Yes, it certainly did. Just yesterday Mr. Stone gave me instructions about his schedule for the week, and now he..." Her voice faltered.

"I'd like to ask a few questions," Brendan said after a moment. "Did anything unusual happen yesterday, or in the past few days? Anything at all, no matter how small or trivial it might seem? Did Mr. Stone seem worried or more nervous than usual?"

Mary Connor shook her head.

"Are you sure?" Brendan persisted. Shifters seemed to have built-in lie detectors, and Brendan always knew when someone was lying or hiding something. He was taking charge of the interview, and I was okay with that.

She pondered over his question, then slowly said, "I wouldn't say he was nervous — excited, maybe. I'm not sure, but I thought it might be because of his new girlfriend."

Brendan raised his eyebrows and asked, "Can you tell us about her?"

"Sure. Her name is Christina Ricoletti. She's a model and actress. They'd been together for a couple of months — I actually thought maybe he was getting ready to propose. They looked so cute together." Mary looked down, trying not to cry.

Carlos, next to me, wrote down her answers, and I studied her. I put her age at no more than twenty-seven, although I suspected she was even younger, maybe twenty-four or so — about my age. She had a pretty, oval face and gave the impression of having a calm and balanced personality. She wore long, elegant pants and discreet makeup. She seemed like the type of woman I could feel comfortable sharing an embarrassing secret with and trust not to gossip about it. I liked her.

"Tell us how your day with Mr. Stone went yesterday," Brendan said.

"Everything seemed normal. I arrived for work around ten till eight — I usually work from eight to five, with an hour for lunch. Mr. Stone arrived around eight thirty and we went over the day's assignments. The usual: sending emails, talking to clients, and updating his schedule for next week. Some additional work came up — Mr. Stone was negotiating a deal with one of the bank's key clients, and I had to send them a detailed email on his behalf — so I stayed until about six thirty. Mr. Stone was still at his computer when I left. He was a true workaholic; he often stayed here until eleven or twelve at night. He loved what he called the tranquility of the small hours, when all was quiet and he was on his own. That was when he could really concentrate." She let out a sob, then continued, "I guess that's why the guards weren't suspicious, and didn't check his office." She wiped away her tears.

Brendan cautiously asked her another question. "Did Mr. Stone have any enemies? Anyone who was angry with him or might have wished him harm?"

Mary Connor shook her head, looking down at the floor again.

"What can you tell us about Mr. Stone's interests, his hobbies — what sort of impression did you have of him?" I asked.

She raised her eyes from the carpet and studied me for a moment before replying. "I don't think Mr. Stone was interested in anything other than his work. As I said, he was a workaholic with a capital 'W.'"

I felt she was telling the truth. The glances I exchanged with Carlos and Brendan showed they thought the same: She didn't know anything else of interest.

Brendan cleared his throat. "Once again, I'm sorry for your loss, Miss Connor, and we appreciate your assistance. One last question: Where were you yesterday evening between ten and eleven p.m.?"

The question startled her. "At home, why?"

Ignoring her question, Brendan asked, "Were you alone?"

"Yes, I was." There was a pause, then she added, "I... uh, I was on the phone with a friend from ten twenty until eleven or so."

Brendan thanked her and we all left the small conference room. The deputy CEO was still working at his computer. "Mr. Larson," Brendan said, "we'd like to ask you a few questions now."

Larson nodded to Miss Connor, and she left the office. When she shut the door behind her, he said, "A terrible tragedy. I can't believe the way Daniel died. I have no idea what sort of people he was involved with, but judging by his death, they weren't very nice." He shook his head and stared at the monitor in front of him.

"What can you tell us about Mr. Stone's interests outside of work?" I asked. To catch Daniel Stone's killer, we had to have a clearer idea of his character and interests, other than the occult.

Mr. Larson coughed. "Well, as I'm sure Mary already told you, Daniel was a workaholic. I've never seen him outside of the office, except for team-building exercises and at the bank's Christmas parties. A decent guy, focused. I don't know much about his private life. I knew he got divorced a few years ago, and he recently started dating someone much younger than him — a model or actress, I think. I don't believe he has children." He looked at his watch, which I interpreted as a prompt for us to finish the questioning and go.

"What else can you tell us about the deceased?" Carlos asked. It was the first time he had spoken since we walked in.

"Unfortunately, I think that's about it."

"And a routine question — where were you last night between ten and eleven p.m.?"

"At home. My wife and children can confirm it." He smiled. He was attractive enough, and in good shape for his age, but something about him repelled me.

"If you think of anything else, Mr. Larson, call me. Your colleague's murder seems to have some ritualistic elements, which could indicate something more complex than a random or privately motivated murder."

Larson went pale at Brendan's words. Brendan handed him a business card, saying darkly, "It would be unfortunate if anyone else was murdered because someone withheld information."

"Thanks." The deputy CEO cleared his throat. "I'll keep it in mind." He rose and shook hands with us, then saw us out.

As we waited for the elevator, I turned to Brendan and Carlos. "So what do you think about Larson?"

Carlos narrowed his eyes and replied, "He's definitely hiding information. I just don't know what or why."

"We'll soon find out. I hope it won't be too late," Brendan said grimly.

Chapter 3

Later that afternoon, we received the coroner's initial findings. According to the report, Stone's murder occurred between ten and eleven p.m. the previous night. We questioned the security staff at the bank in greater detail, but they didn't tell us anything other than what Mary Connor had already said. Daniel Stone often burned the midnight oil in his office; the guards knew this, and it didn't strike them as odd. No one had come into the bank building that night, as the cameras had already confirmed.

Brendan got the number of Stone's girlfriend, Christina Ricoletti, and contacted her. It turned out she was in Milan, Italy, and Brendan had the unhappy job of informing her of her boyfriend's murder. She said she would catch the next plane to New York, and would probably arrive late that evening. We agreed to meet the next morning at her apartment on the Upper West Side.

We spent the rest of the day searching Daniel Stone's apartment in Lower Manhattan. We examined all his personal items and computer but found nothing of interest other than a statuette of a skull with the top sliced off.

"Creepy," I said, turning the skull over in my hands. "This is the second unusual item — this and that horned statue with the inverted pentagram we found in his office. They're similar in style and color." They both had the letter "D" carved into the base, but we'd found that mark on many of Daniel Stone's nonmagical belongings, too.

"I think you're right. Looks like the banker was associated with the dark arts in some way," Carlos said. He seemed nice, and I tried my best to focus my attention on him instead of on Brendan, whose sexy ass and biceps, combined with his arrogance, only distracted me. I was a supernatural — shouldn't I be better than ordinary mortals, in better control of my emotions and passions? Maybe I would have to resort to one of Naomi's potions. We offered anti-love potions as special-order items at the shop; they didn't sell well enough to keep in stock, and besides, they took Naomi more time to prepare than the more popular love potions. But what I really needed, I thought, was an anti-horniness potion.

It was approaching eight p.m. and I was already feeling tired. Brendan was feeling the strain too. "This case is looking much more difficult than I'd like it to be," he said as we prepared to go our separate ways for the evening. Frankly, I'd never seen him so worried and nervous.

"Relax, Brendan. We'll handle it, now that I'm on the team." I winked at him, but he didn't seem amused in the least. Well, if he wanted to be a Debbie Downer, let him. "So that's all for today, right? I'm going to teleport back. What time — "

"You'll *teleport* back? What?" Brendan snarled.

I started — what was wrong with him?

"You have a transport charm?" he continued. "You should have mentioned that earlier. We could have used it."

"I'm afraid it's only got a small charge, barely — " I began, but he cut me off before I could finish.

"Alex, every minute matters. I have to report my findings on this case to the Magic Council, and with the findings suggesting the involvement of dark magic, they're going to be pushing me even harder. You could have saved us some time and transported us all to Milan so we could question the victim's girlfriend. But you didn't even mention you had a transportation charm — you kept quiet about it until you wanted to use it for your own convenience."

"Don't be a fool, Brendan. I already told you it's only got a small charge. It's barely enough to teleport me home. Besides, we put the time to good use searching Daniel Stone's apartment and found that creepy statuette."

"You should have discussed it with me first. I'd like to know all our options beforehand. Don't do that again."

That wasn't a request — oh, magic forbid! It was a downright order. "It *wasn't* an option, asshole. Aren't you listening?" I gritted my teeth.

"Hey, hey, you two," Carlos said. "You're both acting stupid. It's not worth arguing about — we don't need that kind of tension. Can't you just shake hands and forget about it?"

"I won't tolerate you bossing me around," I said, ignoring Carlos's comment. "I came here to help you out, not to be your slave."

"And I'm grateful for it, but I won't tolerate willful and irresponsible behavior. We're working together and you need to keep me posted."

Willful and — ! But I gritted my teeth. "Fine."

"I have work to do so I'm not going to argue with you any longer," Brendan said, "but I expect you to inform me of any spells or charms you have access to. I'll see you at Ricoletti's apartment tomorrow at eleven o'clock." With those words he strode away down the street.

I breathed a sigh of relief — I wouldn't have to see Brendan's stupid face anymore today. When I turned around, I saw Carlos studying me. "What?" I said, baring my teeth at him. He held up his hands and took a step back, and I teleported.

***

"You must be Sergeant Sax." A tall brunette with supermodel proportions, heavily made-up, greeted us at the door.

"Yes, that's right. And these are my colleagues, Alex Shaw and Detective Carlos Delvalle,"

Brendan said. Bastard! He used a title to introduce Carlos, but for me, nothing! I stepped hard on his foot with the heel of my boot. I was wearing one of my favorite pairs — elegant and feminine, but the heel was relatively low, so I could kick monster ass if I needed to. Brendan gritted his teeth and endured the pain.

"Our condolences on your loss, Ms. Ricoletti. I'm sure you must be grieving — " Carlos began as Christina led us into her living room, but she interrupted him.

"Ah, yes. It's not a pretty thing, but that's life — people die all the time." She said it casually, as if her pet goldfish had died. Carlos appeared bemused.

"You possess a remarkable gift for detachment." Brendan made himself comfortable on her couch. Christina's spacious apartment was luxuriously furnished with an artistic flair. The walls were painted in warm colors of yellow and light purple and decorated with pictures of beautiful models, worthy of the cover of *Vogue*. Christina herself was a very attractive young woman in her mid-twenties, with dark hair and beautiful dark eyes which she used to great effect. She had that sultry look that men loved so much.

Well, honey, my voice chimed in, *you have to admit, she's the complete package.*

What does it concern you, anyway? I snapped at it. I felt a bit insecure around Christina, and didn't like the feeling. The voice inside my head laughed, which gave me a headache. I concentrated on Christina's answers, not her appearance.

"Would you like something to drink, sergeant, officers?" Christina smiled at us charmingly, but we all shook our heads. She fixed herself a drink — a martini, by the look of it — then sat next to Brendan, while Carlos and I sat on the sofa across from them.

"We'd like to begin by asking about your relationship with Mr. Stone. How did you meet?" Brendan asked.

Christina sighed and took a sip of her cocktail, then held it in her lap. "Well... it was several months ago, maybe six, at one of *Vogue*'s parties. Daniel's bank was one of the party's sponsors. We struck up a conversation, exchanged phone numbers, and he called me a few days later. He asked me out, and we began dating. We'd been seeing each other for about a month when he proposed we spend a romantic weekend together in Paris. I accepted immediately; I've always loved Paris — romance, history, and the fashion industry! My first fashion show was in Paris ten years ago, in fact. Such wonderful memories."

I wondered at what age she started modeling — thirteen, maybe? Fifteen?

"Our relationship became more serious after that," she continued. "We met mostly on the weekends. He made reservations all over the US and in more exotic places. We went to Bali once; it was wonderful." She said the last words softly and sighed. "Sometimes he finished work early on Fridays, and we would spend the afternoon together, either at my house or in his apartment."

"And did he mention any troubles to you? Personal or work related?" Brendan asked.

"Hmm... no, I cannot think of any." Christina wrinkled her brow, then added, "He complained about his ex-wife once."

"Can you think of anyone who might have wanted him dead?"

She shook her head and sipped at her drink. She seemed completely relaxed — her boyfriend's death didn't seem to have affected her at all, which made me wonder whether she had even liked him. Or maybe Christina Ricoletti had that same attitude toward all her intimate relationships. Perfect detachment, I had to give her credit for that.

"What can you tell us about Mr. Stone's interests? Did he have any hobbies?" I asked.

Just then Christina's cell phone chimed with a message, and she took it out. She read the message, smiled, and then turned her attention back to us. "Pardon me. Where were we? Ah, yes, Daniel's interests. Well, he was interested in the occult, and in magic... Do you believe in magic, sergeant?" She turned to Brendan, a mysterious smile on her lips.

Was it just me, or was she flirting with my ex? Fine — if she wanted him, she could have him. He was bad news.

"It's a rather controversial topic," Brendan replied evasively. "Did Daniel have a mentor or master who taught him?"

Christina sipped at her cocktail and put it on the table before her. "I've never been interested in such things. Give me makeup, clothes, and shoes, and there's nothing else I need. Except men, of course." She winked at Brendan. "I don't have any interest in magic, spells, and potions. God knows I'm no witch," she giggled. "I never questioned Daniel about his interests, just as he didn't ask me about makeup or clothes. Only once did I go with him to a... what did he call it, an 'occult party'? If you ask me, it was just a swingers' party, but we all had to wear trench coats and carnival masks. Sounds kinky, doesn't it?" She trailed her hand down her décolletage.

Brendan's eyes followed the motion of her hand.

"Would you participate in such a party, sergeant?" She asked Brendan, and Carlos cleared his throat. I had no intention of intervening — I sensed that Brendan was uncomfortable with her flirting, probably because he was working, but I didn't mind watching him suffer.

"Let's get back to our topic," Brendan said. "You say you attended an 'occult party'; where did that take place?"

"It was held in a magnificent mansion on Staten Island, and was one of those parties where everyone sleeps with everyone — absolute debauchery. Pardon my questions, sergeant, but are parties of any interest to you?"

Brendan asked, "Did they do any sort of rituals? Sacrifices, anything of the sort?"

Christina laughed out loud. "Sacrifices? Do people do such things?"

"You have no idea what kind of creatures lurk in the dark," I said casually. Christina gave me a puzzled look, then turned her gaze back to Brendan. I half expected her to ask to see our badges.

"Miss Ricoletti, can you answer the question, please?" Brendan prompted.

She gave a slight sigh. "No, I saw no sacrifices. I don't think they've ever done any — though Daniel did mention a week or two ago that they planned to sacrifice a lamb. I didn't pay close attention, but I thought, 'That poor animal.' I mean, if they decided to kill one."

"And who is 'they'?"

"The occult society — the secret club that Daniel and one of his colleagues from the bank belong to. Um, belonged to. I mean, *Daniel* belonged. It has a funny name, something about a skull." She frowned for a few seconds, pondering, then exclaimed, "The Hollow Skull, that's it! A rather stupid name, isn't it? I once mentioned to Daniel — I think immediately after the orgy — that they should change it. Do you know what he said? He told me to fuck off!"

"Hmm. Imagine that." I said.

Christina gave me a dirty look and looked like she was about to snap back, but Carlos interrupted. "Do you happen to recognize this symbol, Miss Ricoletti?" He showed her the picture of the sliced-off skull on his mobile.

"Of course — that's the club's symbol. I think the name comes from it. Where did you get this photo from?"

"We *are* detectives." I smiled at her. "Do you have the address of the house where the party was held?"

Christina looked for it on her mobile phone. Stone had sent it to her a few months ago in a message, she said, shortly before the party in question. After a few minutes of searching, she decided she must have deleted it. "You have no idea how overloaded my mail is. I have to clean it out occasionally. I'm sorry," she said and smiled apologetically.

"Is this by chance the colleague of Daniel's who is also a member of the Hollow Skull?" Carlos showed her a picture of the deputy CEO, Mr. Larson.

"I'm not sure. I saw him only once, but that could be him," Christina said.

Having it be Larson would make sense. I'd probably be nervous to tell the cops I was a member of an occult club, too, especially during the investigation of a ritualistic murder like this.

"Miss Ricoletti, other than the Hollow Skull, did your boyfriend meet with other people with similar occult interests?" I asked.

"You're taking Daniel's penchant for the occult very seriously, I see."

"Yes, ma'am. There are possible ritualistic overtones to his murder," Carlos replied. Brendan and I looked at him in concern: we had to keep our world's existence a secret.

"That is," Brendan interrupted, "while we aren't yet certain what the exact nature of your boyfriend's murder was, we cannot exclude any theories, however bizarre they may — "

"Now that's a surprise!" Christina said. "If Danny was killed in some bizarre occult ritual... wow!" She chuckled. "Who would have thought his magical mumbo-jumbo would have killed him?" She looked at Carlos, curiosity evident on her face. "Do you think the things Daniel believed in are true? I mean, the supernatural — do such things really exist?"

I held my breath — I had no idea what Carlos would answer, but under no circumstances should he tell people about the existence of our world, or even about magic. If one realized that magic was real, then the next conclusion would be that mythical creatures from fairy tales and legends might also be real. And that was what the Council did not want to happen, at any cost. Every investigator signed a confidentiality contract and the Council was very strict in enforcing it. If that contract was violated, heads would roll. "I don't believe in anything, Miss Ricoletti, unless I see it with my own eyes," Carlos said coolly.

Christina was visibly disappointed by his response. She leaned back on the sofa and sipped at her cocktail for comfort. "For a moment I thought Daniel's murder might have had a supernatural angle," she said sincerely. I could see where she was coming from — if my own life were as empty and devoid of adventures as hers seemed, my only interests being clothes, shopping, gossip, and cocktails, I'd be thrilled by a potentially supernatural murder, too.

"Let's get back to Mr. Stone's friends. Other than his colleague, Mr. Larson, can you think of other people in his circles or acquaintances who have shown interest in the occult and magic?" asked Brendan.

"I would need to give that some serious thought. I've been busy preparing for an upcoming review of H&M and didn't pay much attention to what Daniel said recently. Not that he ever said much — he was a rather quiet man." She squinted, straining her memory. Suddenly she stood and went to the other end of the living room, which held a desk and a shelf with magazines and books. Christina selected a thick notebook and carried it back to the sofa.

"Let's see what I recorded in my diary. I write everything down; I have such a poor memory," she said, sitting down next to Brendan. She flipped through several pages in silence, then said, "Ah, here I wrote that Daniel mentioned something to me about a special wizard, a sorcerer." She added, "I have no idea what this means. Is it something like an evil wizard?" She looked at us, apparently expecting confirmation or some explanation, but no one responded. She returned her eyes to the diary and continued, "That was September nineteenth. A few days later, on September twenty-third, he told me he bought some books about magic."

I glanced at the shifters. We had gone through all the victim's belongings, but hadn't seen any books about sorcery or magic. Perhaps someone had taken them before us. Perhaps the murderer.

"What were the books, and where did he keep them?" Brendan asked her.

"I don't know which books they were. As I already told you, that's not really my thing. But he kept all his books in his library."

"Miss Ricoletti, I'm afraid we'll need to review your diary as evidence," Brendan said.

"Of course, detective. For you, anything," she said suggestively. She flipped through a few more pages and exclaimed, "Ah! Here's something; Daniel mentioned a bar he'd been hanging around lately." She pointed at a passage as she passed the notebook to Brendan.

"The Hellfire Club," read Brendan, and his eyes met mine.

"Can you tell us anything else about this sorcerer — a name, anything?" I asked. We would read every note she had written, but I wanted to take the opportunity to test her. If she was playing games with us, she might slip up.

Christina leaned against Brendan as she flipped through a few more pages, then she looked up at me. "No, I'm afraid that's all I've written down. As I said, that sort of mumbo-jumbo has never interested me. At least, not until now." She gave Brendan a sultry look. "But whoever this sorcerer was, obviously his skills didn't protect Daniel. What a pity."

Brendan and Carlos exchanged a quick glance. Christina caught it.

"What?" she asked. "Don't you — Oh!" Her eyes widened as realization dawned on her pretty face. "You think that sorcerer may have killed Danny?"

"We can't exclude any possibility, ma'am," Brendan told her. "Before we wrap things up, we need to know where you were yesterday between ten and eleven o'clock at night."

"Are you asking out of personal interest, sergeant?" Christina said, smiling flirtatiously. I rolled my eyes. The woman was unbelievable.

"Miss Ricoletti, we are investigating your boyfriend's murder," Brendan reminded her.

"Oh, fine. I just wanted to lighten the mood a little. I don't know why everyone gets so tense when a murder is involved," Christina said and sighed. "I was in Hotel San Antonio in Milan, sleeping soundly in my bed."

"Can anyone confirm that?" Brendan asked her.

"Yes. My close friend and colleague Svetla was with me — she's a well-known Ukrainian model. We always share a room." Christina smiled suggestively at Brendan.

He cleared his throat and said, "Thank you, Miss Ricoletti." He stood. We followed his example and said our goodbyes, leaving her with her fabulous model's life.

Outside, I turned to the shifters. "What do you think, guys? I think she was telling the truth. If she was lying, she deserves an Oscar."

"Yeah, without a doubt, she told the truth," Carlos confirmed.

I looked at Brendan, who looked somewhat concerned.

"What is it, Brendan? Wondering how to ask Miss Ricoletti out for dinner, or how to get invited to one of those swinger parties?" I teased him.

He stopped in his tracks on the street and fixed me with a stern gaze. "I know that place, the Hellfire Club. It's a well-known supernatural hotspot; nonmagical creatures aren't allowed in. And since our victim was human, that means he must have known an influential supernatural who helped him gain access."

Which pointed to the sorcerer.

Chapter 4

"It sounds like whoever got Stone into the Hellfire Club was playing him for a fool." Brendan said. "By the way, Alex, the next time you step on my feet while I'm questioning a witness, I will dismiss you from the case. Am I clear?"

"Fine. The next time you insult me in front of a witness by giving everyone a rank but me, I quit. Am I clear?"

Brendan tried to stare me down, but I knew he needed me more than I needed him, and I stared back. After a few seconds, he spun away to face Carlos. "Now, we have a few pieces of key information: the Hellfire Club; Mr. Larson, the deputy CEO; and the mansion in Staten Island. I suggest we leave the club until last — it's closed now anyway, and will remain nearly empty until well after dark. I want to go back to UCB and talk with Larson again. I think we all agree he's holding something back, and now it seems likely to be connected to the victim."

"If I were a member of an occult club and participated in their sex parties, I wouldn't want to disclose it to the cops, either," I said.

Brendan nodded.

"Have you been to the Hellfire Club?" Carlos asked Brendan.

"Yes, I have. It's a meeting place for pretty much all users of dark magic — shadow-casters, dark wizards, sorcerers, all sorts of demons — you name it. Most of them are low-level so they're probably not a threat, but nonetheless there are a lot of them."

"Were you there because of work or... on your own time?" I asked.

Brendan smiled. "When you work as the Magic Council's investigator in NYC, you have to explore every avenue. Since I was transferred here, I've been there half a dozen times, either for information or on a lead, following a suspect."

"Honestly, I've never heard of this club," I said.

Brendan shrugged. "I didn't know about the Hellfire Club either, until I came here."

"So in order for Daniel Stone to be allowed into the club, he had to have either been a supernatural or to have known an influential one?" Carlos asked.

"Exactly. The Magic Council won't like this at all," Brendan replied.

"I didn't feel any magic in the victim. Maybe this sorcerer Christina mentioned is our guy, and got Stone inside," Carlos mused.

"That's what I'm thinking." Brendan rubbed his forehead. "I'm starving — it's already past one o'clock. Let's go get lunch, and I'll call a few people to track down the owner of the mansion in Staten Island, in case Mr. Larson doesn't loosen his tongue."

We walked as we talked, and Brendan stopped by a late-model BMW, unlocking it.

I exclaimed, "The Council sure doesn't pinch pennies on their investigators' cars."

"Obviously," Carlos said with envy in his voice. "In Brazil, I'm driving a second-hand Ford."

Brendan shrugged as he started the car. "I can't help that." Carlos tried to offer me the front passenger's seat, but I insisted on sitting in the back — I didn't want to be too close to Brendan. We had barely fastened our seatbelts when Brendan gunned the engine, the tires squealing on the asphalt.

"Where are we going?" I asked, clutching at the door handle.

"The Lucky Leprechaun," Brendan replied.

***

The Lucky Leprechaun, located on the Lower East Side of Manhattan, served as both a restaurant and a meeting point for the local supernatural community. That is, for the middle-class supernatural community. Just as with humans, our world divided along economic lines: wealthier supernatural beings frequented fancy, expensive places, and the middle-class had their own hangouts. When we entered, the savory aromas of Irish stew and corned beef engulfed me and mingled with a whiff of sweet desserts. Magic of all tastes and colors swirled in the air, further whetting my appetite, and my stomach started to rumble.

As with all magical places, the Lucky Leprechaun was invisible to human eyes. As we settled in at one of the large tables, I looked around, examining the restaurant's customers. All were mystical beings, of course. A few of them didn't appear human: At one of the tables near the bar I saw two hooded figures with tentacles jutting out from under their cloaks. Near them a centaur was pacing nervously from foot to foot near a table; he looked around often, glancing at the front door, apparently waiting for someone. Two witches were seated at the table next to ours. One was attractive and eye-catching; she wore black clothes and a black pointed hat with a sparkling purple band, and heavy makeup — her eyes were ringed entirely in black and framed with thick black lashes. Even her lipstick was black. I could feel her magic, but it wasn't strong — light and hissing, like a potion simmering in a cauldron on low heat. The other witch, casually dressed as an average human, had much more powerful magic. I'd noticed this before: Some supernaturals who weren't very potent tried to compensate with a strong first impression. I thought it rather silly: This trick might work on weaker supernaturals, but anyone who was powerful enough — such as Brendan, Carlos, or me — wouldn't pay attention to mere physical appearance, but would rely on his or her sense of magic.

The waitress came over to take our orders; my magic sense told me she was a hearth witch. She greeted Brendan by name and they chatted amiably. She asked if he wanted his usual and he confirmed — he clearly came here often. Then she looked at Carlos and me. "What I can get you to drink?"

"Brendan, what did you order? Some kind of magic tonic?" Carlos asked.

"Yes." Brendan turned Carlos' menu over to the drinks section on the back.

"Our magic lemonade has a light, refreshing enchantment that will infuse you with a pleasant energy. Something like a light potion. It comes in several different flavors," the waitress added, pointing at the list.

Carlos and I looked over it and the waitress said, "I'll return in a minute, when you're ready."

Brendan checked out her ass as she walked away. He was so irritating. I focused on the menu.

"Oh, look," I exclaimed after a moment. "They have magic milkshakes and smoothies, and raw bars for dessert." The variety of the restaurant's offerings overwhelmed me.

While Carlos and I looked over the menu, Brendan talked on his phone. I listened. From his informal tone, he knew the other party well. He asked them to gather information on the Hollow

Skull Society and get the address for the house in Staten Island.

When the waitress came again, Carlos ordered a Guinness beer with magic flavoring, and I ordered a Sparkling Strawberry Enchantment.

The girl jotted our drink orders down on her notepad. She double-checked Brendan's food order — steak and French fries — then looked expectantly at us.

"Um, I'm a vegetarian," Carlos said. "I see a few meatless dishes listed in the menu, but do you offer anything else?" I almost choked — a vegetarian tiger shifter? I'd never heard of such a thing.

The girl thought for a moment, then said, "I'm afraid we don't have anything other than what's on the menu, and our sides and soups. If I can make a recommendation, though, our pizza Margherita is vegetarian, and it's amazing. It's probably our most popular dish."

"Pizza Margherita — that sounds delicious. One for me."

"Let's make it two," I said.

"Who did you tell to find out about the Hollow Skull thing?" I asked Brendan from behind my smoothie after the waitress left. It was a delicious drink, with a distinctive magic aftertaste. Sizzling fireworks fluttered on my tongue — a very pleasant experience.

"Corrie. She's with the Council, and also in the NYPD. She often helps me gather information for cases."

"This is delicious," Carlos interjected. "A curious combination. I've never tasted anything like it. In Brazil there are a few magic bars and restaurants exclusively for supernaturals, but they're just meeting places for our community," he mused. "They don't offer drinks with actual magic in them."

"I get the feeling you're liking the supernatural pulse of NYC," I said with a smile.

"It's a bit too soon to judge, but so far I do," he admitted.

The waitress soon brought our meals and we all fell on them greedily. The pizza Margherita was hot, thin, and crispy — delicious. Brendan definitely had good taste in restaurants.

We were finishing up when Brendan's mobile rang. "Hello," he said, tossing the last of his fries into his mouth. He had long since devoured the steak. Like most other shifters — Carlos being an exception to the rule — Brendan loved meat, especially steak. "Yes, Corrie, I'm listening. ... Really? This is interesting. Elliott Rumford, right?" Brendan wrote down the name on the napkin before him. "Yeah, thanks, Corrie. Once again, I owe you one. Pardon? ... Well, so far everything's going fine. ... Yes, yes, I know. See ya later. Bye."

He hung up and said, "The Hollow Skull society's headmaster is a man named Elliott Rumford."

I raised my eyebrows. "And how did your *assistant* find this information? Care to share?" I asked and sipped the last of my smoothie. I had a feeling that Brendan had turned his affections to this Corrie girl after he'd transferred to New York.

He said, "A while ago, we captured a succubus charged with draining the sexual energy of a victim in Manhattan. The charges were dropped because she had an ironclad alibi: at the time of the assault she was working at a swingers' party in Staten Island for one Mr. Elliott Rumford. She claimed he was the master of an occult society, the Hollow Skull."

I exchanged glances with Carlos. "Turns out succubi can be useful. They're not known for honesty, though," I said.

Brendan looked amused. "Usually they're not, but it was in that one's best interest to tell us the truth. Anyway, Corrie also found a phone number." He was already dialing it.

Unfortunately, the call was answered by Elliott Rumford's secretary, who cut Brendan off with: "He is very busy." Even the mention of NYPD didn't faze her. Brendan said she promised to relay the message to her boss, but unless Brendan had a warrant, Rumford couldn't meet him any sooner than the next week.

"We could try to get a warrant, but I think it'd be more effective to back Larson into a corner so he convinces Elliott to meet with us," Brendan said. He waved the waitress over and asked for the check.

"Lunch is on the house, Mr. Sax," she said.

"What?" He turned to her, surprised, just as a gorgeous blond woman appeared, looking like she'd stepped out of a Playboy cover. She wore a white apron and smelled of bread, cookies, and spices. Her magic made me think of delicious food eaten around the warmth of the hearth — which made sense, since she was also a hearth witch. Her magic was wholesome and powerful.

"Brendan, baby, where have you been?" She hugged him warmly. "We haven't seen you here for a long time! I was starting to worry about you. I'm glad to see you — and who are your friends?"

Brendan smiled. "Kim, hi. I'm glad to see you, too," he said, and turned his gaze to us. "These are my colleagues, police detective Carlos Delvalle, and Alex Shaw, an independent consultant. I appreciate your offer to treat us, but there's no need — I insist."

"I don't know why you won't let me do something nice for you, hon." She winked at him and turned her gaze to Carlos and me. Carlos had been staring, and no wonder. She looked like a cross between Scarlett Johansson and Jessica Alba, so naturally men drooled all over her. I had to admit she was stunning. I got the impression she had that little extra something that average beauties lacked: wit and soul — a rare gem.

I nodded at her in greeting. Carlos said, in a slightly hoarse voice, "Nice to meet you."

"Well, detective, I don't want to distract you from your official duties. Whenever you have time, drop by my humble restaurant. You're always welcome," she told Brendan flirtatiously, a grin on her pretty face.

"So I see you didn't get bored in New York, *hon*," I said, imitating the sexy hearth witch's tone after she had gone.

"I can't blame you, dude. That's one hell of a sexy lady." Carlos still stared after Kim.

Brendan cast us a disapproving look. "Don't you two have an investigation to rack your brains over? Roll up your sleeves and get to work. We have a culprit to catch," he growled. Then he stormed out of the Lucky Leprechaun, while I tried to suppress my laughter.

***

"Yes, Sergeant Sax? Can I help you with something?" Larson's secretary asked from behind her enormous desk. Brendan had driven us back to Universal Credit Bank on West Wall Street.

"Yes, you can." Brendan leaned toward Mr. Larson's attractive secretary and smiled at her in his typical fashion, showing his white teeth. "We'd like to talk to your boss, Mr. Larson."

The girl looked bemused. "Again?"

"Yes. Some new information has come up regarding the case," I added.

She phoned her boss and, a few minutes later, escorted us into the luxurious office of the deputy CEO of Universal Credit Bank. We found him behind his mahogany desk reading something on his laptop, appearing deep in thought.

"What can I do for you?" Larson greeted us, without bothering to get up from his big black leather chair.

"For a start, you can begin telling the truth," I said, sitting sideways on the mahogany desk.

Larson swallowed nervously. "I... I don't understand you."

"Game over, Mr. Larson. We know about the Hollow Skull society," Carlos said.

Larson's face paled. "How — how did you find out about the, uh... secret society?" His voice was practically a whisper.

"We are NYPD, aren't we?" Brendan said as he studied the paintings on the wall. They were landscapes and pictures of beautiful girls, but nothing obscene or erotic. I liked them, too, and they had no occult overtones whatsoever.

"I suggest you loosen your tongue and start telling us about your involvement in that secret society, and Mr. Stone's. Or would you prefer I get a warrant for your arrest?" Brendan stood over him.

Larson cleared his throat and loosened his tie. His hands shook slightly. "Okay, okay: I'll tell you everything, under one condition — whatever I tell you has to stay between us. I'm a public figure; I have a family and children — I don't want my secrets disclosed."

Brendan smiled. "We can't promise any such thing, and you know that. But assuming that whatever you were doing was legal, you have nothing to worry about."

Larson contemplated Brendan's words, then wiped at the droplets of sweat on his forehead. He said, "Daniel and I were members of a secret society — nothing special, we just participated in their swinger parties. I only did it for the sex. The women — oh boy, you have no idea what the women there were like!" he exclaimed. Excitement gleamed in his eyes. The man was quite a hedonist, it seemed.

"I think we can imagine," I muttered. I was familiar with the succubus species. Succubi were the Magic Council's favorite suspects when it came to supernatural sex crimes, and Brendan and I had even hunted a few of them during my gig as an independent consultant.

Mr. Larson cast me a glance and continued with his story. "That was my reason for joining, but for Daniel, the sex wasn't important. He wanted power and magic. Obviously I don't believe in magic and the like, but Daniel — he believed with all his heart. And maybe that's why he met this kind of end." He sighed and shook his head.

"Did Mr. Stone share anything with you about recent developments in his magical, uh... quest?"

Larson's high-pitched laughter resounded in the office like an echo. "His magical quest? Poor Daniel, he was delusional, the poor fellow, just like his magical pals." He snorted, his eyes gleaming with delight as if he enjoyed this whole magical obsession thing. "I can't believe you law-enforcement agents pay any attention to it."

"Daniel's magical pals may be delusional," I said, making sure to keep my expression neutral, "but *they* believe it. And Mr. Stone's murder did have ritualistic aspects, which we need to make sense of in order to get to the bottom of this."

Brendan cleared his throat. "Mr. Larson, we received information from Mr. Stone's girlfriend that, not long before his murder, he met someone who called himself a sorcerer. We think this may be connected to his murder. Do you know anything about that?"

Larson leaned back in his armchair and ran his hand through his graying hair. "A sorcerer? My God, what kind of world are we living in?" he said, more to himself than anything. "Well, I guess I shouldn't be surprised. Daniel and Elliott, the master, believed in higher forces and energies and all that crap. At my initiation ceremony, Elliott told me a bunch of weird stuff, claiming one can release a 'greater power' — which apparently was the reason behind their orgies — but I never really paid attention to any of that."

"How long have you been a member of the Hollow Skull society, and who invited you?" Carlos asked.

"About a year and a half, maybe." Larson's face became thoughtful, trying to remember. "Daniel invited me to join one night when we were having a drink in his office after work. He didn't talk about spells or wizards or anything; he just mentioned hot women and sex, and asked whether I'd like to join. I said, 'Do you even need to ask?'"

"Do you know how long he had been a member of this society?" Brendan asked.

Larson frowned, glancing at the office door. "I have no idea, but I believe it was at least a few years. I believe he and Elliott may have founded the society together."

"What do you know about Elliott Rumford?" I asked.

"Oh, Elliott." Flames of emotion flickered in Larson's eyes. "A real Casanova — he's always surrounded by the hottest girls."

"Mr. Larson, we have no interest in the women surrounding Mr. Rumford, only in Mr. Rumford himself," I interjected. I couldn't take another minute of listening to this disgusting pig. I knew his type very well: back at the Magica Academy, I'd had to deal with lots of men like Larson.

Larson flashed me a smile and said, "Don't get mad, now. I don't want to see a frown on that pretty face. All I know about Elliott is that he's one hell of a tycoon — filthy rich. He's one of the owners of Texas Oil. I don't think he does any actual work there; he probably just goes to the Board of Directors' meetings to vote on the important decisions. Anyway, I asked Daniel once how he'd met Elliott, and he said it had been at an occult meeting in Manhattan. I don't remember any other details."

So Elliott Rumford and Daniel Stone were both interested in the occult and supernatural stuff. What was it with these wealthy men — why did they suddenly want to become wizards? Didn't they have better things to do than fool around playing Harry Potter?

"Mr. Larson, are these symbols familiar to you?" Carlos showed Larson the photo of the sliced skull on his phone.

"Yes, it was the logo of our club. It's ugly, isn't it?" He grimaced.

"And do you recognize this?" Carlos showed him the picture of the horned statuette with the inverted pentagram encircling it.

"No, I've never seen it before. Where did you find it?" he asked curiously, but Carlos put his mobile phone away as fast as he had taken it out.

"Mr. Larson," Brendan said, "I'd like to ask for your cooperation. We need to speak to the master of the Hollow Skull Society — this Mr. Rumford — as quickly as possible."

"I beg your pardon?" Larson hadn't seen Brendan's request coming. He rose from his comfortable leather chair and moved to the huge glass window, staring at the panoramic view of Manhattan. If I worked there, I'd probably take in the view from time to time, too, either for comfort or as a distraction.

"Mr. Rumford's secretary has explained that her boss will not be able to talk to us until next week, perhaps even later. And today is only Tuesday. I'd like you to talk to him as soon as possible to convince him to assist us. I don't want to bother getting warrants or subpoenas. This case must be solved as quickly as possible. Our time is quite valuable, and I'm sure the same is true for you," Brendan said.

Larson turned to us and I smiled at him, applying all my female charm. *Call your buddy,* I thought, concentrating on the thought. Larson sighed and reached for the mobile on his desk. I smiled — this little superpower of mine came in handy, occasionally. Too bad it worked only on humans and only sometimes: I couldn't control or predict when.

The conversation between the two men was short and to the point. Larson explained that we needed to find the killer as quickly as possible, that we knew about their secret society, and that if Rumford didn't talk to us as soon as possible, we'd get a warrant.

"Elliott says to meet him at his Staten Island mansion tomorrow at nine a.m.," he said after he ended the call.

"What's the address?" Carlos asked, his notebook and pen in hand.

"My secretary will provide that. I hope that's enough for you."

"If we need your help further during the investigation, we'll be in touch," Brendan said as we walked out.

I looked at my watch as we left the UCB skyscraper — it was a little after four-thirty. We had the address of the secret society's master and would question him tomorrow. "We have more time today. Do you want to visit the Hellfire Club?"

Carlos and Brendan turned to me in surprise.

"Oh, come on! Isn't that where our victim probably met his sorcerer? Where's your adventurous spirit, guys?"

Brendan glanced at his watch. "It's a bit early — it probably won't get busy for a while yet — but Alex is right. It won't hurt to go to the club."

"I'm glad you agree." I smiled and took a few steps, then hesitated. "Where exactly is this club, and how do we get in?"

"I thought you'd never ask," Brendan said. "Let me have your transport charm." He held out his hand demandingly. I felt the urge to turn my back on him and walk away.

Instead I said, "Here it is." I handed him the small metal container containing the magic substance. Naomi and I called it "fairy dust," although it wasn't really. Fortunately, I'd anticipated his request, so I'd brought more today.

Brendan opened the lid and took a pinch of it.

"Envision the place we want to transport ourselves to," I instructed him just in case: each transportation charm worked differently; some required mental visualizing, others — not. Brendan sprinkled the dust around, and a large glittering silver cloud appeared. Magic began to pulsate in the air around us. I closed my eyes and felt the familiar tug in my chest taking me through the ether.

Chapter 5

We found ourselves in a dingy alley. In front of us, a large neon sign with the words *Hellfire Club* illuminated the dim space. Brownstone buildings loomed on both sides — the club was somewhere in Brooklyn. I took a deep breath of the cool fall air and felt it refresh my lungs.

"So this is the infamous club," I said, just before stepping into a puddle. "Shit. This stupid club is going to ruin my favorite boots." At five hundred dollars, the boots were one of my most expensive accessory purchases — but they were worth it. I loved boots, especially leather ones, as well as all-black leather clothes. This outfit now came very handy: it turned out the Hellfire Club had a particular dress code. When I was working in my bookstore instead of as an independent consultant for the Magic Council, I wore ladylike clothing. In my heart of hearts, though, I preferred the badass outfits.

"With the money the Magic Council is paying you, you can buy a dozen pairs of boots — name-brand, at that," Brendan said.

Yes, if we left out the fact that my bookshop was dead in the water and I had to pay its bills first.

"Brendan mentioned that you run your own business," Carlos said, as he headed toward the glowing sign. I must have been projecting my thoughts without realizing it. "What exactly is it?"

"An occult bookshop. We also sell love potions, spells, enchanted objects, stuff like that. And we offer tarot reading and divination, and prepare all sorts of herbal potions," I replied, following him.

"Cool."

I was about to reply that it *had* been cool until competition had turned up, when a hoarse voice called, "Stop! Identify yourself."

In front of us, at the club's entrance, two centaur guards had appeared as if from the void and stood in our way, crossing two long, sharp spears. Their spearheads shone light purple, indicating enchantment. If we got stabbed by one of them, the consequences would be very unpleasant.

"Um?" I looked around, perplexed — the voice we'd heard certainly hadn't belonged to the centaurs. Peering into the dim space, I finally distinguished a small figure standing next to the centaur on the right — it looked like a leprechaun. The little man looked intently at us, his green clothes and funny hat matching the neon sign above.

"Who are you?" I asked.

"I am Peter Raibach, owner of the Hellfire Club. And who the hell are *you*?" When he spoke, I saw that his teeth were yellowish and sparkling.

"Did you see that?" I whispered to Carlos. "Are all his teeth really golden?"

"I can hear you, young lady," the leprechaun said, annoyance clear in his voice.

Brendan intervened hurriedly. "Excuse me, Mr. Raibach. My partner is new to Manhattan; she's not familiar with the way we do things here. I'm Brendan Sax — a werewolf; my partner Carlos Delvalle is a tiger shifter."

"And the mouthy woman?" The leprechaun directed his gaze at me.

"I'm an elemental mage," I said, raising my chin slightly. I was uncomfortable revealing anything about my magical powers, but I had to get in.

The leprechaun's lips stretched out in a smile. "Good. My mother was a half-mage, too. Well, ma'am, gentlemen, I am delighted to welcome you to my humble club." He nodded to the two centaurs and they lifted their spears, letting us pass through to enter the cryptic club.

"Does he really let people into his club this easily? I thought it was supposed to be secret and strictly guarded. Doesn't he worry that ordinary people can get in here?" I whispered to Brendan as we descended the narrow steps of the winding staircase. He pretended not to hear me, and I cursed him mentally. On the stone walls on both sides hung flaming torches burning with a bluish-green fire, invoking associations of hellfire. My sense of magic told me it was also a protection charm.

After a few moments, Brendan said, "The club is invisible to nonsupernaturals. Besides, its greedy little owner has one of the best noses for magic in all of NYC."

"Interesting fire," Carlos said, staring at one of the torches.

"It must be how the club got its name," I said. "It looks exactly like hellfire."

"Could be. The torches are actually a special protective charm: If someone causes trouble here and tries to escape, they form a fiery net and block the club's exits. It's terrifying. I've seen it a couple of times during investigations."

"Why *did* the leprechaun name it the Hellfire Club?"

"A good question," Brendan said. "But I don't know. Maybe because a lot of dark wizards and supernaturals gather here?"

"They seem to be quite an interesting lot," Carlos remarked. "Do they cause a lot of trouble?"

"Nah, most of them are low- or mid-level supernaturals. But, of course, you have to be careful not to give in to a succubus' charms." Brendan grinned at the tiger, and I rolled my eyes at Brendan.

At the bottom of the long winding stairs we found ourselves in a huge underground hall. Crystal chandeliers hung from the ceiling and lights illuminated the vast space, coloring it in shades of red, green, blue, and yellow. Spaced throughout the hall were several dark brown columns around which ornamental ivies coiled. As we drew nearer to the columns, I noticed runic symbols inscribed on them, and a few carvings of legends and myths about demons and vampires, presumably from the Old World. A hint of magic flowed through them, and my skin prickled. It was dark magic, but nothing too gruesome or abominable. The club was more crowded than we expected, despite it's being only five in the afternoon and still daylight. We weaved our way through the diverse crowd that filled the dance floor, swaying their bodies to the heavy beat. A bit farther down the hall, near the restrooms, I noticed a separate room with a sign above it bearing the inscription *Debauchery*. Making out near the entrance were several couples — and a foursome.

The club's customers were exactly as Brendan had described them — low-level wizards, quite a few vampires, and the occasional succubus. I even thought I spotted a few incubi, though I wasn't sure about that — incubi tended to conceal the nature of their sexual magic from women.

We approached the bar, where the logo of a skull and crossbones was painted very realistically on the bar wall. I asked the bartender for a martini.

"Just a martini?" He smiled at me and I saw his fangs. My magic sense told me he was either a panther or a puma shifter. "We've got Hell's Pleasure, which is very popular with our female regulars, as well as the Devil's Little Joy. Both are with Baileys. Do you want to try one of them, babe — or how about both?"

"Which one would you recommend?" I tried to ignore him calling me 'babe.' I hated when guys did that. Usually, I either kicked them or ignored them completely, but neither strategy was feasible right now, so I gave him a false smile.

The bartender winked at me. "I'll make you the Devil's Little Joy — you'll love it." He poured some alcohol from a few bottles into one glass, mixed the contents, and served me the cocktail. "Cheers, babe!"

I suppressed my frown and tried the drink. It was good, though a bit strong for my taste. "Delicious," I told the bartender. He grinned.

"You're some sort of cat shifter, aren't you?" Carlos asked the bartender, leaning on the counter. "I'm a tiger shifter. Carlos." He held out his hand. "Nice to meet you."

"I'm Norwik — panther. So are you guys looking for anything special tonight? Dark magic? Sex? Whatever you need, I've got you covered." He smiled at us.

"Nah, we're just checking out the supernatural scene here in Manhattan. We're from out of town," Brendan said. "Two beers, please."

Norwik took two bottles from the shelf behind him, opened them, and set them on the counter before Brendan and Carlos. Then he leaned toward the werewolf. "Haven't I seen you here before? You were here about six months ago — you caught a succubus."

Brendan burst out laughing. "Dude, you have a wild imagination. But we are looking for something. Or should I say some*one* — a sorcerer."

The bartender grinned and whispered to Brendan, "For the right amount, I'll tell you everything I know. I've met plenty of sorcerers in this club. I've been working here for over three years and know most of the patrons by heart."

I was just about to protest — I didn't like the idea of paying for information — when a man's deep voice called from behind my shoulder, "New faces! What's your name, baby?"

I turned around and saw a tall, attractive man with chiseled features beaming at me. I felt the rush of hormones heating my belly and cheeks as I blushed. Before I realized it, I was smiling, silly as a teenager, the alcohol making me a bit dizzy and even sillier. Had they put something in my drink? Some strong, dark magic?

"I'm... Maggie," I said, barely remembering the fake names we had agreed on. "And these are my friends, Steve and Johnny. Who are you?"

He leaned against the counter and smiled broadly. "You can call me Roy. So, babe, why haven't I seen you here before? I would have certainly remembered you." His eyes ran up and down my body, and I felt the heat rushing up through it, warming my insides. His magic was intense and devouring, like a delicious dark chocolate or well-aged wine. Instinctively, I licked my lips. "Oh, you know — I'm new to the city, haven't had the time to look around or have fun," I replied, grinning ever so widely. Something about this guy intoxicated me.

"Really? Well, you can have fun with me," Roy said. "Where are you from?"

He was close enough that I felt his magic on my skin — strong and dark, permeating and obsessive, with the additional flavor of beautiful but rotten fruit. His face was only a few inches away from mine, and I couldn't help wondering what it would feel like to kiss him. The voice in my head called, *This is not good, Alex, don't do it!* but I pushed its advice aside.

"We're here visiting from San Antonio," Brendan interjected. "You ever heard of a place called 'the Hollow Skull'?"

"Nope." Roy's eyes never left mine. "Sounds sexy. What brings you here?"

"We're looking for an Elliott Rumford. He was a friend of Daniel Stone. Do either of those names ring a bell?"

Roy dragged his gaze away, and pondered for a minute before shaking his head. "No, sorry. Why? What business do you have with him?"

"We'd like to talk to him," Brendan said.

"Well, good luck then." Roy smiled and directed his attention back to me. "So, baby, are you dating anybody?"

I glanced at Brendan. He had a thunderous expression on his face, which pleased me immensely. "No, I'm single," I replied, and leaned closer to the stranger. His magic alone was an incredible turn-on.

"Good." He leaned over me and smoothed a few unruly strands of hair. "You're beautiful."

All of a sudden I started feeling dizzy, as if I were going to black out.

"Are you all right?" Roy's voice sounded anxious.

"No, she's not all right — why don't you back off?" Brendan said irritably.

"Don't talk about me like I'm not here," I said. "And I can make my own decisions." I took a deep breath and began to feel a little bit better.

"I'm glad to hear that, babe." Roy ran his hand over my waist and lowered his head to kiss me. But before he could do it, I was overwhelmed with a feeling of being in danger, strong enough to make me feel sick. Without even thinking, I instinctively summoned a fireball and hurled it straight into his chest.

He went crashing into the next chair, taking the person who had been sitting on it down with him. I looked at my hand in astonishment — why had I used magic? Something must have threatened me; I hadn't acted deliberately, but rather instinctively in self-defense. And whatever I did had sobered me up.

"Hey, calm down," the bartender said. "Don't attack our clients."

"I have no idea what happened," I muttered. A small crowd of supernaturals gathered around me, Brendan, and Carlos. I could see clear bloodlust in the eyes of the vampires among them, and somewhere among the crowd I spotted a bogeyman. Damn. Supernaturals could get very touchy when their sense of security was threatened, and the fact that we weren't regulars here and that I'd had an uncontrolled magic outburst wouldn't be reassuring to them. If they all suddenly attacked us, we would have a hard time fighting them off.

"What are you? Mages, wizards?" someone asked.

I turned to Brendan, worried, and he gave me a silent sign to stay quiet.

"Wow. That was amazing. I love aggressive women." Roy got back up and started to move toward me, but I backed off and Brendan blocked his way.

"Dude, the lady doesn't want to talk to you. Come on Maggie, we're leaving." He took my elbow and we began working our way through the crowd around us, Carlos following in our wake. Some of the supernaturals watched us suspiciously, and in the eyes of a few others I recognized the desire to attack.

"What the hell happened?" I asked Brendan as we reached the exit.

"I have no idea, but you should know better than to mess with an incubus."

I nodded, embarrassed. Right after my attack somehow brought me to my senses, I'd realized that's what Roy was. *That's* why I was so attracted to him. His raw sexual energy had lit up my libido, making me respond to him, even though I wasn't the type of girl who picks up random strangers at bars. I could only half blame it on that drink.

"What's the plan now? Are we leaving?" I asked.

"We have no choice — your fireball drew attention to us." Brendan opened the door and we stepped outside into the dark alley. "We'd better lie low for a while."

"What? We drop the search for the sorcerer just like that, just because I made a silly mistake?" I asked in disbelief. My emotions were still high after the spontaneous magical outburst, and part of me didn't want to leave.

"I'll drop by again in a few hours," Carlos suggested. "Hopefully, everyone will have forgotten about the accident by then."

"Do whatever you think is appropriate," Brendan said. "I have to go; the Magic Council just summoned me. A piece of advice, Alex: Stay away from any incubi. I don't think they have a good effect on you. And be on your guard; I didn't like the look of those vampires in there. Just keep your eyes open, in case any of them decide to follow you."

I nodded, feeling a little foolish for not having recognized the incubus.

Brendan turned his back without uttering a single word, and strode away down the dark street. I stared at him for a moment before turning to the tiger shifter. "Well, what are we going to do?"

"I think I'm going to go back to my room and take a nap for a couple of hours, then I'll come back around ten. There should be a new crowd by then, and they'll probably be even busier. I think Brendan is right — you should stay away from the club, at least for tonight."

"A nice plan," I grunted. "Well, tonight's not going to be a fun night for me, obviously." I was reaching for the metal container with the transport charm when I heard a cracking noise, and something hit me hard in the back. I crumpled to the ground as my vision went black.

Chapter 6

"Alex, are you all right?" Carlos asked, his voice sounding rough and strained as I came back to consciousness. I was dizzy and my legs had given out at the surprise blow. For a moment, I thought I might pass out again, but I quickly recovered.

"I've been better." I stood up as quickly as I could. My back throbbed — it felt like I'd been struck with a heavy object, maybe some sort of rod. And yet there was no attacker in front of us. The space behind me, though, was glowing slightly.

Then something whizzed by my face, passing inches over my left shoulder as I ducked. I connected with the invisible thread inside my center and a big fireball appeared in my right hand, illuminating the space around me. Two men stood only a few yards away. One wore a fedora hat, tilted low to obscure his face, and carried a large wooden rod. The other was dressed in black leather pants and a hooded leather jacket. That one directed his gaze at the wall behind us, his eyes glowing with a blue brilliance, and the wall exploded.

Sand and gravel swirled in the air and poured over our heads. Great — a telekinetic! I immediately extinguished the fireball in my hand to focus on the more immediate problem, and ducked as several dozen bricks flew past our heads. A few struck us, but more were coming. I summoned the element of air and a gust of wind swished to life on the tips of my fingers. I hurled the wind, and the oncoming bricks were flung back in the opposite direction. Meanwhile, Carlos had transformed into a tiger, his eyes glowing yellow like two burning coals in the darkness.

I summoned fire again and hurled a gigantic fireball at our attackers with all the force I could muster, then seized one of my enchanted knives and flung it too. They ducked the fireball and it missed them by inches, burning the brim of the first guy's fedora, but the knife hit its target. It struck the telekinetic in the upper right arm, near his shoulder, and he cried out in agony.

I called the knife back and the guy screamed again, falling to his knees. In the meantime, Carlos, in tiger form, had flung himself on the man with the fedora hat, who'd dropped his rod in all the commotion. Carlos roared, standing with his front paws on the man's chest. The man's fedora had fallen off, revealing blond hair.

Carlos shifted into his human form and, clutching the man's shoulders, bellowed, "Who are you working for? Who sent you?"

But before the blond could utter a word, the telekinetic focused on a nearby trash can, using his powers to hurl it straight into Carlos's upper back. With a cry of pain Carlos transformed back into a tiger, the better to ease his suffering and help him heal faster.

I instantly began summoning another fireball — this guy was going to pay for hurting Carlos!

In his tiger form, Carlos was already charging the telekinetic, so I went for the blond guy. But the bastard had recovered his rod and now, with a swirl of his hand, he mumbled an incantation in Latin and the rod transformed into a gigantic three-headed snake. It hissed at me, its eyes glowing red with promises of pain and suffering.

I heard the telekinetic guy give a painful cry — I hoped Carlos had bitten him.

But I couldn't take time to check — the snake attacked me, two of its heads lunging for my flesh. I launched into a double flip in the air, but the third head shot out and buried its fangs deep in my left thigh. I screamed in pain, fury washing over me.

The ghoulish creature had just ruined one of my favorite pairs of jeans!

That was it — the last straw. I screamed bloody murder at the snake. It was about to attack me again, but I focused on finishing my fireball. I put all my emotions into it — all the anger, fatigue, jealousy, hatred — everything I'd been experiencing these past few days. It paid off: I hurled the enormous fireball at the snake's heads. Red-orange flames exploded in the air, and Carlos and the telekinetic guy were knocked to the ground. The air filled with smoke and dust, and flames engulfed the surrounding space. I tried to get to Carlos, but the chaos was complete — I couldn't see a thing. A pain seared my thigh from the snake's fangs, and I choked on the dust and smoke. I had to get out of here if I wanted to survive, but I couldn't leave without Carlos. I glimpsed him lying unconscious near a wall, and I headed that way. Debris clouded my vision and fire singed my arms. Just like the three-headed snake, the flames wanted to bite and devour me. I gritted my teeth and connected with the thread in my center: a strong gust of wind stirred within me and I released it against the burning mess around. It quickly extinguished the fire and blew the dust aside. Once the space was clear, I opened my eyes and reached the wall. Next to Carlos was the telekinetic, a trickle of blood running down his cheek; my magic sense told me he wasn't alive. A pity — I'd have loved to beat the crap out of him and learn who had sent the two after us. But it was too late for that.

    I took out the transport charm, sprinkled it around the shifter and me, and visualized the Steaming Cauldron. The air around us vibrated and the familiar magic pull began, taking Carlos and me away from the smoking mess I'd created.

***

Panting and still bleeding, I found myself in our occult bookshop, Carlos lying unconscious next to me. I coughed and took a deep breath of the fresh air in the shop. Only now did I realize just how terrible the air had been in that dark alley that I'd set on fire.

"For magic's sake, Alex, what happened?" Naomi hurried toward us. Thank magic no customers were in the shop. The last thing we needed was to scare off what few clients we still had. Naomi took one good look at us and raced to the shop's front door, turned the sign to 'closed,' locked the door, and rushed back to my side.

"Are you all right? Who's this?" she asked, examining my wound and eyeing the shifter on the floor.

"I'm fine — I'll heal in a few hours at the most. The bleeding's already slowed down. I just have to change my jeans: that'll give me time till my healing powers kick back in and I can do something to help Carlos." I looked ruefully at them — another pair, gone. "This is Carlos. I think I mentioned that Brendan has an assistant investigator? Well, that's him. He's a tiger shifter."

"Is he okay? What happened?" She leaned over him and took his pulse. Once she had reassured herself that he was alive, we moved him to the nearest chair in our shop, behind the cash register. While Naomi tended to his wounds, I went up to my room and changed my clothes. I put on a clean top and an old pair of jeans, which were already faded and frayed at the hems. At least I wouldn't regret it if they also got destroyed.

"So, what happened?" Naomi said when I came back.

I tried to collect my thoughts, which proved difficult. "Carlos and I were outside a supernatural spot for dark magic users called the Hellfire Club, when two guys jumped us. One was a telekinetic, and I think the other one was a dark wizard or something. Maybe a mage, I dunno. He spoke to his rod in Latin and it transformed into a gigantic snake... Oh, I need some water," I panted, my head suddenly feeling extremely heavy. My back didn't hurt too much — honestly, I'd totally forgotten about it, and my healing powers had started to kick in anyway. In less than a week, my powers would reach their zenith with the full moon. My healing was slower than if the moon were full but I would manage.

"Here, I have a better idea." She slipped out of the room while I sank into a chair. "Drink this," she said when she came back, patting me on the shoulder and handing me a mug of some hot herbal concoction.

I took it from her and sipped, no questions asked. It had a slightly weird taste, but I swallowed it nevertheless. "What's in it?" I asked casually.

"Nothing special," Naomi said with a wave of her hand. "Vervain, sandalwood, pine, peppermint, blackberry, and some frog's leg and bat blood."

"What?" I cried, almost choking.

Naomi burst out laughing. "You should have seen your face, Alex! You know I didn't put a frog's leg or bat blood in it," she scolded playfully. "I'm a hedge witch, not a sorceress."

I was relieved. "You scared me out of my wits, girl. Don't joke like that, especially not when I come home exhausted from a fight," I replied.

"I'm sorry, Alex. I didn't mean to upset you. I just wanted to lighten your mood."

I waved my hand dismissively and went to check on Carlos. The explosion had knocked him unconscious and he was injured, but we weren't terribly worried. A shifter's inner animal would protect him from a lot of harm, although it didn't make him invulnerable. My adrenaline and Naomi's concoction had given me an extra power boost, so I decided to use my own powers to help him heal faster. My healing powers worked slowly on me, but they were always faster when applied to others.

I touched the shifter's chest and concentrated. Flickering light yellow waves flowed from my hand to Carlos' skin. I concentrated harder and the healing energy went deeper into his body. Gradually, his chalk-white face regained its natural, healthy color, and in a few moments, he opened his eyes. Seeing me and Naomi, he jumped.

"What happened? Where am I?"

"Calm down, Carlos, you're in my bookshop — I told you about the Steaming Cauldron, right? This is my best friend and business partner, Naomi Mitchell. Naomi — Carlos Delvalle."

Carlos visibly relaxed. He smiled amiably at Naomi and they shook hands, exchanging the usual courtesies.

"It seems I blacked out back there. What happened?" he asked me. "I remember biting the telekinetic guy hard, then an enormous explosion knocked me off my feet. That's where my memory ends."

"I'm responsible for that enormous explosion," I said. "I teleported us here, where it's safe. I caused too much damage and chaos over there."

"Aha." Carlos rubbed his temples and said, "I have to get in touch with Brendan and tell him about the attack. I have the feeling it's linked to our investigation."

"Or it could be that the incubus was somehow involved," I suggested.

"I don't think so, but anything's possible. At any rate, I didn't like that club — something was foul over there, apart from its name. If you'll excuse me, ladies, I'll call Brendan." With these words he stepped over to the shelves near the love potions, leaving Naomi and me on our own.

She turned to me and said, "What's bothering you? I can see there's something."

I frowned. "To be honest, I don't know what to think of that ambush. I guess it could have something to do with the murder we're investigating, but I feel like it's something entirely different."

"Well, you'll figure it out soon enough, I'm sure."

I was pondering the issue when Carlos interrupted my thoughts.

"Alex, Brendan wants to talk to you."

Before I could reply, though, Brendan's all-too-familiar voice sounded in my own head. *"Alex, Carlos just told me about your little adventure."*

"Come on — little?"

"Okay, a big one. Are you satisfied now?" he snapped.

"Not yet, but it's better not to minimize things."

For a second, Brendan remained silent, suppressing the angry outburst which I felt sure would be coming soon. *"Did you get a good look at your attackers' faces? Any impressions of them?"*

"Well, one was a telekinetic and the other was a dark wizard or something. I'm sure Carlos already told you that. The wizard was blond and had a magic rod, and the telekinetic wore a hood. I can't remember anything else."

"Okay, that's enough for now. Get some rest, both of you. Tomorrow morning at six we have a high-profile meeting with the Courts of Heaven and Hell at the Veil — Carlos has the details."

"What the fuck?" I protested, but Brendan had cut off our mental communication. Damned shifters and their supernatural abilities!

"Did you talk to Brendan?" Carlos asked.

"Yes. He cut off the connection just when I was going to ask him about the Veil and tomorrow's meeting, though. What's all that about? Brendan said you'd know."

"Yes. Kai, the chief of the demons, is furious because of his devotee's murder. So he's called a meeting between the Courts and us — the investigators. It seems we're in for a party tomorrow," Carlos said gravely.

"Just when I thought it couldn't get any worse," I muttered.

"I don't want to upset you, Alex, but something tells me more murders are in the cards." Carlos looked at me thoughtfully with his beautiful green tiger's eyes, and I shivered.

Chapter 7

Before falling asleep that night, I tried to imagine the Veil. I pictured it as a posh place decorated in dark colors and filled with magical runes, guarded by dragons or perhaps ferocious three-headed dogs, but I wasn't prepared for what lay in store.

At ten minutes to six the next morning, Carlos and I waited in front of a futuristic-looking glass building located in a quiet Brooklyn neighborhood. A six-foot-tall ogre with a strange tattoo on his neck guarded the entrance, his biceps bulging even through his meticulous suit. He looked at us as if he had eaten glass for breakfast. When Brendan appeared, he showed his Magic Council ID badge and the ogre let us in. Passing by I got the feeling he was made of either steel or marble. His magic felt like massive ocean waves — a tsunami. I understood why the Council had hired him — he seemed invincible. Even I would probably have a hard time winning a battle against him, unless it was during the full moon.

We walked down a narrow, blue-painted corridor. It led us to a magnificent hall, as brightly lit as any splendid aristocratic house. The hall was lined with flaming torches, and in the center of the marble floor rested a large cherry wood table. A few supernaturals sat behind that grand table. Strong, ancient magic hit all my senses. It felt like taking a bath in a magic fountain: every supernatural's power was unique and gave me a different feel or taste, but the one thing they all had in common was potency.

"I didn't expect this," I said to myself., but Brendan nodded at me as we took our seats at the very end of the table with a nameplate bearing the inscription "Magic Council." Farther along the table I saw nameplates for "Court of Heaven" and "Court of Hell"; most of the seats were empty.

I couldn't deny it: I was excited. Never in my life had I attended a meeting between the two most powerful courts in the universe. It was a definite privilege to be here. Many supernaturals would kill to witness such an historic event. Tales of past meetings had become the stuff of legends and myths.

I looked around, examining the large hall in more detail. Runic symbols on the walls emanated extraordinary power which prickled like needles on my skin. Some of the runes were for protection, others for strength and concentration, and a few for peace, mutual understanding, and accord. With the types of supernaturals who were about to gather here, peace and agreement would definitely be needed.

Seated next to me, Carlos asked, "What do you think?"

"I'm dazed, to put it mildly," I replied, still not able to divert my gaze from the runes carved into the walls around us.

Carlos smiled. "I felt the same way the first time I was here."

"How many times have you been here?" I asked him.

"Three, including today."

I was about to ask him about his previous visits to the Veil when the door opened and a dozen supernaturals burst in. The first thing to hit my senses was the taste of the newly arrived creatures' magic: Never in my life had I experienced such a diverse mix. It was as if someone had mixed the gentlest, softest magical vibrations with dark, monstrous, even killing magic — the feeling was unbearable, bordering on insanity, and I tried to turn off or blunt my magical radar. Awen and Brendan had told me that, in times of need, a supernatural could dampen their sense of magic, but I'd never done it before. I lacked the training. Maybe if the moon were full, the strange and unusual powers that manifested within me at that time would protect me, but that was still nearly a week off. I began to feel sick — my heart rate quickened and I nearly fainted from dizziness.

Sensing my discomfort, Carlos whispered, "Connect with your center and imagine it as a shield against the magic around us."

I closed my eyes and connected with the thread inside of me. I felt the ancient magic surging within, more powerful than ever. It built a high wall between me and the supernaturals around us. I immediately felt better — my heartbeat normalized and the tingle in my head disappeared, along with the vertigo. I gave Carlos a thankful smile and he beamed at me. I did like this guy.

"I think everyone is here, so let's get started," said a tall, thin man, dressed all in black, as he took his seat. Although extremely good-looking, something about him repelled me. From behind my protective barrier, I felt his energy — a wild, tumultuous, dark magic. I had never experienced such a strong energy before; even behind my mental wall, my hair stood on end. Something was unsettling about his magic — maybe that was what had made me feel so ill a few moments ago? This man was definitely a demon — their power always had a very negative effect on me — and judging by the strength of his magic, he was a high-ranking one, at that. I knew I was safe, though.

A second man rose from his place next to Brendan — his magic was more potent than average, but it felt nothing like the black-clad man's, and I was relieved. He smoothed his suit down and began to speak.

"I am Tomas Meyer, and I represent the Magic Council. We will serve as arbitrators between the two Courts. We are here at the request of the Court of Hell, to discuss the murder of Daniel Stone. I now give the floor to the Master of the Court of Hell, Kai Hellster." He sat down next to Brendan, and the same tall, thin man in black stood up, his magic power mounting then breaking over me like a tsunami. It was a good thing I had a strong shield up; otherwise, I wouldn't have lasted long in his presence.

"Thank you all for responding to our request to attend today, and thank you to the Magic Council for your prompt response and your efforts regarding this investigation. As I suppose you all know, one of our low-level worshipers — Daniel Stone, the CEO of Universal Credit Bank — was killed the day before yesterday. As the investigators can attest, it was a supernatural murder. The symbol of the Holy Order of Shadows was carved into the victim's chest. Correct?" He turned to our end of the table, and Brendan nodded with an inscrutable expression on his face.

"So." Kai cleared his throat and glanced at the papers in front of him, then continued, "Given the prominence of the murdered human, as well as recent tensions between the demon Sukshmilla and the god Dibba, and — last but not least — the use of the symbol of an ancient order whose mission was to exterminate demons, I believe this murder was ordered by the Court of Heaven."

He had barely spoken the words when a wave of protests filled the room. Chaos reigned for a few moments before the Magic Council's representative rose to intervene. He held up a hand for attention, then spoke. "Master Kai has made a serious accusation, but let's all remain calm. I'm giving the floor to the Mistress of the Court of Heaven, the Morrigan, to address the issues."

Everyone's eyes turned toward the middle of the table, where a tall black-haired woman in silver-white robes sat. I'd rarely seen anyone carry themselves so gracefully and with such dignity as this woman — but 'woman' was a misnomer. She was a goddess, I reminded myself, and I shouldn't forget it.

"Thank you, Tomas." She didn't rise as Kai had done, but stayed in her seat. "If it weren't for the formality of this meeting, Kai, I wouldn't even bother addressing your groundless accusations. It is typical of the demonic nature to create conflicts and strife, but our Court had nothing to do with that lost soul's murder. Moreover, your Court has no evidence to support your allegation."

More commotion and heated comments followed, the loudest coming this time from the Court of Hell. The Magic Council's representative intervened again, and gave the floor back to Kai.

"I'm sure we will find evidence, Morrigan. The Holy Order of Shadows' symbol hasn't been seen for nearly a hundred years, so it stands to reason a supernatural was involved. Since it wasn't one of our ranks, it must have been someone from your Court."

Protests arose from the Court of Heaven. This was reminding me more and more of a ping-pong game.

"Then find the evidence and present it!" the Morrigan replied, a challenge in her voice, once Tomas had established order again. "Your theory is sheer insanity. Why would we want to break nearly one hundred years of peace between our two Courts? Maybe it's you who wants to break the peace." Angry shouts arose from the Court of Hell, but the Morrigan's voice sounded over them. "I say it is more likely that one of your own demons killed the man."

At these words, chaos again erupted. Demons were verbally attacking gods, hurling accusations at them and vice versa. After a few minutes of effort, Tomas established a temporary order.

"Your words alone spell war," Kai growled. His magical energy had intensified and was more powerful than ever. I wouldn't want to cross him for the world, I thought; only a goddess would stand a chance against him. For some unknown reason, in that moment my magic spontaneously tugged at my center, and I had to subdue it. This was unusual. I needed to have that talk with Awen, and soon.

"Isn't it true, though?" The Morrigan's voice soared like a hawk in the stillness of the hall. "The Magic Council has informed me that the victim was a member of an occult club, the Hollow Skull. Any comments, dear?"

I couldn't help but smile at the sarcasm in her voice. Her magic felt very serene and, at the same time, powerful, like ocean waves — gentle and playful, but with the clear impression that they could turn into a deadly storm if need be.

"Yes, Morrigan, *dear,* Daniel Stone was indeed a member of that club, but no evidence so far indicates that he was killed by his fellow members. Isn't that correct, Mr. Sax?" Kai turned to Brendan. Had the question been directed to me, I would probably have stuttered like an idiot in front of all those important supernaturals. Thank magic I wasn't in charge of the investigation.

"The investigation is still ongoing, and we are not ruling anything out. This case is more complicated than it seems," Brendan said.

"Perhaps you need additional help, sergeant, is that the problem?" Kai sneered.

"Kai, you're very rude today," interjected the Morrigan. "First you accuse me and my court of murdering your insignificant devotee, and now you're insulting the man leading the investigation."

"I'm giving you and your petty Court a week, in which time I expect Mr. Sax and his team to solve the murder and find the culprit. And I demand that an independent supernatural help them on this case. It's clear they are not able to handle it on their own," the demon said.

"Oh, you *demand?* Or what?" The Morrigan bared her teeth and magic surged from her, tasting of poison, destructive and ruthless. It hit the protective wall I'd summoned around me and I hoped the meeting would be over soon, that we'd all be safe and sound and the end of the world would be averted. A girl can dream.

"Or I'll assign some of my own staff to investigate the case — and I believe neither you nor the Magic Council will like the results."

"But that would violate the peace treaty!"

"So it would," Kai said, gloating.

Raw magic flashed in the goddess' eyes for a moment, making them gleam with a strange golden light. Then it disappeared as quickly as it had surfaced. "Why are you so obsessed with this murder?"

"As I already said, we think it was a political murder, having a greater purpose and meaning."

The Morrigan sighed. "You're insane, Kai, I'm telling you."

"If that's true, then there's no reason to worry, right? I request you comply. Now." He wasn't begging; he was demanding, as only a demon could.

"I need some time to discuss your request with my court," the Morrigan said.

Kai nodded in agreement, and with that, a magical wall of air rose up to enclose the Court of Heaven and keep their discussion confidential. The conversation lasted not more than a minute or two, and the Morrigan, of course, was the central figure. When they were done, she removed the wall with a glance.

"Kai, we have reached a decision. Given the complexity of the assassination, the Magic Council needs at least fourteen days to solve the murder. We don't mind calling in an independent supernatural to monitor the investigation, but there will be one condition: The Magic Council will choose him or her."

Kai exchanged glances with the demon sitting to his right and accepted the terms.

Tomas Meyer nodded to Brendan curtly and said, "The Magic Council believes the fae Kagan Griffith is the most suitable supervisor for this case."

I recognized the family name — the Griffiths were one of our world's dynastic families. The magic dynasties were families of ancient supernaturals, the most powerful ever to grace the earth. They had immense power over the rest of us magic users, and exerted massive influence on the human world. Of course, the general human populace didn't know they were magical — ordinary humans knew them by their wealth and influence, but thought they were humans just like anyone else.

Kai and the demons didn't mind the choice of Kagan Griffith, but I cast a look at Brendan and could tell he was unhappy. His male ego and sense of authority as the head of the investigation would clearly suffer.

Although I was, like all supernaturals, aware of the Griffith family, I had never heard of this particular member. But just the name 'Kagan' was making my skin pulsate with strange magic. Names, especially supernaturals' names, held vast magic powers; one had to be cautious how and where one used them. For instance, for the sake of the universe, I wouldn't dare mention Kai's name idly.

Kai's lips spread in a grin and he added, "Know, though, that if the culprit is not caught within fourteen days, I will charge a demon with finding the murderer."

"If you violate the treaty, Kai, it can mean only one thing: a war between the two Courts," the Morrigan said quietly.

A strange light gleamed in Kai's eyes, making my hair stand on end. "So much the better," he said. "It's high time for the fun to start."

Chapter 8

Brendan cursed aloud.
We were back outside the building, the meeting between demons and gods concluded. "Oh, come on — it wasn't so bad, was it?" I asked.

Carlos glanced at me skeptically, and Brendan wore his typical discontented look. His brows were knit, and the twitching of his upper lip indicated he was thinking hard. He looked like a storm cloud.

"Great. Just fucking fantastic," he cursed under his breath.

I tried again. "I'm sure this Kagan person will be helpful."

Brendan pushed past me, his eyes gleaming a furious yellow, indicating he'd connected with his inner animal.

From personal experience, I knew that when Brendan was angry it was better to stay out of his way, so I didn't say anything.

It was a little before eight o'clock, so we had an hour until our meeting with Elliott Rumford at his Staten Island mansion. Before then, we had to meet with our new supervisor. The Council, anticipating the need for an independent investigator to join our team, had made arrangements with the fae ahead of time. Tomas had contacted him to inform him of the assignment and to ask that he get started without delay.

I was excited by the prospect: something about his name prickled my skin and made me feel like a six-year-old waiting for Christmas morning.

I glanced at Carlos, who stared ahead vacantly. Brendan stood a few feet away from us. I sensed him having a mental conversation with the Magic Council — I assumed they were giving him details about our first meeting with Kagan Griffith.

He finished and came over to us. "Okay, guys, we're set to meet Kagan at his office on the Lower East Side."

"How are we going?" I asked. "Transport charm, or do you prefer to drive your expensive toy?"

Brendan gave me a dirty look. Trying his best to sound nonchalant, he said, "It's almost eight; better to avoid the rush hour traffic if we want to make our meeting with Rumford. Let's use your friend's teleportation charm."

"Sounds good to me," Carlos chimed in.

"Me, too," I said, "but under one condition: I need some coffee first." I headed down the street and into a small café, the shifters following me.

Over coffee, I thought about my financial situation. When we solved this murder and my gig with the Council ended, could I go back to being a full-time shopkeeper? Or should I ask Brendan for a permanent job with the Council? That would improve my finances, no doubt, but the idea of begging him for work got my panties in a bunch.

Let's solve this case first, then we'll think of what to do next, my inner voice advised me.

A valid point. I tried to relax. The fragrant aroma of coffee and freshly baked cookies filled my nostrils and invigorated me. I glanced at Brendan with mixed feelings. When I first arrived the day before yesterday, I was angry with him because he'd stopped calling me, but now, with this latest turn of events — the investigation we were both part of — I was mollified.

While Brendan and Carlos finished up their coffee and donuts, I pulled out my phone and went online to see what I could learn about Kagan Griffith.

He was owner of Griffith Enterprises, which manufactured and sold steel and iron. Strange — fae were usually averse to iron. But he didn't need to touch it to sell it, so that might explain it. I also learned he was born in Ireland, where his family normally resided, though they had homes in NYC and London as well. That made sense — the fae originated in Ireland, which was the homeland of half the supernatural species.

Once they were ready and we were out of the cafe in a deserted street, I took Naomi's teleportation charm and sprinkled it around. Before that, just in case, I cast an invisibility spell so that no passers-by would notice us. A sparkling silver cloud appeared and we stepped inside of it. Brendan envisioned the place we had to go, the magic grabbed us, and we stepped through the portal in front of an imposing skyscraper.

"Wow! Stunning," Carlos exclaimed. The building looked new, and the suites would probably be in the seven-figure range. A small but beautifully maintained garden encircled the skyscraper and I breathed in the fresh scent of flowers. I took a better look at the surroundings — most of the buildings were relatively new, with their own encircling grass lawns, but the fae's skyscraper really did stand out — it was taller and looked more expensive. The Manhattan Bridge was not far behind us.

"So, was he supposed to meet us here or...?"

"The Magic Council just gave me the address," Brendan replied gruffly.

I let my thoughts drift to the fae we were about to meet, the heir of a magic dynasty. Several of the families held multinational, billion-dollar companies. I'd always wondered what filthy rich people did with all their money. Some of them donated to charity organizations and causes, sure, but they still had a lot of cash to burn. I sighed and wondered how much good karma it took to be born into such a family. Probably a lot.

"Sergeant Sax?" said a male voice. We turned our heads and saw another ogre. This one had softer features than the last, and a multitude of tattoos drew attention to his bulging biceps. "I'm Mr. Griffith's assistant," he introduced himself. "If you'll follow me, I'll take you up to his office." He led us through the building's lobby and into the elevator, and then at the correct floor to the fae's luxurious office suite. The ogre ushered us into a large reception room and left us, closing the door behind him.

I caught my breath.

A very tall man — probably six foot six — awaited us with a muscular, athletic body and chiseled features. He towered above all three of us. He wore a dark gray T-shirt, tight on his perfect body, and I wasn't sure whether the sudden heat I felt came from the sun streaming through the window, or from his looks. What really held my attention, though, was the feel of his magic: it smelled of fragrant spring flowers in full bloom, tasted of fresh early dew, and sounded like roaring wind. No, more like a tornado. This guy was powerful — I wouldn't want to have to fight him, that was for sure. His energy invigorated my senses, caressed and played with my own magic. He was not only smoldering hot, but full to the brim with power: It practically sizzled in the air around him. I instinctively bit my lower lip. His energy felt unusually good — quite the opposite of the incubus I'd encountered the previous day in the Hellfire Club.

"Greetings." He spoke in a sonorous male voice with a mild Irish accent.

"Kagan Griffith, I presume?" Brendan said. He was trying hard, poor guy, but his magic had nowhere near the raw prowess of this fae's.

"That's correct. You must be Brendan Sax." Playful sparkles glowed in the fae's eyes. He clearly enjoyed the effect his magic had on people.

"Yes, I am. These are my partners, Carlos Delvalle and Alexandra Shaw."

Kagan nodded and studied us. When his scrutinizing look rested on me, I felt his magic intensify, pouring over me like an ocean wave. He lit up all my senses and I suddenly felt thirsty for more.

This guy was sure to be a magnet for the ladies.

Brendan cleared his throat and looked at me questioningly — my attraction to the fae must be pretty obvious. I realized I was gaping at him. Or, to be more accurate, I was straightforwardly ogling him.

"Uh, I apologize for staring — I've never met someone from one of the magic dynasties," I managed to stammer.

He smiled, and I figured he must often experience situations like this.

"Please, take seats so we can discuss the case and make plans," Kagan said. We obeyed, sitting on an enormous sofa, soft to the touch and quite comfortable.

"So, how far have you progressed with the investigation? The Magic Council filled me in briefly, but I'd prefer it if you acquaint me with the details yourselves," he said.

"To be honest," Brendan began, "we haven't progressed much. We know that the victim, Daniel Stone, was a member of an occult club, the Hollow Skull, and had participated in orgies, and that shortly before his death he'd also met with a mysterious sorcerer. He had an interest in dark magic, which was why he was a member of that club. Probably nothing too serious, just orgies and debauchery, but we have to follow the lead anyway. It is quite possible that this sorcerer might have been the killer, or at the very least known the perpetrator. The murder was clearly a supernatural one — we all felt a powerful dark magic lingering at the crime scene — and it's possible Stone had company that night. If that were the case, whoever he was entertaining might have been the killer, but we have no way of knowing if anyone was even there. There are dozens of plausible scenarios," he finished. "It's all very shady and unclear."

"What about the sign of the Holy Order of Shadows?" Kagan asked. "The Court of Hell is on fire because of it. No pun intended."

"It seems to me they're just looking for excuses," I said, "and that sign is a good one. I doubt it's a genuine clue. If you ask me, the culprit wanted to divert attention from his true identity."

"Why do you think so?" Brendan asked me.

"It seems almost certain that the perpetrator knew the victim — there were two glasses of wine and no sign of force or someone breaking into Stone's office. This mysterious symbol seems like a distraction — anyone investigating the murder will focus on it, and might not look too closely at Stone's circle of friends."

"That makes sense to me," Kagan said. "Since we don't have much to go on, this case may be a challenge. What are your plans for today?"

"We're going to Staten Island to question Elliott Rumford," Brendan said. "He's the president of the Hollow Skull, the occult club I mentioned."

"Interesting. Humans have started to show great interest in otherworldly matters and the paranormal lately. What do you know about this Rumford?"

"Not much. Only that he's stinking rich and interested in the occult," Carlos said.

I added, "I did some research on him last night, and the victim's girlfriend told us a bit about him yesterday. He's chairman of Texas Oil, a billion-dollar corporation; he's thirty-nine years old, divorced, with no criminal record. He's a very generous man — he's donated tons of money to various charitable causes. He lives in a mansion in Staten Island, which reportedly cost him ten million dollars." I'd been feeling quite excited about the meeting at the Veil, so I had decided to research some of the leads from the previous day

— not that they were any direct help at this point in our investigation.

Carlos smiled. "Good work."

Kagan grinned. "I like working with you guys already. Being a supernatural investigator has always been one of my favorite activities."

"Don't jump to conclusions," Brendan murmured, and eyed Kagan suspiciously, mistrust written over his face. Watching these two interact would be more interesting than any TV show.

I smiled and took out my transport charm. I was about to hand it over to Brendan when Kagan forestalled me. "There's no need to use your charm. I'll take care of the transportation."

Then he connected with his magic, unleashing it. It felt simultaneously gentle yet strong, subtle yet persistent. The air around us vibrated with yellow-white light, then grew into a big swirl that took us through the ether and into the void.

**

The swirl of magic deposited us in front of a lavish four-story mansion of white limestone with a marvelous lawn, worthy of a royal summer residence.

"That was impressive. How did you do that?" I said to Kagan. He hadn't used any charms or spells, not even an incantation.

He shrugged. "It's fae magic. For the record, though, I know the mansion; it's one of the largest in the area — on the whole island, in fact. I knew exactly where I had to transport us."

"Impressive," Carlos muttered.

"Yes, it certainly is," I said, still looking at Kagan. I had known a few fae, of course, but never had I witnessed a display of their magic prowess.

This is good, Alex. Watch this guy closely. You can learn a few things from him, the voice in my head advised.

"No, I meant the hedge and the figures in it." Carlos pointed at the topiaries that surrounded the garden and the different figures cut into them: a horse, a dolphin, the sun, and many other similar symbols. The hedge was tall, about five feet high, but well trimmed, and the grass below was perfectly maintained.

We took the path leading to the mansion doors, and for a few moments I was transported to another world. Images of people dressed in clothes from the twenties and thirties and the atmosphere of jazz parties filled my mind. They were laughing, chatting idly, and dancing. This mansion had a history and I was peeking into it.

This gift only manifested occasionally: I could see the pasts of places, objects, or even of people. Of course, as with all my magic, it was most powerful at or close to the full moon. I had no idea why the gift had kicked in now, when the moon was just past the first quarter. Then it dawned on me — perhaps it was because of the fae's potent magic. I had noticed that when close to a very powerful supernatural like Awen, my powers increased and intensified.

"Alex, are you all right?" Brendan's voice took me out of my reverie.

I shook my head to clear it, pushing away the mansion's memories, and replied, "Yes. Sometimes I can see into the past, and it happened just now — I saw this place as it was in the nineteen twenties."

"Wait, what? You have the ability to see into the past?" Carlos asked incredulously.

"Sometimes; it's unpredictable. It isn't usually this powerful, though, especially when the moon isn't full."

Kagan fixed his gaze on me for a few seconds, and I felt a surge of heat seething inside of me. His magic caressed mine gently, trying to draw it out, but I resisted and pushed it away. He frowned and commented thoughtfully, "Hmm. I'll figure you out eventually."

I flashed a skeptical glance at the fae. This was going exactly where it shouldn't. Of course, I was flattered and thrilled by his attention — what girl wouldn't be? — but I didn't like drawing the attention of such a powerful supernatural. Awen's words echoed in my ears, telling me I shouldn't reveal my true colors to strangers; it was dangerous. I trusted his judgment. I began to regret taking this job.

"Here we go, guys," Brendan announced when we'd climbed the dozen steps to the mansion's front door. The oak door alone looked like it had cost a small fortune. "Let's drop the idle chatter —

we'll have plenty of time for that later. We need to focus on questioning Rumford."

"Got it, chief," Kagan said dryly.

Brendan glanced at him and pressed the buzzer. After a moment a butler opened the door. Brendan introduced us, and said we had an appointment with Elliott Rumford.

"Yes, of course. Mr. Rumford is expecting you. This way, please," the butler said. Entering the house, we found ourselves in a black-and-white tiled corridor, like a gigantic chessboard. The servant led us through huge halls hung with opulent chandeliers, worthy of the French elite. The walls boasted portraits of aristocrats with old-fashioned clothes dating back to the eighteenth and nineteenth centuries.

The butler stopped in front of a dark mahogany door and knocked. We heard a muffled "Yes," and he opened the door, ushered us in, and introduced us to his master.

Elliott Rumford nodded curtly, and the servant left the room as quietly as a mouse.

A second man also occupied the room, with a pen in his hand and a notepad on his lap. I concluded he was Rumford's lawyer. The room itself was relatively small and cozy, holding a desk with a laptop on it, a fireplace on one side, a few chairs, and a sofa against the wall. Elliott Rumford stood up and came over to greet us. He looked to be around forty, with a beautiful, oblong face and cold blue eyes. For a second, a blade gleamed before my eyes, then was replaced by a stack of money. The vision made me feel like vomiting.

I hated these sudden visions — they threw me off balance, coming spontaneously like that, without even the smallest warning or sign.

"Alex, are you okay?" Brendan took my hand and turned to Rumford. "She needs water."

Rumford pressed a buzzer on his desk and requested a bottle of water, and in only a few moments a young woman appeared and handed it to me. Strangely enough, I sensed magic. Was it possible that Elliott Rumford was a supernatural? When I took the bottle the girl handed me, I glanced at her and caught my breath. She was definitely non-human. I looked at my colleagues and exchanged glances with the shifters, who nodded in confirmation.

Staring at the girl, I could feel her magic tempting me, raw and enticing. It took me a few seconds to realize she possessed sexual magic. I caught an amused look on Kagan's face. She was definitely a succubus. But what the hell was she doing in here?

"Are you feeling better, miss?" Rumford hesitated. "You seem... confused. Is everything all right?"

I cleared my throat. "Yes, I'm much better, thank you."

Rumford nodded to the woman, and she left the room. Odd — despite his interest in the occult, he seemed unaware he had a succubus working for him, living under his roof. If he did know, then he was a marvelous actor, but he didn't strike me as the type. He seemed to have a cold, calculating personality, and judging by the quick vision I'd experienced, he'd probably committed some crime to climb up the financial ladder.

Rumford introduced us to his lawyer, Mr. Weber.

"So what can we help you with, inspectors?" the attorney began. "My client is rather pressed for time, so we'll appreciate it if we can get through this quickly."

"As you know," Brendan began, "we're here to question your client about Daniel Stone's murder. How long had you two been friends, Mr. Rumford?"

Rumford thought for a moment before saying, "For quite some time. I met Daniel through UCB, where I was a client. We clicked and started hanging out, practicing sports together — tennis, soccer, that sort of thing. We didn't become very close until the past few years, though."

"Did the two of you share any other interests?"

The lawyer and his client exchanged quick glances.

"Well, we were both members of a club named The Hollow Skull," he replied somewhat hesitantly.

"What about the club's occult purpose?" Carlos asked.

Rumford chuckled a bit nervously. "I wouldn't describe our society as 'occult.' We're just a bunch of intellectuals who gather to play cards and drink whiskey. Sometimes we discuss politics and similar matters, but that's all."

He was definitely lying, though he was good at it: he maintained eye contact and didn't hesitate or flinch. I wasn't surprised. He was the occult club's president, after all; he had to have practice in keeping his cool.

"Right." Brendan suppressed a frown. "But according to Larson, you and Mr. Stone were interested in supernatural matters."

"I'm afraid the poor man is delusional. Perhaps he was in shock, confused after the murder. As I said, my club is quite boring and ordinary."

"Is this also delusional, Mr. Rumford?" Carlos had taken out the sliced skull statuette. It seemed to me Rumford's face paled a shade, but he regained his composure quickly.

"That is mine, yes. My ex-wife bought it in South America — Peru, I believe. The indigenous tribes use such statuettes for protection against evil spirits and the like."

We all exchanged looks — the bastard was on his guard and clearly didn't intend to reveal anything to us. This would be as hard as we thought.

"Do you know whether Mr. Stone was interested in the occult?" I asked.

He darted a look at me. He contemplated a second before replying, then looked straight into his lawyer's eyes and nodded curtly.

Mr. Weber said, "My client can't comment on Mr. Stone's private life and interests, detectives."

"Mr. Stone's girlfriend, Christina Ricoletti, said that shortly before his death, Mr. Stone had been obsessed with dark magic and had met some sort of a sorcerer."

Elliott Rumford chuckled. "You mean someone actually convinced Daniel he was a sorcerer? I didn't think Daniel was so gullible."

"Where were you on October fifth between ten and eleven p.m., Mr. Rumford?" Brendan asked.

A faint smile tugged at the corner of his mouth. "I was in a restaurant — Gatto Nero — at a business meeting."

"Can anyone confirm it?" I asked.

"The restaurant staff, I suppose, and Laura Clark, the colleague I met with."

"Mr. Rumford, this is a serious matter. Needless to say, we won't be happy if you're hiding important information or impeding the investigation into Mr. Stone's murder. I'm asking you once more, Mr. Rumford: Do you know anything at all about the victim's occult inclinations?"

"As much as I'd like to help you, I'm afraid I cannot. I've already told you everything I know. Now, if there is nothing else I can help you with, you'll have to excuse me. I have some work to do."

He was definitely lying, but why? Was he afraid to say what he knew, or was he trying to cover for the culprit?

"You're lying, Mr. Rumford," Brendan said quietly. He leaned forward, his eyes gleaming the light-yellow shade of his inner animal.

Elliott Rumford cringed slightly. "I've told you everything I know, inspectors. I must ask you to leave my property at once," he said adamantly.

"You must be making a hell of a lot of money, aren't you?" Kagan intervened. Until now, he had stayed silent and watched Brendan lead the questioning, with Carlos's occasional intervention.

Rumford was taken aback. "I don't see what that has with Daniel's murder."

"Mr. Rumford, I am Kagan Griffith, chairman and CEO of Griffith Enterprises. In case you're asking yourself what the hell am I doing here — and you are — I add color to my everyday life by helping the police. I have no idea why you're lying to us or what you're hiding, but if you don't start talking and tell us everything you know about Daniel Stone, I promise you will regret it. Now, what else do you know about Stone's murder?"

Kagan walked toward Rumford as he talked, and now leaned toward him slightly over the desk. His potent, ancient magic pulsated tangibly in the air around us, giving me goosebumps. It felt like a thunderstorm brewing. I looked at Carlos and Brendan, and saw them on alert, their senses sharpened, ready to attack at any moment should the need arise.

"Very well." Elliott Rumford rested his hands on the desk, but his attorney intervened.

"Elliott, I strongly suggest — "

"Shut up, Max." Rumford took a deep breath and turned to us. "I'll tell you everything."

We all nodded and Rumford continued reluctantly. "Okay, you're right. The Hollow Skull is an occult club, but we haven't done anything illegal. There's no dark magic, no sacrifices — not even animal ones, for that matter. Daniel joined our club a year or so ago, along with the deputy CEO, Jamey Larson. During the last month or two, though, Daniel was asking me a lot of questions about sacrifices and dark magic. He found some books about it and really got a bee in his bonnet. I know such things exist, but I've never wanted to get involved — it's too dangerous. Frankly, it scares the shit out of me. I tried to dissuade Daniel, but he wouldn't hear a thing. Even his stupid girlfriend talked to him, but he wouldn't listen to anyone."

He took a deep breath and sighed, then continued, "So about two weeks ago he mentioned he'd met a sorcerer. He never told me his name — he said 'names are very powerful' — but he kept calling him the Rune Keeper."

"The Rune Keeper," Kagan repeated, thoughtfully. The name didn't ring a bell with me.

"And that's pretty much everything I know. From what Daniel told me about this guy, the sorcerer, it freaked me out. He was talking about revolution, a totally new occult society, glorifying demons and the dark side. He sounded like a zealot, to be honest. I didn't know how to keep him on the right track."

"In that case, it seems you had a motive to kill him — to get rid of him and his obsession with dark magic," Kagan mused.

"Don't be ridiculous. Why would I tell you this, if that were the case? It would be cutting my own throat."

"Did Mr. Stone tell you where he'd met this sorcerer?" Brendan asked, rejoining the conversation for the first time since Kagan took control of it.

"No, he didn't. But I believe it might have been at the Hellfire Club."

The Hellfire Club again! First we were attacked there, now the sorcerer turned up in connection to it. But one couldn't help but wonder how Daniel got in the club in the first place. I exchanged looks with Brendan. We'd have to go back there immediately and dig up all the information we could.

"And how did he find his way to the club? From what I understand, it's a very exclusive venue," Kagan said.

Rumford's eyebrows drew together as he thought. "I think... Daniel mentioned once having visited another occult club — some kind of Wiccan coven or something." He put his hands on his head, as if to help him remember. "This is all a bit too much for me. You may not believe in supernatural powers, but I'm convinced they exist. I've never wanted to meddle with them, though. I treated it like a parlor game, but when Daniel started getting deeper into it, I got nervous." He looked up, meeting my eyes. "Daniel invited me once to attend a meeting with him, but I didn't want to get involved. Maybe he would still be alive if I had gone with him."

"There's no point in blaming yourself. What's done is done," I replied.

"What was the name of that Wiccan coven?" Brendan asked.

Rumford shook his head. "I'm sorry, I don't remember. I'm not good with names. However, I have the feeling he got his books from there. He must have — I can't imagine where else he could have gotten them." He thought hard for a few seconds, then added, "Maybe I should have gone to that Hellfire Club too, to get to know that sorcerer. But I was — and still am — afraid of all that supernatural stuff. You know, the past few times Daniel and I got together, he seemed different, and not in a good way. He was starting to scare me."

He sounded sincere and we all felt it.

***

As we passed through the hallways on our way out, we saw another maid cleaning one of the large rooms; by the magic I felt inside her, she was a succubus as well. She caught my gaze and looked at me intently. I looked away, burying my magic deep down inside of me, and continued walking down the black-and-white corridor.

"Well, we got off to a rocky start but at least we managed to get some information out of him," I said once the butler had shown us out.

"Yeah. I thought it was going to be a dead end until Kagan threatened him. Good job, by the way," Brendan said.

The fae nodded to him.

"He was trying to play the innocent because of the Hollow Skull's orgies," Brendan remarked.

"There were strong sexual vibrations in the air," Kagan agreed. "They attract the succubi, and then the sexual vibrations compound. You know, the law of attraction." He looked at me and smiled.

Why the hell was this guy staring at me?

"I think you felt it too — or, rather, saw it. I'm very interested in your ability to read environments and places. Only the most exceptionally powerful supernaturals can do so. I see you're one of the few who can."

"What are you talking about?" I stopped in my tracks and turned to face him. This guy was up to something. I had always known I was different, not merely an elemental mage as I claimed to the outside world. If he knew something more, I wanted him to tell me. For magic's sake, I was almost twenty-five and still didn't know my heritage! I had the right to know about my real magic.

"Easy there, lass. I'm just making an observation, nothing more. That's why they've assigned me, after all — to supervise your investigation." He smiled and walked past me.

"I suggest we all head to the Hellfire Club and look for that mysterious sorcerer. We need some answers from him," Brendan said.

We looked expectantly at Kagan, thinking he would teleport us. But he had stopped in the middle of the lawn and his face took on a serious expression. I knew that look very well: Brendan wore it, too, when he was communicating with the Magic Council. We tactfully moved aside and left him alone.

I studied the beautifully maintained roses and violets in the garden. The energy here was quite gentle and innocuous, a strong contrast to the predatory sexual magic that prevailed inside the mansion. There was a lot of debauchery at the Hollow Skull parties, no doubt. I let my thoughts wander freely, taking in the opulent nature of the landscape around us.

In a few minutes, Kagan rejoined us.

"What's up with the Council?" Carlos asked.

I glanced at Brendan — he had a grumpy expression on his face. It must have wounded his pride that he wasn't the leader of our investigation any longer, and that the Council didn't communicate with him first. I hoped his ego wouldn't make him do or say anything stupid. In many cases, alpha males like him have large, fragile egos.

"Bad news, indeed," Kagan said, making me forget about Brendan's ego. "There's been another murder. Just like Daniel Stone's."

Chapter 9

"What?" I exclaimed. Even though Brendan and Carlos had both hinted this might happen, I was still surprised. The two shifters exchanged worried glances as well. This whole case was heading steeply downhill and a dread feeling settled in the pit of my stomach.

"What in magic's name is going on?" Carlos said, solidifying my premonition.

"I don't like this. I don't like it in the least," Brendan said, more to himself than any of us. I could tell he was agitated: His eyes had acquired the light yellow color of his inner animal, and the taste of magic radiating from him was like waves just before a sea storm.

"The victim is a homeless man this time. He was killed in a back street of one of the poorer districts in Queens. No witnesses, and the sign of the Holy Order of Shadows is on this victim's chest as well."

"We have to put an end to this," Brendan said. His jaw clenched and he balled his right fist. His eyes also began to gleam in their peculiar yellowish light when he got high on emotions or in danger.

"I wholeheartedly agree," Kagan said. "It sounds like the Courts of Heaven and Hell are on the worst terms since the Second World War. Alex and I will go to the crime scene, and you two should go to the Hellfire Club."

"I beg your pardon?" Brendan raised his voice and I felt my heartbeat speed up. I hadn't expected him to do something stupid so soon!

"Alex and I will go to the crime scene, and you two should go to the Hellfire Club," Kagan repeated, as if Brendan actually hadn't heard. "We have to manage our time wisely, and act quickly. There's no need for everyone to be at the new crime scene or see the victim. Two people are more than enough for that."

"But it's too early for the Hellfire Club. It won't even be open yet."

I glanced at my wristwatch — it showed almost ten a.m. Brendan was probably right.

"Then stake it out," the fae said. "I want to know what's going on over there. This club has come up in several of your lines of questioning, always connected with some mysterious sorcerer. Someone needs to watch that place closely."

"In that case, let Alex accompany Carlos, and I'll go with you. I insist."

Kagan tilted his head. "Alex is going with me."

"I am a senior investigator of the Magic Council." Brendan stood his ground, coming over to the fae and looking him straight in the eyes.

"And I'm in charge of this investigation. Now go, before I ask to have you replaced." Kagan waved him away negligently. The fae was getting slightly annoyed, and I knew I didn't want to see him really angry. Bearing in mind his powerful, ancient magic, I imagined his outburst would resemble a volcano, or a dragon breathing fire.

Brendan didn't move, and they stared at each other intently. The werewolf looked ready to attack at any moment.

I didn't want to see him make a total fool of himself. Kagan *would* replace him if he didn't go now. "Brendan, don't be an ass. Do what he says."

Startled, Brendan looked at me, and that broke the tension between him and Kagan. With a sour face, Brendan let his shoulders drop. "Give me the transport charm, then."

I did, and the fairy dust took them through the void.

"That was a bit difficult," the fae commented. "Is he always like this?"

I shrugged.

"I thought so. Why did I bother asking?" he said, more to himself than to me. "Okay, never mind. Let's get to the crime scene." He concentrated and his magic intensified, creating a vibrating field of power around us. I heard an ancient rhythm, and magical runes seemed to pulse in silver-yellowish light in the air. A vortex appeared and grabbed me by the waist, and I heard myself yelp before I disappeared into the void.

***

The magic spat us out on a miserable street in a poor part of town. All sorts of noises reached our ears, from rap music and jangling kitchen utensils to the chatter of police radios. I saw a couple of police cars, and braced myself for what I was about to behold.

"Ready?" Kagan asked, standing next to me.

Was he reading my mind? But he didn't wait for an answer, merely smiled and began walking toward the crime scene. I had to rush to catch up with him.

We crossed an intersection and saw, on the right side of the sidewalk, the familiar yellow crime-scene tape. A group of police officers stood around the body. When Kagan and I came close enough, one of the officers stopped us, but Kagan showed his ID. It was an enchanted NYPD badge and worked the same as Brendan's, casting a glamour so that whenever a human police officer saw it, they would believe we were detectives assigned to that particular case, and let us pass.

"Hello, Lieutenant Griffith," the officer said, respect evident in his voice.

"What do we have so far?" Kagan asked as we approached the corpse. The flavor of magic reached my senses — it was the same as at the first murder scene, a very distinct dark magic. This was sorcery, as clear as day, and in that instant I knew both murders had been committed by the same perpetrator. The pit of my stomach tinged and I resolved to catch the murderer before he killed again.

One chubby middle-aged cop heard the fae's question and turned to us. "Apparently, the victim has been homeless in Queens for years. We have to wait for the coroner's report, but it looks like he was stabbed in the chest. No one seems to have seen or heard anything. We're looking over the footage from surveillance cameras to see what we can find." The cop hesitated before adding, "Some kind of symbol is carved into the victim's chest."

"Do we have a time of death?" Kagan pulled out his cell phone and snapped a picture of the victim's face.

"Probably in the early hours of the morning. The body was discovered around half an hour ago — it was hidden in a dumpster. After we get the autopsy results, we'll know more."

"All right. Call me when the medical examiner's findings are in," Kagan told the policeman and handed him a business card. The cop glanced at it and nodded, then Kagan turned and headed quickly down the street.

"Wait, where are you going?" I called after him and had to scurry to catch up with him yet again.

"I want to question any other homeless people in the area," he replied, still pacing forward and looking around.

"The cops probably already have, or are working on it. Can't we just ask them?"

"I prefer to question them myself. I have my own methods."

"Even if we find anyone, do you think they'd have any information?"

"It can't hurt to try. I find it particularly strange that no one has seen or heard anything. I would imagine the poor man screamed blue murder."

About three blocks later, we saw a few beggars sitting on the sidewalk. One of them, a woman who appeared to be in her forties, was drinking beer and speaking to one of the others, a man.

"Oh, what do we have here?" the woman said, raising her hoarse, husky voice and then cackling with insane laughter. She seemed to be as nutty as a fruitcake and looked like a hag, but had no trace of magic. I didn't like the feel of her energy, but at least she was a human. If she'd been a supernatural, she would probably have been a pretty nasty witch.

"Spare some change?" One of the men beside her stood up and came over to us. He was almost six and a half feet tall, about the same height as Kagan, and burly.

"Lieutenant Griffith. Officer Shaw and I are investigating the death of a man who we believe lived around here for quite some time. He was killed early this morning. Did you know him?"

Kagan held out his phone, giving the man a glimpse of the picture of the victim.

The big man froze on the spot, then grunted, "I don't do no business with cops. I don't know nothing," and walked away. The woman, however, smiled at us, showing blackened and broken teeth.

"I'll talk to you — in exchange for a dollar or two."

I glanced at Kagan. Chances were she knew nothing, and besides, who knew how reliable she was? But Kagan ignored my look and showed her the picture.

"Do you know what he was doing last night? Or did you notice anything unusual in the small hours?" the fae asked her.

She gave another bellow of insane laughter and said, "I might know or I might not. Who knows?" The woman clasped her hands, her eyes gleaming with delight.

I pulled Kagan aside and whispered, "Leave her — I seriously doubt she knows anything. She's completely nuts."

"Well, a little bit of charity won't hurt, will it?" he replied in a low voice, and turned to the woman, taking out a ten-dollar bill out of his pocket. "Will this help you remember?"

She licked her lips and reached to take the bill, but Kagan drew back his hand, keeping the bill out of her reach. "Uh-uh. First you tell us what you know, and then you get your reward."

She swore, then reluctantly said, "His name was Craig — at least that's what we called him. Poor guy — he'd lost his memory, didn't remember anything about his past life. Anyway, we fucked now and then." She laughed again, and Kagan urged her to continue with her story.

"Last night, though, he took off somewhere, said he had some business. Simon was looking everywhere for him. Never did find Craig, but he found a couple of boxes full of food dumped about five blocks from here, over on Brown Street. He called Larry" — she pointed at the tall man — "and told us to come over and eat up. So we weren't around here last night."

"Called him? You have mobile phones?" I asked in disbelief.

"Honey, *everybody* has a cell phone," the woman said with a chuckle.

"That's not of much interest to us." Kagan glanced at me and went on, "At what time did you go over to Brown Street?"

She thought hard for a few moments before answering. "After midnight. Probably around one."

"And that's all you know?" I asked, my disappointment clear in my voice.

"Shh," Kagan said, then handed the woman the bill. "You earned your money," he said, and motioned for me to follow him.

"Are you nuts? She lied — she said she knew something but she didn't know anything at all," I snapped when we had moved away, leaving the woman with her reward.

"I beg to differ. We know now that Craig left his friends for some reason. Maybe the culprit lured him away with either money or food, and then, when one of the homeless guys went to search for him, distracted the rest of the group with a few packages of food."

I didn't know what to say. I hoped Brendan and Carlos would have better luck in uncovering something of interest to the investigation. That thought had just crossed my mind when Kagan stopped in his tracks, his face sterner than it had been a moment before. I'd seen this look twice today; it meant he was receiving a new mental message, either from the Council, or from Brendan or Carlos.

Chapter 10

Kagan told me the call was from the Council and he had to go, so I joined the shifters.

Brendan and Carlos hadn't seen anything of significance. They'd arrived at ten-thirty, and kept an eye on the premises until the establishment opened at noon, just before I arrived. Except for the bartender and a few drunken low-level wizards, no one else was in the club. The club wasn't as impressive as in the evening; there were no sparkling lights on the ceiling, and the runic symbols looked dull. Everything seemed very different — almost ordinary.

A different bartender was on duty. He was a mage too, though a weak one. The shifters had already questioned him about the sorcerer known as the Rune Keeper, but he claimed he had never heard the name before.

In the late afternoon, much to my relief, we went to get lunch at the Lucky Leprechaun; I was famished and I ordered a pizza Margherita, a magic pastie, and a few magic raw bars. Even Brendan stared at me in disbelief as I devoured all this food — as a werewolf he could devour lots of food but wasn't accustomed to seeing me eat that much. He also asked about the new murder, of course, and I described everything Kagan and I had seen at the crime scene.

"So it seems like the same culprit," he said thoughtfully and sipped his beer.

"I'm afraid so," I agreed.

On our way out, Brendan questioned some of the supernaturals in the restaurant about the Hellfire Club, but with no luck — the clientele was entirely different. Only one witch said she'd been there, but she hadn't ever heard of the Rune Keeper.

We went back to the Hellfire Club, and soon the fae joined us.

For the next few hours now we sat in the club, watching and occasionally chatting with the growing number of supernatural patrons. Brendan was still in a shitty mood; I knew Brendan very well and his face told me everything. Although he would never have admitted it, my ex had a fragile ego — yet another reason not to be dating him anymore — and having Kagan boss him around drove him crazy.

The fae was also under pressure from the Council, just as Brendan had been; they'd contacted him mentally to inquire how the investigation was proceeding, and wanted him to check in three times a day. The stark neon lights in the hall made my eyes hurt and gave me a mild headache. Something about this place — aside from the name — was deeply hellish.

By eight p.m. the club was packed. A dozen vampires were here — their fangs showing while they conversed with each other or with other customers — as well as incubi and dark wizards; but I didn't see any sorcerers. One vampire came over, probably to flirt with me, though he would have been disappointed. He definitely wasn't my type. I was about to tell him to get lost when Kagan intervened, and asked if the vampire knew of any sorcerers here.

"Are you fucking kidding me? I'm a vampire. We're not the most social of species, if you know what I mean." His eyes gleamed a deeper reddish color. When a few of his buddies approached us, the fae repeated the question to them. The reply, as I expected, was negative. The vampires, however, seemed determined to talk to me, and two of them ordered me a martini.

"Now look what you've done," I scolded Kagan under my breath. "How are we going to get rid of them? If I don't drink it they'll be pissed off."

He chuckled and said, "Just watch."

Moving nearer to the vampire who had first spoken to me, Kagan put his hand on the monster's shoulder and, concentrating hard, connected with his magic. I felt it too: Potent and ancient, like songs about dragons or forever-lost old worlds, but this time quite soothing, like a lullaby or rhythmic ocean waves at night. It calmed my strained nerves. The fae exchanged only a few words with the vampire before the latter nodded, his energy and the expression on his face completely changed. He went away, his cronies in tow.

"Wow, impressive," Carlos muttered. "Good job, bro."

"A piece of cake," Kagan said. "I like this place, actually. It's rather fun here. It reminds me of Michael Jackson's 'Thriller.'" His eyes gleamed in the dark blue-brown light of the club. "Most of the magical creatures here are mediocre, but together their powers become strong."

Weird, I thought.

Kagan turned to me and said, "I know you like me, Alex." He smiled at me.

Hell! He really *could* read my mind!

"Good news. The bartender we talked to last time came on shift," Brendan said, interrupting my surprise. Heading to the bar, he said, "Hey, dude, how's it going?"

The bartender's face lit. "Ah — the fellow with the lady who blasted Roy!" He glanced around and saw me. "If you're looking for him — "

Brendan cut him off. "No, we're not looking for him. We're looking for a sorcerer who goes by the name of the Rune Keeper. Does that ring a bell for you?"

"Depends on how badly you want to know," the bartender chuckled, showing his teeth. "I'm a hard-working guy. As we discussed yesterday, I'm happy to share my wisdom with you — in exchange for a small monetary reward."

"Is a thousand dollars enough?" Kagan took out a wad of hundred-dollar bills and put several on the bar. The bartender's eyes gleamed with excitement and greed.

"I think I know someone who can help you," he said, reaching for the bills like a predator going after his prey — which suited his nature as a big-cat shifter. Sticking the money in his pocket, he looked around. "Do you see that slim guy over there? His name is Jimmy. I've seen him talking to some creepy guys you wouldn't want to cross paths with, and I may have heard him drop that name once or twice." He nodded, reached for a bottle of whiskey, and began preparing a cocktail for another customer.

I turned my gaze toward the guy he indicated. Calling him slim was an understatement — the guy was as thin as a stick. He was also quite young — he didn't look a day over twenty-three.

"That guy?" Brendan asked, mistrust clear in his voice. He turned to the fae. "I think you just wasted a thousand dollars."

"He wasn't lying, was he?" I asked glancing at Carlos.

"No, but he could be wrong, anyway," Carlos replied.

"Let's go and check it out. I'd like to ask him a few questions. Shall we?" Kagan made his way through the overcrowded dance floor, bumping into supernaturals left and right. I noticed that nearly all the women in the club turned their heads toward him. A few succubi tried to talk to him, their magic dangerous and alluring, but he was unfazed. He pushed them away with a strong hand, their magic no match for his. I was glad — I didn't want him getting distracted, like I had when the incubus tried to seduce me. Damn it! Who was I kidding? I didn't want Kagan to have an interest in anyone else in here. The realization that I had a crush on him struck me like a thunderclap. Shit! Wasn't there enough going on already, with two ritualistic murders? Did I have to add falling for a powerful fae?

You don't even know this guy. Better keep your guard up, the voice in my head told me. I agreed with the advice, but didn't know if I'd be able to follow it.

"Hey, how's it going?" Kagan asked the skinny boy when he drew near enough, putting on a false American accent which made me chuckle inside. The boy turned to Kagan, surprise evident in his eyes.

"Who the hell are you, and what do you want?" he snapped. Politeness wasn't his strong suit, obviously. I sensed nervousness and anxiety in him, though. And he wasn't a supernatural. This was getting more and more interesting. He had to have a sponsor. Had his sponsor left him here unattended? Was that allowed? Or was his sponsor here, somewhere?

I started to look around at the crowd, but Kagan said, "We're looking for someone called the

Rune Keeper, and we heard you know about him. Can we talk about this in private?"

I saw a faint smile flash in the boy's eyes. The next instant he flung a stool at the fae and ran away faster than I'd imagined possible for such a skinny guy. Then again, maybe that was how he was able to move so quickly — he had no excess weight.

We all took off, hot on the boy's heels. To chase someone in such a tightly crowded spot was quite a challenge, especially when the customers included vampires, dark wizards, incubi, and succubi. A few times, as I pushed someone aside, I felt electricity go through me.

Brendan and Carlos shifted into their animal forms and raced across the hall, but the skinny boy ran like the wind.

He left the club, Brendan and Carlos close behind. Kagan and I followed them out to the street, the sounds of echoing footsteps and panting serving as a guide since it was pitch dark. Odd — last time there were neon lights outside the club and, besides, we were in NYC. Suddenly, it hit me: The guy must have used magic to black out all the lights. I could create a fireball so we could see, but I was in a hurry and didn't want to pause.

"Can you see?" Kagan asked. He didn't slow down, but in the next moment a white light appeared in his right hand, illuminating the dark space around us.

"How did you do that while running?" I asked, curiosity getting the better of me, then hastily added, "Never mind." We were in hot pursuit with no time for chit-chat.

We crossed a few more intersections, then Carlos and Brendan, who were slightly ahead of us, stopped. Brendan shifted back to his human form in the middle of the street, and turned to us, quite puzzled. "I don't understand what happened — one second he was here and I was about to throw myself on him, and the next moment he had disappeared. Poof! Just vanished into thin air."

Before anyone could respond, we heard a sinister cackle, and a gang of vampires came at us. I counted fifteen, their eyes full of bloodlust and rage, gleaming crimson. Their skin, though, wasn't as pale as I would have expected. These were definitely not normal vampires — so what were they? Shapeshifters, summoned vampires, or something entirely different?

I tried feeling their magic: they didn't smell of rotten meat and corpses, like common vampires, which only increased my concern. Suddenly a wave of fear and anxiety washed over me. Was that coming from me, or were the vampires causing the negative emotions?

"What was that?" Brendan said, looking at me and Kagan. I didn't have to be a shifter to read his mind; I was thinking the same thing. This was a trap.

"I have no fucking idea, but I don't like it at all," Carlos said, drawing his gun. Brendan followed his lead, pulling his as well. I noticed that these guns were different from the ones they usually used — the handles were encrusted with a silvery metal. Given the type of vampires we had bumped into, I was ready to bet the guns were loaded with silver bullets, which was a sure way to kill vampires. Good; at least we had ammunition against these monsters. Wooden and silver bullets have always worked against vampires — at least, against common vampires. Hopefully, they would work against these creatures as well, whatever they might be.

"Stay positive, guys. Don't let the fear creep in. They feed on it," I said and wished my stare could kill all of them.

"Well, well. Nice to meet you, especially you, Miss Positivity," the vampire in front of the gang said, saliva dripping from his fangs. Why did vampires always have to be so gross?

To make you want to kick them faster and harder, the voice in my head said.

"I hope you enjoyed your stroll, because it was your last one." The vampire nodded to one of his comrades, and they charged us.

This is going to be fun, the voice in my head chimed in. I had to agree.

Chapter 11

As soon as the vampires attacked, Carlos and Brendan started shooting, one bullet after another, aiming for their hearts. Two vampires screamed in pain as the potent silver seared their bodies. The creatures' bodies glowed a deep green, then exploded satisfyingly and turned to ash. Two down, I noted with contentment. Now to get the rest of the bastards. I already had my chakram and one of my enchanted knives out, and I stabbed the ghastly creatures with all the force I could muster. That should teach these bastards some manners. But to my dismay, my weapons didn't take down the vampires — they only scratched them lightly. These monsters were more powerful than I had expected — frighteningly so. I immediately regretted not bringing the enchanted silver knife Awen had given me — truth be told, I hadn't even been thinking of it as a weapon, but as a keepsake from my mother.

    Kagan blasted the vampires with a gust of wind. It threw them back a few feet, but they came again, more determined than before. Two vampires came straight at me, their lanky arms swirling toward me. I took a few steps backward and the vampires' eyes fixed on me, glowing like eerie red lasers in the night air. I had to push them back, so I blasted a cloud of dust right into their eyes. That should give me some time.

The vampires stopped in their tracks, trying to disperse the dust magic I had hurled at them. I took the opportunity to look around me. The rest of their gang didn't slow down, though; one hit Brendan hard in the arm while another went for Carlos, and the others charged at me and the fae. Brendan growled at the vampire before him and fired. He was still in his human form, though the yellow-green color of his eyes wasn't human at all, and I distinctly felt the pull and song of his magic bubbling inside him.

Kagan blasted a new gust of wind against the vampires, this time using fairy dust. It dizzied them and threw them off balance, but I knew they would soon recover. We needed to take advantage of the situation — I had to use my magic. There was no other way to beat these monsters.

I reached for the magic thread inside my center, calling it. The vibrations of its song caressed my ears and the fire element intensified in me. But I needed a much bigger fireball than usual, so I let the magic build in me for a few more moments. Even if those vampires were coming straight out of hell, which didn't seem that hard to believe, a huge fireball was bound to destroy them. I glanced at Brendan as he shot one of the vampires in the heart, then spun around to shoot another at close range, the vampire's fangs almost touching Brendan's bare neck. The creature fell to the ground, and out of the corner of my eye I saw his body glowing in the same deep green color, just before it exploded into ash.

I ducked a new vampire blow to my right and, putting more force into my blow, stabbed my crescent knife deep into his heart: the bubbling anger inside me filled my entire being and I drew energy from it. The creature screamed, his crimson eyes darkening. Along with the bloodlust and rage, I recognized insanity in them too. The vampire pulled himself together but before he could charge at me again, someone shouted, "Alex, duck!" I did and someone shot the vampire in the heart. He fell to the ground, the smoke from the silver bullet drifting away in the air. He gleamed and then exploded like his cronies.

Another scream pierced the night and I whirled. Carlos had shot a vampire in the abdomen and its blood was splattered everywhere, all over us and the remaining vampires. It only enraged the monsters more. Their leader, the one who had talked to us, went straight for Carlos, and a few more followed him. I'd already summoned a gigantic fireball, drawing all my magic. A new vampire charged at me, but I flung an elbow at him — thank magic the moon was waxing. Before the monster could strike me again, I hurled the fireball in my palm toward the leader and the minions surrounding him. It struck them like a lightning bolt, painting the night in shades of red, orange, and yellow, making the air sizzle. They cried out, the flames consuming their clothes, yet the fire didn't swallow their flesh — and even worse, they didn't fall down as any decent vampires would have done in their place: the monsters simply fell back a few feet, then headed for us again, slower.

What the hell? "How is this even possible?" I cried, my voice turning high-pitched, and I swiped at the sweat on my forehead. I'd dealt with a lot of vampires, but never had I seen anything like this before. Another wave of fear and anxiety — stronger this time — crept over me, freezing my heart and soul. That was definitely the doing of these ghoulish monsters.

The leader swung around to face me and sneered, "Bitch, fire doesn't work." One of the vampires pounced at me, but I ducked at the last moment and his momentum carried him past me. A second vampire rushed me, and I punched him straight in the chest, knocking him flat. A third vampire hit me hard in my abdomen, sending a piercing pain through my body, and I bit my lower lip hard. This bastard was really infuriating me. I slashed with my enchanted knife, stabbing him straight in the heart. Blood dripped from the gash in his chest as I called back my knife and wiped it hastily on my jeans. Another pair trashed! At least they weren't as new as the pair the three-headed snake had ruined. This job was hard on my clothing.

"Fire may not work on you, but silver bullets do," Brendan said as he fired several consecutive shots straight into the leader's skeletal body. He dropped to the ground, his crimson eyes gleaming in the dark night and sending chills down my spine. The whole thing was freaking eerie.

"Alex, summon another element to combine with your fire. Set up a magic barrier around them. There are too many of them — we need to hurry," Kagan said, almost panting in my ear. His breath gusted against my neck, giving me goosebumps.

Of all the times to let your hormones distract you, Alex, why now? I scolded myself.

Alex! Pay attention! the voice cried.

Just then a vampire punched Carlos in his chest, knocking him to the ground, and another bit him hard on the neck. Carlos screamed. But it was his skin color and facial expression that terrified me: he was white as chalk. More vampires gathered around him, drawn by the blood and terror. He had to call on his inner animal, and quickly, or he'd lose a lot of blood. But to do that, he had to break free from the vampires and their magic.

Brendan began shooting frantically at the gang of vampires, which now numbered only eight. Kagan blasted another gust of fairy-dust wind at them, then he turned to me and nodded. "Do it now, Alex!" A vampire tried to land a blow on me, but before I could react, Brendan shot him with a silver bullet. I reached inside myself for the other element I felt most comfortable summoning: air. I felt its power and song calling me, playing with my magic and my senses.

The sensation air gave me was even more enticing: Fire could burn, sure, but wind was unpredictable and invisible. I reached for it and when it surged within me, I unleashed it. A wind barrier with flames burning on its borders appeared in the space before us and I threw it at the vampires, just in time. Brendan had just wiggled free from the monsters' grip, and Carlos was fighting for his life, his right knee and neck bleeding heavily. Once we made it out of this mess, I'd heal him again. If he was still alive.

The wind barrier closed around the vampires, keeping them at bay though they tried to break out, beating soundlessly against the wall. They weren't harmed, unfortunately, but they were prisoners.

"Good," Kagan muttered next to me. He knelt down and put his hand on the ground, concentrating hard, slight wrinkles forming on his handsome forehead. And then I felt it: the song and magic surging from Mother Earth. The raw magic intensified, making my hair stand on end. He was drawing power from the earth element, pumping himself up. The vampires kept kicking and punching the barrier, the muted thundering sounds echoing in the space around us. A few more minutes and they could possibly break free, even more enraged than before.

"Move away," Kagan shouted, and when Brendan and I darted behind him, dragging Carlos between us, he poured all his magic into the enclosed barrier. The earth beneath it crashed down, swallowing the vampires. Gravel, dirt, and rocks rained down, quickly filling in the hole he had created as the vampires disappeared into it. Within a few minutes there was no sign of the abyss or the vampires that had gone into it.

I watched Kagan with astonishment — he controlled the elements and drew strength and magic from nature with enviable ease and speed. He wasn't done, though: He drew another portion of magic from the moon and a gleaming white light sizzled in the air above our heads. He concentrated his energy onto the place where the earth had swallowed the vampires and drew a pentagram over it. It glowed for a moment and then an explosion crackled, scattering dark clouds of rocks, sand, and debris. The earth beneath our feet shifted a bit, but otherwise we were all alive, at least for now.

"That should do it." Kagan turned to us, his face covered in sweat.

"That was... amazing," I panted, and the fae beamed at me.

"I was hoping you'd like it," he said with a sly grin.

Ugh! I was too quick with the praise.

I ignored his reaction. "I don't understand why the fire didn't hurt or kill the vampires," I said, glancing at Carlos.

He didn't look well. He had transformed back into a tiger, in order to connect with his magic and boost his regenerative powers, but he was weak and wounded. His knee and neck still bled profusely. Damn vampires! I needed to heal him, but first we had to get out of here. A part of me was afraid another attack might follow, with magic knows what kind of monsters this time.

Kagan read my mind, and he reached for his raw fae power. The wind swirled around us, caressing my hair and skin. The air vibrated with yellow-white light, then grew into a big swirl that took us through the ether into the void.

Chapter 12

The portal took us to a luxurious apartment. My exhaustion from the day's events had taken its toll. As soon as we stepped through, I collapsed onto a couch that looked as expensive as it was comfortable.

"Wow, this looks like it could be Mark Zuckerburg's place," Brendan muttered as he laid Carlos's limp body on a fancy light blue sofa that had probably cost more than all the magical artifacts in the Steaming Cauldron. At the thought of the shop, I felt a tight knot forming in the pit of my stomach. I resolved to think about how to save our business venture as soon as I could think straight.

Kagan chuckled. "I don't know about Mark, but this is my home here in the States. We were in my office suites a few floors down this morning."

The fae's NYC residence was gorgeous. I gazed at the apartment in awe: a spacious living room with fine, expensive furniture, everything sparkling clean, overlooking Manhattan Bridge through a big window that provided a magnificent view. I could definitely picture living here and waking up to that panoramic view each day. Fae sure knew where to live!

"And where do you live in your native Ireland? In a castle?" I asked him, envy discernible in my voice. I tried hard to conceal it, but failed. This place was so damn gorgeous, and completely out of my reach. I had better chances of dating Chris Hemsworth than ever being able to afford such a classy apartment. It wasn't fair: I worked my ass off and barely made ends meet, but here he was — a privileged fae, owing his wealth to the benign destiny of being born to one of the magic dynasties. Life really sucked — or karma, whichever.

Kagan looked amused. "Yes, Alex, as a matter of fact. My family owns a castle in Dublin and another in Belfast. If you behave, I might invite you there sometime."

I wanted to apologize for my remark, or at least tell him that I didn't judge him for his privileged birth — after all, he had just delivered us from that gang of vampires — but Brendan cut in.

"You and your family are pretty stingy with your money, though. A lot of less fortunate supernaturals could benefit from even a tiny part of your wealth." I could distinguish notes of envy in his voice too. It was a small relief that I wasn't the only one who envied the fae, though Brendan's bitterness was not only because of Kagan's power, wealth, and influence, but also — mostly —

because the fae was our new team leader. Men and their macho competition!

"Belonging to one of the magic dynasties is both a blessing and a curse," Kagan said coolly. "It's not so easy when the rest of the supernatural world hates your guts."

Brendan couldn't muster any reasonable response to that.

I rose and went to Carlos, who was lying half-conscious on the other sofa. His foreleg was badly injured, the vampire bites glistening; there were also bite marks on his neck fur, though not as big as the wound on his leg. The worst problem, though, was his decreased energy level — the monsters had drained a considerable part of his life force.

"Don't worry, Carlos, I'm gonna heal you," I whispered. I put my hand on his fur and concentrated, half-closing my eyes to call my magic thread. Its beat surged inside me. A light blue circle of light appeared in my hand and I poured it into Carlos's body, trying to be as gentle as possible. He howled and bared his fangs, but let me do my thing. Seconds later his pain as well as his injuries were gone. He lay still for a few moments, then transformed into his human form with his clothes back on him. Only powerful shifters could keep their clothes on. He stared in disbelief at his perfectly healthy body then looked at me.

"Jeez, Alex, that was... unbelievable!" He got up — gingerly at first, then moving with more confidence — and hugged me. "Thank you so much. I thought those bastards had gotten the better of me." He let go of me and I saw the gleam in his eyes. "I had no idea you were a natural healer. Brendan once told me you could heal yourself, but I didn't know you could heal others also."

"She's pretty extraordinary for a simple elemental mage, isn't she?" Kagan said, drawing nearer to me. There was a gleam in his eyes that I didn't like.

I wished he'd just say whatever was on his mind, or leave me alone; but, facing him, I said only, "Well, it's been a rough day. That battle exhausted us all."

Kagan looked so ridiculously confident and sexy that I couldn't help but feel attracted to him. I got mad at myself for having such feelings: he was too dangerous for me, too prying, too... powerful.

"I agree with Alex — it's been a hell of a day," Carlos chimed in. "Thank magic we're all safe. Speaking of which, dude, you've got an awesome apartment here. Do you happen to have any brandy or whiskey? I think we could all use a drink right now."

"Sure, help yourself," Kagan replied absentmindedly, gesturing to the wet bar in a corner of the room and holding my gaze like a predator waiting for his prey to make a mistake. I didn't know what he expected me to say or do, and it made me nervous.

"Can we talk somewhere privately?" I asked.

He looked at me, amusement evident in his eyes. His lips twitched slightly. "Why?"

"It seems to me you know something about me that I myself am not really aware of. Seriously, can we speak privately, just the two of us?" I said in a quiet voice.

The fae smiled and put a hand on my arm. Even though his touch was light, his magic intertwined with mine, setting fireworks off in my mind and making me think of delicious champagne and forbidden pleasures. It took all the self-control I had left not to show my weakness for him as he led me to a smaller room.

"So, now we're alone. Your wish is my command — anything else you want me to do?"

I wanted to kiss him then and there so much that I could hardly suppress my desire.

"Yes," I said, and to my credit I maintained a poker face. "You've made several vague comments now, and I want you to just come out with it. Who do you think I am?"

"I know you're not just a mage as you claim to be. A mere mage — even an elemental mage with full control over all four elements — can't heal herself or others, or see into the past like you do," he said quietly.

"Well, I've always been different."

"No, this is not just different. This can only mean one thing." He came over to me and I inhaled his scent. It intoxicated me. He took my hand and caressed my palm. "I think you know, deep down inside you, what you are. I want you to realize it yourself, instead of me telling you. Don't you think that's better?" he said, practically whispering in my ear. It felt so good it made me dizzy.

Don't give in to his charms, Alex, the voice in my head warned me, and I instantly sobered.

Kagan was insanely powerful, rich, and belonged to the magic dynasties. What would he ever want with a girl like me? Awen's words echoed in my head: *"Don't ever reveal your powers to strangers, child."* But he had meant the caution for other supernaturals in general, not for my working partner. After all, Kagan was on our team.

You still don't know him at all. Give it more time, the voice said.

I don't think he means ill, I replied.

He is powerful, and you ought to be careful with such people. The voice was firm, unshakable, and convinced me.

I shook my head and took a step backwards. I had been way too intimate with him in the past few minutes.

"I gotta go," I mumbled, avoiding eye contact with him. "It's getting late."

"Where to? It's already past eleven o'clock. Why don't you stay here for the night?"

"I'd rather spend the night in my own bed. I'm sure you guys will do just fine without me around to disturb you." I opened the door and saw Carlos and Brendan sipping their whiskey on the sofa, chatting amiably. I pointed at them. "See?"

"All right, but whatever you do, stay alert. I don't want anything to happen to you. We seem to be dealing with a very cruel and dark individual."

"Thank you."

"And don't go anywhere on your own. We'll visit the Hellfire Club again tomorrow. Be back here at ten o'clock. You'll be able to envision my place, won't you?"

"Of course." I had already taken out Naomi's transport charm when I had another thought: The moon was two days past first quarter, and I was feeling it in my veins. I no longer needed Naomi's charm. But considering how curious Kagan was about my abilities, it didn't seem like the best idea at the moment to show him my other special talents. True, some mages could teleport themselves, especially telekinetics, but I was labeling myself an elemental mage.

Kagan raised his eyebrows, and for a split second I thought he had read my mind again. But I had no time to ponder the issue; I just wanted to get into my own bed and call it a day. I sprinkled the fairy dust around me, and a glistening golden cloud rose in front of me. I stepped in and envisioned my home, my room on the third floor of the house in Ivy Hills above the occult shop.

"And be on time tomorrow," Kagan said, just before the magic took me.

Chapter 13

"Good morning, sweetie. How did you sleep?"

Naomi tickled my back with her fingertips and I turned away from my bowl of cereal to see her. The clock on the kitchen wall read just past seven-thirty. "For once, excellent. I missed being home." Last night I'd gone straight to bed and fallen asleep with my clothes still on. Exhausting battles cured insomnia.

"Aw, that's adorable." She hugged me, then sat down and asked, "But tell me, is everything okay between you and Mr. Werewolf?"

"Oh yeah. Sure, it's fine." Now that I was convinced I really wasn't interested in him any longer. I resumed munching my breakfast. "How are things in town? Any big sales recently to get us back on our feet?"

Don't be mean, the voice in my head said.

I'm not, I replied, stung. I didn't intend to be sarcastic, just realistic. Thank magic Naomi hadn't yet noticed my internal conversation — my lunacy.

"It's the same, sweetheart, honestly. And Des continues to bewitch our clientele. His charm and good looks go a long way with the ladies."

I looked at her for a while before saying, "Not only with them, it seems. So he's 'Des' now?"

Naomi blushed, confirming my hunch. I wasn't about to stop teasing her. "All right, tell me what you've been up to while I was off fighting crazy vampires in New York, girl! You can't hide the truth, especially not from me, the Magic Council's big shot."

"Really? You had a fight with vampires? What happened?"

"Uh-uh, you're not going to distract me that easily, Noe. Come on, spill the beans!" I poked her.

"Okay, okay." She got up and spread her hands in the air helplessly. "It started the day you went to work with Brendan. He came by just before closing and invited me for a drink at Atomic Hound. One thing led to another and... you know."

Atomic Hound was our favorite bar, just a few miles away from our occult shop, owned by a cousin of one of the Atomic Kitten's band members. It was a traditional English-style pub house, where one could go to meet half the neighborhood, hear and share gossip, shoot pool and play darts, and, on Friday nights, sing karaoke. Naomi and I had been regulars there for over a year until my gig at the Magic Council had started.

Seeing the look on her face, I asked, "What, you slept with him?"

Naomi looked horrified. "For magic's sake, Alex, of course not!"

"Noe, we're not living in the nineteenth century. Don't get all virgin on me," I said, suppressing a giggle. Sometimes Naomi could be such a puritan, although she wasn't usually prudish by nature. I didn't know what had come over her.

"How can you think I'd sleep with a guy I barely know? I'm not a slut!" The indignation in her voice was as clear as day.

"Sorry, I didn't mean — "

"Gotcha! You should have seen your face!" She giggled, and I grabbed an apple from the bowl on the table and threw it at her. She caught it in midair.

"So, did you sleep with him or what?" I repeated my question, slightly annoyed.

"No, I didn't. We just kissed. And he is *really* a good kisser. But like I said that night after his gathering, party, whatever — there's some kind of dark energy inside him, I can feel it. I can't put my finger on it, but it's there nonetheless. It worries me. So, as nice as the kissing was, I told him I'd rather be friends."

I nodded thoughtfully. "How did he take the rejection?"

"Oh, he was fine. He even walked me home."

So, there were still nice guys nowadays, guys who would make sure you got home safely even if you refused to date them or have sex with them. That made me optimistic.

"But enough about my pitiful love life — how's that murder investigation coming along? You mentioned vampires and a fight; did you find the killer?"

I sighed. "Not yet. We know we're after a dark supernatural and there's a mysterious sorcerer involved in the case somehow. Whether he's the supernatural we're looking for, we don't know, but he's at least linked. One thing became clear last night, though. The sorcerer's minions hang out at a place called the Hellfire Club, and apparently the killer can summon some really shitty vampires — I don't even know what kind they were. I need to talk to Awen about that." He had quite a few useful old books describing nearly all the types of monsters and supernaturals in the universe. If any information was available about the vampires I'd encountered, it would be in one of his books.

Naomi raised her brows. "Shitty vampires? You mean even shittier than the normal ones? Wow! That *is* hard to beat. Tell me about them."

I shrugged. "There's not much to tell, other than that they were quite obnoxious. But at least they weren't as dangerous as the demons and gods I met in the Veil."

"You've been to the Veil? The motherfucking *Veil*? The place that's only open to the highest-ranked supernaturals?" Admiration and envy flashed in my best friend's eyes. "For magic's sake, how did you get in there in the first place? And what were you doing there — snooping about the case?"

A smug smiled tugged at the corners of my mouth. "I had to go. There was a meeting between the Courts of Heaven and Hell. Kai, the leader of the demons, was furious; he wants the person who murdered his worshiper — the bank CEO — to be caught, and an end put to the occult murders. There's been a second murder committed by the same perpetrator, in the same style. We all agree the killings were done by a supernatural." I took another sip of my tea and mused, "And it's not only Kai; we *all* want the culprit behind bars. I just don't understand why the killer's targeting ordinary humans. Of all the magic creatures available, why choose humans? What does he have against them?"

"Maybe he has some issues — perhaps he was bullied by humans when he was a child?" Naomi suggested and silence fell over the room. Back at Magica Academy, a lot of bullying had gone on, and we both knew how one's life could be ruined because of it. Then Naomi glanced at the clock and realized she was going to be late, so that was the end of our conversation.

She headed for her room on the second floor, and I was finishing my cereal when she reappeared, dressed for the day.

"Do you have a lot of work today, too?" she asked, and came to the table to pour herself a cup of hot water from the kettle.

"I'm afraid so. Thanks to Kai's paranoia, we have a deadline; if we miss it, there'll be a magic apocalypse."

Naomi giggled, and I pretended to be annoyed as I scolded her. "It's not funny at all. We don't know yet who the murderer is. We'll have to work every day until we find him, so I have to be at Kagan's apartment in Manhattan by ten this morning."

Naomi frowned, and slight wrinkles formed on her lovely face. Hedge witches had an amazing natural beauty. My best friend made awesome skin potions and creams for smoothing wrinkles, skin regeneration, and so forth. Naomi's magic could make a granny look like she was in her twenties — but she was so pretty she didn't even need to use it, and I sometimes envied her for that.

"Kagan?" Naomi asked. "Who the hell is that?"

"The Magic Council assigned a fae to be our new supervisor. You can imagine how pissed Brendan is."

"Wait, girl — are you talking about Kagan Griffith?" Her pupils dilated.

"Yes, that's him. How did you — "

But my question died in the air because Noe suddenly shrieked, "Alex, do you know who you're working with?" She obviously didn't expect a response from me, because she got up, raced to the shop storeroom, and hastily came back with a copy of *Forbes* magazine clutched in her hand. "Is *that* the Kagan you're talking about?"

She tossed the magazine to me and I gasped: Kagan's handsome face stared at me from the cover, his lips forming a faint smile. I stared, and it took me some time to regain my powers of speech.

"Since when do you read *Forbes*?" I asked, still finding it incredible that Kagan had made the cover of one of the most influential magazines in the world. I'd known he was rich, of course, but *that* rich?

He looked pretty sexy in a suit, but I shook my head to banish the thought. Now was not the appropriate time for romantic sentiments.

"Someone must have left it — oh, wait, I think I took it from Des's shop. Yes, that's right: I stopped by Magica World — the magazine was by the cash register, and there's an article I wanted to read. Des said one of his coven's members had brought it, so he said I could have it."

This Desmond guy is odd, the voice in my head said.

So what? I asked.

The voice was silent for a moment, then said, *I don't like his energy. He's just weird, you know? Be on your guard around him.*

"So that's the Kagan you're working with?" Naomi cut into my internal dialogue and brought me back to reality. I didn't know about Desmond, but the mental conversations I was having with myself were getting pretty freaking weird. But Awen knew best, and he had advised me to listen to my inner voice. For magic's sake, why did I have this gift — this thing, whatever it was? Why did I have to be so different?

I cleared my throat and turned to Naomi. "Yes, that's him." I suddenly felt a lump at the back of my throat. "What is he doing on the cover of *Forbes*, anyway?"

"Griffith Enterprises is one of the country's richest companies, and your fae boss is — let's see here... number fifty-seven on the world's billionaire list."

I almost choked.

This guy is so out of your league, girl, the voice in my head said very distinctly.

"Wow — the Magic Council has some pretty powerful allies," I commented. "And yet it's a bit odd ..." I muttered, looking at the magazine. Then I shifted my gaze back to Naomi. "Of all the people in our small town, you found a magazine at Desmond's shop with the fae I happen to be working with right now on the cover. Don't you think that's suspicious?"

Naomi stared at me and said, "No, not at all."

"It gives me some food for thought," I said.

She shook her head energetically. "No, no — what's the matter with you Alex? Have you lost your mind? It's a coincidence; it means absolutely nothing. It's true that Des is interested in the occult, but it's all Wiccan stuff. The witches we met at the lecture possessed very little magic indeed."

"Don't let any Wiccans hear you say that. Not all of them are so low-level, you know." My best friend's remarks put me off a little, even though I wasn't Wiccan.

"Of course, darling. I know some do have strong magic, but that's not my point. Anyway, about Des — he's nonmagical, too. And he lives here, in Ivy Hills, not in NYC, remember? All your hard work has really taken a toll on your brainpower, Alex — you're imagining things that don't exist."

She raised valid points, I had to admit that. And yet... "Okay, maybe he isn't involved, but someone from his Wiccan coven is? Maybe the person who gave him the magazine?" I mused. Then I remembered something: Elliott Rumford had mentioned that Daniel Stone had joined a coven, and may have gotten his entry to the Hellfire Club that way.

"That's more likely," Naomi said and patted me on my back.

I didn't respond; I was still dazed by Naomi's revelation. I cleared my throat and tried to gather my thoughts. "For someone who claims not to be romantically interested in Desmond, you seem kinda partial, don't you think?"

"Are you teasing me or what?" Her eyes gleamed with amusement.

"Just making an observation."

Naomi arched her brows and turned to leave the kitchen, so I said, "All joking aside, Noe, I think this is important. Can you ask Desmond which member of his coven bought the magazine?"

Naomi shrugged. "Okay, if you think that'll save the world, I'll ask him."

"And when Desmond answers you, would you be so kind as to call and tell me also?"

"Well, aren't you demanding."

I chuckled. "Just a little, but you still love me."

Naomi grunted instead of responding, but I knew her well — she would do it. She headed for the door, leaving me alone with the *Forbes* magazine, Kagan staring at me from the cover. He looked incredibly sexy in his suit, the arrogant look in his eyes giving him that bad-boy vibe women loved so much.

Oh, this is not good, Alex.

I didn't need my inner voice's opinion on this matter — I thought the same thing.

***

It took me about fifteen minutes to get to Awen's house at the edge of town. His Victorian home looked peaceful and untouched by time as usual, unlike my current state of mind. Ever since Naomi had shown me the magazine with Kagan on the cover I'd been feeling agitated and apprehensive. I hesitated for a moment before I took out the key. My head swarmed with questions burning for answers, yet I didn't feel up to sharing my troublesome thoughts with anybody.

Awen was here; I could feel the taste of his magic, like an excellent, mature wine that caresses your tongue and senses, and makes you want to drink more and more of it. Although Awen's magic initially seemed light, it was unusually powerful and tugged at my own magic power, calling it out to play. The only supernatural I'd ever met whose magic might be a match for Awen's was Kagan.

I became irritated with my own stupid mind and sentiments — thinking about the fae again! Now was the least appropriate time to be thinking of romance. I was in the midst of an investigation and the future of our occult shop was uncertain — as was my own.

I cleared my mind of all worrisome thoughts, unlocked the front door, and went in. I hoped he hadn't gone out. I went to his living room and turned on the lights. As usual, a gust of peaceful energy enveloped me, calming me right away. Suddenly, all my troubles seemed insignificant — even the vampires from last night and the unsolved murders we were investigating. I heard my mentor's steps approaching, and soon enough he appeared in the living room.

"Alex, is everything all right? I thought you were in New York City," he said, his voice concerned.

"I am. Well, I mean, I *was* in New York; I just came home for a little recharge, and I wanted to ask you a few things."

"Has something happened? Or did you just want to spend time with your old mentor?" His smile warmed my insides, and all the remaining tension died out.

"I was just wondering..." I sighed. "These past couple of days have been crazy. I've been in all sorts of strange places." Images of the Hellfire Club and the Veil flashed before my eyes. All this stuff was new to me, and only now did I realize the changes I'd been subconsciously experiencing.

Awen smiled at me paternally. "It's okay, Alex, take your time. Do you want a cup of coffee?"

I nodded and Awen went to the kitchen. In the meantime, I prepared myself for my confession.

When he returned, I began with my story. "So, last night we fought a bunch of real crazy vampires. I've never met anything like those monsters — I mean never, ever. I was hoping you'd let me look through some of your old magic books for information about them."

"Sure. I have two books that might be especially helpful. Whatever you're looking for, it'll be somewhere in there." The kettle began whistling in the kitchen as he retrieved the books for me. "The water's boiling; I'll fetch your coffee. What's your flavor?"

Kagan, the voice inside my head said before I could suppress it.

Damn it, you are not helping! Why were my silly hormones making things so complicated? He was way out of my league, and I knew it all too well.

"Kagan is your flavor?" my mentor asked, perplexed.

Had I said that aloud? I blushed and added hastily, "Cappuccino, please."

Awen nodded, handed me two old tomes, then went back to the kitchen to prepare the coffee. I impatiently opened the pages of the first book, going straight to the vampire section. I found the types I was already familiar with: common vampires, then shapeshifter vampires, followed by the nastier ghost vampires, and finally the psychic vampires. This book said they were descendants of the Aztec and Mayan gods. According to the description, they were human in appearance, fed on negative emotions — primarily fear, despair, and anger — and they could be killed by fire.

That wasn't the case with the vampires from last night, the voice in my head said.

I leafed through a few more pages, desperate to figure out the type of monster I'd fought, but the information just wasn't here. Then I looked through the second book.

"What's not here, sweetheart?" Awen's voice pulled me from my thoughts, and he handed me a cup of cappuccino, then sat down on the couch next to me.

"Sorry. I didn't realize I said that part out loud," I mumbled, and sipped cautiously from the hot cappuccino. It was delicious — Awen always made awesome coffee.

"Tell me what's bothering you about..." He lowered his gaze toward the book in my lap and finished, "the vampires? Is that it, my child?"

I told him all about the attack from last night. "That's the first time I've seen vampires that weren't affected by fire. And the fireball I summoned was *gigantic*, but didn't affect them at all. I read over all the types listed here, but the ones I fought last night aren't here," I said. I waved my hands helplessly in the air. "Basically they had normal skin complexion with crimson eyes, and crazy magic abilities, as if someone had pumped them up with raw power — with evil."

Awen took a deep breath, closed his eyes, and seemed to contemplate my question for a long moment. Opening his eyes he then asked me slowly, "You've met a lot of monsters and evil supernaturals during your gig at the Magic Council, haven't you?"

"Yes, indeed, but I've never seen anything like those vampires."

"I know." He paused as if searching for the right words, and I noticed the slight wrinkles that had formed on his forehead. As old as Awen was, he didn't look any older than thirty-five. I'd always viewed him as my father, though — a mentor with vast experience and knowledge.

"Alex, have you noticed that lately your magic has been attracting different kinds of supernaturals, monsters in particular?"

I'd always known that my magic seemed to attract all types of supernaturals. I tried hard to remember. Kicking monsters' butts is the everyday life of any supernatural consultant but, come to think of it, I had been doing a lot more of it on this job than on previous jobs.

"Kind of, but that's part of the job, right?" I told him.

"It's not only that, child. See, your magic and power are... let's say *enticing*. They attract other supernaturals to you like a magnet. That's the reason why I personally wasn't thrilled about you working as an independent consultant for the Council. I never said anything, of course."

I stared at him, not quite following his reply. "Okay, but what does that have to do with the vampires I fought off last night?"

He smiled at me indulgently, like a parent to a child. "I believe your magic has attracted a very accomplished sorcerer. From what you described to me, it sounds like this sorcerer summoned demon souls into vampire bodies and was controlling them. At least, that's what I think is happening."

I gaped at him and he continued, "It's a pretty advanced dark magic, so the mastermind is very powerful, no doubt." He stood up and took another thick tome from his library, skimmed through the pages, then showed me the demon section. "It's explained here. Read it for yourself." He placed the book into my hands. I stared at the pages, which featured drawings of various kinds of demons.

I hate these creatures, the voice in my head said, calmly but unmistakably. I hated demons just as much as my inner voice did.

I gathered all my mental strength and searched in the book for summoned demonic souls. I scanned a few pages, then found what I was looking for. I read aloud, "A very rare type of demon is the one unleashed by a powerful evil wizard or sorcerer. Such a supernatural can summon incorporeal demonic souls from hell and place them into ghosts or into the bodies of vampires, thus creating a fearful supernatural monster having the attributes of both a demon and its original monster soul." I skipped a few passages describing the incorporeal demon-powered ghosts and continued reading about vampires. "A vampire, on the other hand, upon connecting with the demonic soul, can retain some of the physical appearances of vampires like red eyes or pale skin, but it is exceptionally intelligent and coordinated. The demonic soul also makes the body very resilient and resistant to physical harm and injury. If the summoned demonic soul is a powerful one, the vampire may have a normal skin complexion and lack the characteristic smell of rotten meat. An important note is that the wizard or sorcerer transfers their abilities and whatever elemental magic they may have to these demon-powered vampires and can control them. The monsters can be easily killed with silver — a silver bullet or a drawing of a benevolent occult symbol like a pentagram over them is the only way to slay such creatures."

After reading the last sentence, I shut the book, and looked into Awen's beautiful blue eyes. "This description portrayed the type of vampires we fought off last night, down to the smallest detail. Kagan must have known this, or else he has powerful intuition, because he drew a pentagram above them." I furrowed my brows. "But I'm not quite sure whether it was the vampires' special abilities or the killer who was protecting them from the fireball I hurled at them. If it was the killer, he must be a dark wizard or a sorcerer — the vampires' magic tasted really vile," I mused. I drank my remaining coffee in a single gulp.

"Most likely. If the sorcerer or wizard has control over fire like you, he would have made these creatures immune to it. It all has to do with his abilities. Does that answer your question?"

"Yes. Thank you for everything, Awen. You're awesome." I hugged him and got up. Time was running out, and I needed to teleport myself to Kagan's place. He would probably be pissed if I turned up late. "I have to go, though. Thanks again; the cappuccino was delicious, by the way."

"You're most welcome, my dear," he replied.

I was headed for the door when Awen's melodious voice made me stop in my tracks.

"Before you go, Alex, tell me something: Since you started this assignment, how many times have you been attacked?"

I sensed something I had never before heard in his voice — hesitation.

"A couple of times; that's why the Magic Council's wages are so high." I envisioned the big pile of cash I would receive at the end of my assignment and smiled.

If you make it that far, the voice remarked.

Oh, shut up! I snapped at it. I wasn't in the mood for such grim comments and teasing.

Awen sighed heavily and stood up. "Alex, I'm afraid it is more than just your regular workday routine. A word of caution: I have the suspicion that the mastermind behind the vampire attack has targeted you and may be trying to kill you, so he can take over your magic."

Chapter 14

Awen's words echoed in my mind, my heartbeat speeding up. I heard myself say, "Isn't that what all villains do?" I chuckled nervously and tapped my foot on the squeaky floor. There was no point asking him if he was certain: Awen never spoke unless he was sure.

My mentor squeezed my hand reassuringly. "Don't worry, Alex. I didn't want to frighten you; just be alert."

I nodded. "I'd better be going." I left his house and shut the door behind me. However, before teleporting myself, I had to do one more thing: I went straight home and took my enchanted silver knife from the cupboard shelf. Awen was probably right. Somebody was trying to kill me or at least harm me — I recalled the ambush in the street right after our first visit to the Hellfire Club. But what Awen suggested was worse: they might want to take my magical powers. I had no intention of simply surrendering to them without putting up a good fight.

The knife's blade glinted in the daylight, taking my breath away. It was so beautiful, and frighteningly powerful. The runes engraved on the blade only intensified the prickle of magic on my skin.

A quick glance at my watch reminded me I needed to hurry in order to arrive on time; it was already nearly ten o'clock. I reached for my magic, which was now bubbling in abundance inside me. The moon was waxing and my peculiar powers pulsed and vibrated in me, wanting to be released. It felt so good to connect with them and unleash even a tiny part of them that, when I arrived back at Kagan's apartment, I was grinning from ear to ear.

"Hello, gorgeous!" the fae greeted me. "You must have had a hell of a time back at your place. You're beaming with happiness." *No, it's just connecting with my inner power,* I thought, but said nothing. He was clad in a tight dark gray T-shirt that accentuated his muscular chest and biceps.

I realized I was ogling him just as my inner voice said, *Don't drool over him, girl! Don't let him know you like him in that way.*

Good luck with that.

Kagan smiled. "I could help you master your magic with some special training, if you'd like," he offered. But before I could think of a clever response, Brendan came out of the bathroom, naked to the waist, with a towel hung loosely over his left shoulder.

For magic's sake, why was he half-naked? I thought in irritation. I looked around and saw

Carlos dozing on a couch. I turned my head in Brendan's direction and said, "Don't tell me you've just woken up! How is that possible? We're on an investigation. I rushed here to be on time, and you guys aren't even fully dressed!" I had to admit I was exaggerating, but it was very unprofessional for Brendan to be running late.

I felt Brendan's murderous glare on me but before he could snap back, Kagan intervened. "Easy, Alex. Brendan and Carlos had vivid nightmares last night, probably because of the vampire ambush yesterday. I let them sleep a bit longer than normal." He looked over at the shifters. Following his gaze, I saw that Brendan's expression was impassive, and I sensed that he had calmed down.

I sat on the sofa and tried to sound nonchalant as I asked Kagan, "So, chief, what are the plans for today? By the way, I'd like to share something with you regarding the investigation."

His face lightened and I saw a faint smile tug at the corner of his mouth. "We'll roll up our sleeves and get back to work, that's for sure, but not before we have a good brunch. I won't be able to think straight until I get something to eat. Let's have a decent meal and then we'll talk business, okay?"

I had no option but to agree. In half an hour we were out of Kagan's apartment. He had teleported us to Temptation, a cozy — and expensive — restaurant in Lower East Manhattan.

It was a hotspot for upper-class supernaturals and, like all other magic restaurants and bars, it was invisible to humans. And pretty much to lower and middle-class supernaturals too, I thought bitterly. The entrance looked ridiculously elegant and magnificent: Golden letters on matte glass spelled out the restaurant's name, sparkling with all the colors of the rainbow, though red predominated. Potted pines the height of a man stood on both sides of the entrance and, next to them, three-headed dogs and venom-spitting snakes guarded the door.

But what pushed the security over the top were the monsters handling the dogs and the snakes — two gigantic bogeymen that looked as if they had been taken from the set of a horror movie. Dressed all in black, their faces hidden behind big black masks, they emanated pure horror and dread.

I saw Brendan's and Carlos's eyes glint to the distinct yellowish color of shifters, but Kagan was unflappable. He nodded at the two bogeymen and they stepped aside to let us pass. Once we were inside, enticing magic tickled my senses and I suddenly felt ravenous. Now I understood why they called this place Temptation. The restaurant owner hadn't spared any expense. The floor was made of marble, the tablecloths of silk, and golden chandeliers sparkled on the ceiling. I took a look at the clientele too: first-tier mages, a few shifters, and a bunch of fae.

Temptation was the type of place where a meal cost more than a pair of designer jeans or boots, and I would much rather spend my money on those things than on a meal, no matter how delicious. Given the fact that my bank balance was in the red, I could hardly afford anything before I got my paycheck from the Magic Council. But, of course, before I could collect a paycheck, we first had to catch the culprit. I hated this vicious cycle. Why did everything have to revolve around money? I turned to the fae, slightly worried.

"Uh, Kagan, I don't know about you, but my pockets are quite thin at the moment. I can barely afford a cup of coffee here," I said, then glanced at the menu board and gasped. A cup of coffee here cost forty dollars. This was insane!

"I agree with Alex — even if we billed the Magic Council, it'd be considered an over-the-top indulgence," Brendan chimed in.

"Wait, you expense your meals?" I asked incredulously. Apparently the Council not only paid very high wages and provided their investigators with BMWs, but also covered their expenses.

"Yes, but it applies only to regular employees," he said.

Which I wasn't.

"No need to worry," Kagan said offhandedly, "it's on me. I'm the one who suggested the restaurant." He motioned us to a table and we took our seats. If he wanted to pay for our brunch, I was perfectly fine with that. The place looked to have delicious cuisine and frankly, I wanted to try it — and I could never afford to eat here on my own.

When I opened the menu, I wasn't disappointed. Temptation offered all kinds of food: steaks, pork, burgers and fries, Asian, Latin-American, Middle Eastern, Chinese, and Italian. Italian was the cuisine I most adored, so I picked a big green wizard pizza with extra pepperoni, mozzarella, and mushrooms, and a magic smoothie called Crescent Moon Magic. I smiled inwardly, recalling my own hidden magic. Brendan ordered a big steak, and Carlos a vegetarian meal, while Kagan said he'd have "a boxty."

"Dude, what the hell is that?" Carlos asked. I was curious to learn also.

The fae smiled and said, his Irish accent more marked, "It's a traditional Irish potato pancake. We have to keep our culture alive. I am a fae, after all, am I not?"

The waiter returned with our meals, interrupting our conversation. I was astonished that anyone could prepare a meal so fast. Then it dawned on me: magic. Of course!

"So they make all those dishes with magic, right?" I asked, sipping my smoothie. It was delicious — milk and ice blended with a strawberry mixture that gave the drink a divine flavor. And then the magic came, rippling on my tongue: First a sizzling lightning, followed by a gust of wind and finally the sensation of the ocean tides. I could swear I saw the silver light of a crescent moon gleaming on the ocean water. It was an amazing experience, and it did refresh me.

"It's excellent, isn't it?" Kagan asked. I tried not to blush, but I did — and I had no idea why.

"It sure is," Carlos said in between morsels of his vegetarian meal and salad. Brendan nodded in confirmation, too busy with his own dish to speak. The pizza I had ordered was marvelous. It cost an arm and a leg, but oh, boy, was it worth it! — at least, since I wasn't the one paying. After Kagan signaled for the bill, he said, "So, now let's talk business. First, I got the coroner's report on yesterday's murder."

He described its findings. Basically it showed that the homeless guy had been killed between one and two in the morning. The surveillance footage didn't reveal anything of interest.

Then Kagan turned to me. "Alex, you mentioned that you had news?"

"Uh, yes." I cleared my throat. "I know what type of vampires we fought off last night."

"I hadn't intended to discuss the issue, but since you've mentioned it, would you mind elaborating?"

I told him what I'd read in my mentor's old book. He listened to my explanation carefully, nodding from time to time. When I finished, he said, "Yeah, that's pretty much what I figured, too. Someone definitely controlled those vampires. I went with the silver pentagram on a hunch — there was something eerie and dark about them, so... I dunno. I always trust my instincts, and so far they've never betrayed me. I knew the vampires weren't common ones after you blasted them with that fireball and they remained untouched."

"You have great instincts," I remarked, trying not to get distracted by his masculine scent. Besides, I had more to say. "I've got another lead, too."

Kagan's eyes showed interest. "Go on."

"It's about a Wiccan coven in my home town — Ivy Hills, Connecticut."

"What about it?" the fae asked, a shade of doubt discernable in his voice.

"The leader of the coven, Desmond, owns an occult bookshop just like ours. My business partner and best friend, Naomi, showed me an issue of *Forbes* with you on the front cover, and when I asked her about it, it turns out she obtained the magazine from his shop. Naomi said that according to Desmond, one of his Wiccan brethren had probably bought and given the magazine to him."

"And that's it?" Puzzlement was evident in Kagan's voice. The shifters were still picking over the remains of their dishes, only half paying attention to what we were saying.

"Do you recall what Elliott Rumford said? That the victim joined a coven, and that he might have met the sorcerer who might be the killer there?" An uneasy silence fell over the table at the word 'sorcerer,' and I went on. "Also, don't you think it's a strange coincidence that a guy interested in the occult has a magazine with you on its cover just at the moment you're involved in the case?"

He regarded me for a moment, then said condescendingly, "Alex, do you know how many covens there are in America? It's rather naive to think that a coincidence like that qualifies as a 'lead.'"

Carlos and Brendan had pushed their plates away and watched us expectantly. Did they expect Kagan or me to let our tempers flare? I wouldn't give them such a show, and I doubted Kagan would, either.

"It's not only that." I tried to quickly think of a way to explain to him about my inner voice's advice. Things couldn't get worse than they already were, so I began by saying, "I had a hunch, and my hunches are part of my... my magical package, so to speak. I am sure there's something strange going on with this coven." Although I said it quite firmly, intellectually I wasn't so sure. I hoped the voice knew best about that Desmond guy and his coven; otherwise I'd make a fool of myself.

Kagan studied me for a few more seconds, then said, "Is this part of your special powers, like healing and occasionally seeing into objects' pasts?"

I nodded.

He sighed and said, "Okay, you win. Brendan and Carlos — get the address for that bloody coven from Alex and check it out, and do it quickly: you have her teleportation charm, right?"

They nodded and he went on, "Right after that I want you two to head to the Hellfire Club and watch out for our lad from last night, the skinny one. You should probably wait outside the club. It's quite possible that our man may not go in, if he even turns up at all. That boy is important — he's our only link to the sorcerer who I believe is responsible for these murders. Remember," he said, "we have limited time — thirteen more days to catch the culprit before a supernatural apocalypse showers the earth."

"And threatens the very existence of humans and supernaturals alike," I added. At Kagan's look, I explained, "It's more melodramatic that way."

Kagan smiled briefly at me, though his eyes remained serious.

No one else at the table seemed to have anything to say, so I continued, "I gave some thought to our murder cases and I came to the conclusion that maybe someone from the inside is trying to stir up this 'magic apocalypse,' as you put it. What if someone from the Court of Hell — or even Kai himself — is behind all this?" I mused aloud, and looked Kagan straight in his beautiful eyes. For a moment I forgot where I was; I felt like I could stare at him for hours.

"The lady has a point," Carlos said. "The chief demon did look pretty full of himself and seemed to want nothing but revenge on the Court of Heaven at all costs. It's a bit suspicious."

"Or…" I thought for a moment, then said, "What if the murderer has an inside person among Kai's minions? Someone powerful enough and high enough on the hierarchy ladder to inform him of the ins and outs at the Court of Hell — and the Court of Heaven."

"But why would they want a supernatural war?" Brendan asked.

"That's the million-dollar question," I said. "Someone must see some benefit from it. Either that sorcerer or someone like him."

Silence fell over the table for a few moments, then Kagan said, "Okay, enough conspiracy theories, guys. We need evidence." He looked at the two shifters, and Brendan reluctantly got up from his chair. I wrote down the address of Magica World — Desmond's occult shop — and gave it to Brendan. Once the shifters were there, they could get more details about Desmond's so-called coven.

"And what about you guys?" Brendan asked Kagan. "What are you going to do while we check on the Wiccan coven and stake out the Hellfire Club?"

"That's no concern of yours. Now get moving." He waved them off.

Brendan shot Kagan a dirty look, but the shifters headed off, and once out of our sight, Kagan turned to me, a faint smile flickering across his mouth, "So now we're finally alone."

Uh-oh. I didn't like the sound of that at all.

Kagan burst out laughing. "Don't worry, Alex. I'm not a predator — especially not with that special enchanted knife of yours around." He grinned at me playfully and I suddenly had the urge to kick myself for falling for the arrogant fae. Instead, my hand slipped down to the silver knife, Awen's gift, which was sheathed at my thigh. As if the fae read my mind, he straightened his facial expression and said, his tone all business, "I do want to talk to you in private. I have something to discuss with you. Come on, let's get going." He stood and motioned at me to follow, and we left Temptation through a back entrance. Kagan's familiarity with the restaurant convinced me he was a regular customer, which, with his exorbitant wealth, didn't surprise me.

Once we reached the street, Kagan concentrated on summoning his magic. His power prickled on my skin. Tiny golden threads appeared in the air before us, pulsing and vibrating. They looked like teeny tiny stars, so beautiful I wanted to reach out and touch them. Before I could, though, I felt the all-too-familiar magic tug, and darkness engulfed us.

***

The magic portal delivered us in front of a magnificent old castle, perfectly preserved. A tall hedge and garden on either side surrounded us, as far as the eye could see. From one of the towers I saw a flag fluttering: the seven-pointed faery star within a circle, somewhat resembling a lotus. This had to be Kagan's home.

"You live here." I stated. He nodded and headed to the wooden gate, climbing up a dozen stairs, and I followed him. When I reached the landing, he had already gone inside.

From the top of the steps, I had a much better view of the grounds. Two lions sat on either side of the huge oak door. Though carved from stone, they looked alive. I was looking away when the face of the right one came to life. It yawned, showing me its teeth. I instinctively took a step backwards and shook my head — that had to be a magical illusion. After I blinked in surprise, the lion seemed again merely a stone statue, no sign of life.

I sniffed the air; a strong magical energy surrounded the castle, encasing it like a huge bubble. It intoxicated and, to some degree, titillated. The magic was too strong to resist, but any weaker supernatural would have had a hard time tuning into such a high voltage, and couldn't draw on its energy to boost their own. They couldn't ignore it, but would only get drunk on the strength of the magic. Looking around, I spotted another intriguing stone statue — a huge dragon in the center of the hedge garden. I made a mental note to I ask the fae about it later — it intrigued me.

I hurried into the castle and caught up with Kagan speaking to a housemaid in the hallway. She apologized for her appearance — she had a smudge of dust on her apron. I rolled my eyes — she definitely looked much better than my usual working self, especially these days, with my clothes often quite dirty or torn. She told Kagan his parents were away, but he assured her he was here for something else. After he dismissed her and we were left alone inside the huge mansion, he turned to me.

"Did you see the dragon statue in the garden? That's our family guardian. Upon attack or threat, it comes to life, with flaming nostrils, flapping wings, and thrashing tail. It's quite a terrifying sight."

Despite his serious expression, I still found it hard to believe. "Really? The most powerful and mythical of all supernatural beings is out there in your garden as a family guardian?"

Kagan nodded. "Stick with me and I'll show you more fancy stuff than you could possibly imagine." He turned and headed to a corridor which led straight into a large hall. I followed him, awestruck by the hall's appearance. Wow — if, as the singer proclaimed, heaven were a place on earth, it had to be here! Temptation had been fancy and magnificent, but here I was in the heaven of riches: cherry wood floor, huge elaborate chandeliers, the finest furniture I had ever seen, beautiful enormous framed portraits of family members, and a panoramic view of the garden and the stone dragon. I was quite taken with the dragon, to be honest, and wondered what it was like when he came to life. Fascinating and terrifying at the same time, no doubt. And to my eye it seemed that every single item in this grand hall sparkled, like gigantic Christmas decorations. The appearance of this whole space was rather surreal, like the inside of a fairytale, and the hall was even more opulent than Versailles. My initial shock gave way to realization: I was in the grand castle of one of the most powerful fae who had ever graced the Earth.

"Don't get distracted by the guest hall. My parents designed it to show off for the other magic dynasties," Kagan said flatly, without a hint of emotion — not even pride. I realized this was merely a fact of life for him.

"It certainly works."

He smiled. "I didn't know you belonged to one of the dynasties."

It took me a second to realize what he'd just said. I couldn't help but laugh and replied, "I've been hiding it." A huge painting on the wall caught my attention. "Isn't this your family crest? I saw it on the flag waving from the castle's tower."

"Sure is. This is actually the symbol of the fae, as you may know. Since my family prides itself on being the first fae in the world, we have adopted the crest." Kagan came over to me.

Holy moley, did they really hold themselves in such high esteem? Apparently so.

"Do you like it?" he asked, his face dangerously close to mine. His gaze fixed on me and tiny waves of his magic caressed my skin.

I felt the need to keep my distance so I moved slightly to one side. "Yes, I do." The colors were shades of light blue with the fae star in orange. The color combination and vibe of this picture really appealed to me. "What's written in these runes?" I asked, pointing at the inscription below the fae star.

"Two worlds, one earth, one hope."

A beautiful motto, and I found it hard to avert my eyes from this captivating painting. I cleared my throat and asked, "Aren't you and your family independent fae? You don't belong to the Seelie *or* Unseelie Court, right? Neither light nor dark?"

He nodded. "Yes, we're above all notions of duality — we simply exist the way we are."

"So what's the purpose of the inscription? I mean, it seems to be in keeping with the spirit of the Seelie, but if your family belongs to neither court...?"

"Oh boy. No, hold on." He shook his head. "The Seelie and Unseelie fae aren't as black and white as you imagine them to be. I'd say both courts have their perks and their downsides. We Griffiths, on the other hand, have been entrusted to keep the balance on earth between the two courts and two worlds — the supernatural and the human. We serve as protectors and peacekeepers. That's why the Magic Council appointed me to this investigation. Someone wants to shatter the established order on earth and create chaos. We need to stop him at all costs, before it's too late."

I felt humbled, and a little ashamed. I had been thinking Kagan's arrogance came from his wealth, but it seemed more a part of the great responsibility he bore. And I had been afraid to share the nature of my magic power with him! How stupid of me.

You weren't stupid. You were cautious. Don't be so hard on yourself, the voice in my head said.

Are you telling me he's okay? He's safe? I asked.

Mmm, not exactly. I can't tell that yet. Caution is always good.

"Alex, are you okay?" Kagan asked, sounding somewhat concerned. "From time to time you seem sort of lost, as if you're in conversation with somebody else."

That was because I was, actually, but I only replied, "I'm okay, really. I just get a little distracted sometimes. I, uh... was communicating with Brendan." I chuckled nervously and the fae forced a smile. I hoped I'd convinced him. I didn't want him to know about my peculiar... thing, whatever it was.

I'm not a 'peculiar thing,' Alex. I am your destiny, the voice said in irritation.

I cleared my throat. I would have to finish this conversation another time, another place. Definitely not before Kagan's watchful eyes. "Now, what did you want to discuss with me? We're in private, in your castle, on your territory."

He smiled in his mischievous way and said, "I want to show you something." He touched my shoulder and guided me to the far right side of the hall, where a few rows of library shelves stood. They were full of ancient tomes, similar to Awen's, as well as some newer editions and books. I sensed that the books on these shelves contained powerful knowledge, knowledge that could either heal and create or hurt and destroy.

His masculine scent reached my senses, giving me the taste of ripe summer fruits and his distinctive potent magic. Although I was trying to block out his power and prevent it from coming into contact with my own magic, small waves of it reached and caressed mine, titillating it. The taste of divine nectar at the back of my throat intensified: this was much better than the magic smoothie I had back at Temptation. My entire body craved his power. Then I shook myself: I was giving in to his charms! I stepped backwards tentatively.

His smile grew wider, and I realized he knew exactly what he was doing. The bastard didn't even have the decency to apologize or even look abashed. He seemed amused by my discomfiture. "What are you afraid of, Alex?

"Kagan, please, this has to stop. You promised you wouldn't be a predator. Or do you want me to take out my enchanted knife?"

A flash of excitement sparkled in his eyes, but he soon regained his serious, businesslike composure. "I'm sorry, Alex. It's just so... *refreshing* to tease you."

I glared at him and he hurriedly added, "Anyway, I wanted to have some time alone with you so I can show you a technique for keeping your power if the killer attacks you with your weakness. I'm afraid he might throw us a challenge like this. You do have a weakness, don't you?"

I narrowed my eyes. "Most supernaturals do," I admitted. "I'm sort of allergic to iron," While it was true that I didn't like the cold surface of iron on my skin or in near proximity to me, I could nevertheless tolerate it to some extent. However, the larger the quantity, the more difficult it became for me.

"That's unusual for mages," the fae mused aloud.

"Fae are susceptible to iron as well, right?" I asked him, trying to steer the conversation away from me. It worked this time, thank magic.

"In general, yes, but my family has found a way around it. A few ways exist, and all are described in detail here." He handed me a tome he'd taken from one of the upper shelves and continued, "However, I'm going to summarize and show you." He summoned a pair of iron cuffs and held them in his right hand. I could feel the effect on my skin, just from being so close — it wasn't pleasant, but I didn't feel particularly sick.

"What did Magica Academy teach you? I hope they gave you techniques for overcoming your weakness," he asked.

"Is this a test, teacher?" I said.

Kagan raised an eyebrow, so I answered his question. "I should withdraw my magic to block the negative influence of iron," I said and coiled my power deep inside of me. When I did, the slight dizziness and feeling of sickness I had felt a moment earlier were gone. That was much better.

Kagan nodded. "That's what trained supernaturals have been doing for hundreds of years. And yet, if you were captured or in danger and had to fight to save your life, how would you do it without using your magic?"

I had no answer. They'd never covered it at the academy, and, despite the fact that I had worked as an independent consultant on dozens of cases, I had never been threatened with iron in any of my fights. Luck of the draw, I guess.

"Now, it's true," he added, "that in most fights, monsters and magic rebels fight without using iron. In our case, though, we have to win over a dark supernatural, probably a sorcerer, and our adversaries will most likely pull out all the stops and try to exploit all our weaknesses, just like we used silver and a pentagram to kill the demonic vampires."

"Then it'd be best if you train Brendan and Carlos also. You know, as shifters they're susceptible to silver," I said.

"I'm not worried about them. They've had enough experience and training as supernatural investigators; and, besides, our culprit and his evil minions are after strong magic. And frankly, yours is the strongest. Monsters are drawn to powerful magic like moths to the flame.

"Now, Alex, imagine you're in a closed room with thick iron walls, or that you have iron cuffs with runic symbols on your hands and they block your magic." He concentrated and runic symbols appeared on the iron cuffs, which now appeared on my wrists, locked. They gave me a headache and nausea. I inverted my remaining magic, burying it deep inside of me. Much better — except now I was entirely powerless.

"So far so good, but how are you going to get out of them, using your own magical abilities?"

"Can't you just remove the cuffs? I'd rather see you perform a breaking spell or whatever you're going to do. I can learn from watching you."

"I think you can get out of the cuffs using your magic," Kagan said.

"True, I can melt them with fire, but it'd hurt me. And right now I'm in no mood for exhausting my healing power."

"Shame." He grumbled and raised his hand slightly, and a matching pair of cuffs appeared on his wrists. "Satisfied?" he asked. Truth be told, I didn't give a damn whether he had iron cuffs or not — I just wanted the shackles off my skin, period.

"Normally a fae could last at least a couple of hours shackled with cuffs like these before they started affecting his or her magic abilities."

"But you, of course, are not just any normal fae," I interjected and Kagan grinned. I was coming to seriously hate how his sexy smiles melted me. I wanted both to punch and kiss him.

Okay, maybe more the latter, but that wasn't the point.

"You have devised a technique to neutralize the pain of iron, although it makes you lose your magic. But we fae cannot do that," he said.

"So you're feeling pain?" If he did, he hid it pretty well.

"As a matter of fact, quite a lot. But I was taught how to tolerate pain, so it's not debilitating. But it does require a lot of energy and after some time — maybe five to six hours — I'd feel exhausted and my guard would be lowered. Then the iron would affect me in other, more serious, ways."

That was impressive. Even Brendan, with all his machismo, wouldn't be able to tolerate silver on his skin — a shifters' inborn weakness — for more than a few hours. It would kill him.

"But that wasn't enough for your family. You found a better way," I said.

Instead of answering me, he summoned his magic, concentrating. Silver sparkles appeared in the air, swirling around his cuffs. This lasted for a few minutes, until the cuffs finally clicked open and fell, broken, to the cherry wood floor.

I raised my eyebrows. "How did you do that?"

"For every action there is an equal reaction — you know that law of physics, don't you?"

I nodded.

"Well, it's similar with the elements: Fire is the opposite of water, earth of air, and wood of iron. I summoned wood in a quantity great enough to neutralize the iron. Now you try it."

I looked at my hands locked in the iron cuffs. The runes glowed with a pale silver light. They looked beautiful and eerie at the same time, but weren't as powerful as they seemed. True, it was a hindrance, but I had overcome much greater things. I closed my eyes and took in a deep breath. I relaxed my protective mechanism and allowed my magic to reach out. Even though I'd buried it for only a few minutes, I had missed this vital aspect of my being. I instantly felt whole again, but the awareness of pain hit my senses hard. Worse, the runic symbols neutralized my power. I concentrated harder, digging deeper for my magic and summoning the element of wood as Kagan had advised me. The power of it surged inside me and my pain started to fade. The element burst to life, overpowering the power of iron. My handcuffs burst open, just like Kagan's had done a moment ago.

However, in my magic I also found something else: the energy that was always present around the full moon. Now that the full moon was getting close, this magic sang to me in its own way, begging me to release it. I felt that I could do whatever I wanted with it; I felt invincible, like a god. I reached deep for this strange and unique but, unfortunately, repressed energy of mine, and it filled my whole being. *I must be in heaven.* This time, for a change, I didn't intend to bury it. Instead, I closed my eyes and devoured it. The sensation of heat filled me up and the song of fire called me. I had just reached for it when someone else's magic snapped at me and interrupted my play: Kagan.

"Alex, for magic's sake, have you lost your mind?" he shouted. I opened my eyes and saw the huge fireball in my hand, and smelled the smoke permeating the entire hall. My lungs screamed for air and I coughed. There was charcoal on the floor beneath my feet. I didn't even remember burning anything. I snapped the fire shut and hurried to bury my strange magic deep back inside me, where I usually kept it.

"What just happened?" I stuttered, inhaling deeply.

"You summoned a gigantic fireball and the whole room was about to explode before I broke off your spell. And it wasn't just elemental magic — oh, no. As a fae I know very well about that: something else was at play in you, something much more powerful and dangerous. In the name of magic, do you really have no idea what you are?" Kagan stared at me expectantly.

I shook my head.

He continued, saying, "You've been avoiding answering this question even to yourself, but think about it: I believe deep down inside of you, you know what your true nature is." He took my hands in his and stared deeply into my eyes.

I didn't know how to respond, what to say to this. Fortunately, destiny came to my aid just then and I heard Brendan's voice in my head.

"Alex, the bastard from last night is in front of the Hellfire Club. He's talking to another guy, and it isn't a human being. Get your ass over here, now!" With that the mental communication ended.

Chapter 15

"What happened?" Kagan let go of my hands but the look in his eyes was still hard. "Why did you unleash the fire element? You were drunk on magic — your own magic." He waited.

As if I needed him to tell me this. "I know that, Kagan. I'm not a five-year-old."

"Then tell me what happened."

"Later. But Brendan just called me mentally and said the guy we followed last night is at the Hellfire Club. We have to join the shifters." I didn't intend to answer his question, especially not now. Maybe I could try to do it later.

With what, Alex? You don't know who you are. Besides, let's be honest — this sexy fae only distracts you, said the voice.

I ignored it. "Do you want me to teleport us or...?" I couldn't finish my question, nor could I summon the power to look into his eyes. All I wanted was to stay as far as possible from him so that I wouldn't be tempted, which wasn't possible given we worked together. Ugh.

Kagan frowned and grumbled, "We must have that talk, Alex, sooner or later. We'll postpone it for now, but don't think you'll get away from it — or me."

Of course not. When had I ever been that lucky?

He summoned his magic and initiated the teleportation ritual. We stepped into the sparkling magic portal that had appeared, and it brought us to a wall near the Hellfire Club. I saw the two shifters a few yards away.

Walking over to them, I asked, "What's up, guys? Where's the suspect?"

Brendan pointed at the club. "They went inside. They've been in there for about fifteen minutes."

"Any ideas what they're doing?" Kagan asked. "Did you see them exchange anything?"

Carlos shook his head. "Nope. But Brendan and I both felt that our little friend from last night was in the company of a supernatural — and a dark one, at that."

"We couldn't determine whether he was a vampire, but I think not," Brendan added.

"Great. It's just getting more and more interesting," I remarked: my intuition told me, if he wasn't a vampire, he'd turn out to be an even nastier creature. "And what happened with the Wiccan coven in my hometown, by the way? I wanted to ask you earlier, but you cut off the connection."

Brendan shrugged. "We searched for them, but as it turns out, they only meet on Thursdays and Saturdays, every other week. They're called the Temple of Isis. I talked to their leader, Desmond Cohen — nice guy — in his occult shop. Also quite a nice place. If we hadn't been working, I might have wanted to see their goods. Anyway, he looked surprised when we asked about the magazine. He said a friend of his also asked him about it, but he couldn't remember the details. Desmond thinks he probably got it from this young guy who recently started coming to their meetings."

"Well, that could be our boy — the suspect."

Brendan regarded me for a few seconds and said, "Seriously, you believe that?"

"Why not? It's an odd coincidence that a *Forbes* issue with Kagan on the front cover ends up in the hands of a young, gullible occult lover, don't you think?"

"You are unbelievable, Alex. That issue was printed more than six months ago and bought by thousands of entrepreneurs and business owners — not to mention the fact that there's not even a hint of magic in it."

"My magic sense tells me there's something about this lead," I said.

"Really? What, then? Can't your 'magic sense' just solve the fucking murders and save us the trouble?" Brendan snapped.

I was about to use harsher words when the fae intervened. "You two — cool it. Brendan, I trust Alex's intuition. Alex, you might have a point, but nothing's proven yet. Now, both of you, shut up and let's focus on our stakeout."

After Kagan's scolding, Brendan and I kept silent and watched the club entrance from our hiding place for several more minutes. Finally the suspect came out. Next to him was a supernatural who must have been the one the shifters had mentioned — he definitely wasn't a human. He was carrying a cloth-wrapped item, and I felt dark magic prickle on my skin. I thought he was probably either a dark wizard, a warlock, or something in between, but — thank magic — not a particularly powerful one; more on the low to mid-level scale.

The two men parted ways as the supernatural handed the boy the wrapped item. The fae told Carlos to follow the supernatural. Our suspect, the skinny boy, headed straight down the street. We followed him, maintaining our distance so he wouldn't notice us. Fortunately he was too wrapped up in himself to pay much attention to anything else. He crossed to a busier street and got into an old Ford Mustang. Kagan selected a relatively new Volvo model and, breaking its locks, climbed in.

"What in the world are you doing?" I asked him. "This is theft."

"Just get in." He motioned to me and the shifters. "I'll pay for the damage, don't worry. A fae always pays his debts."

If it weren't for our tense situation, I would have laughed: Was he serious or had he just made a reference to *Game of Thrones*? He pressed the accelerator and we were off. Our suspect was a few intersections ahead of us, making no effort to evade us. That was good: he hadn't noticed our presence.

"I could have summoned a car," Kagan added, "but it'd have taken more time than we have." I glanced at him — his face was stern and he seemed to be concentrating.

The chase passed in silence. Kagan maintained a safe distance, but we didn't let him out of our sight. After about half an hour or so, the guy turned left and pulled up in front of an abandoned factory on the outskirts of Queens. The building looked run-down and battered. Kagan drove a little farther down the road in order not to attract the suspect's attention, then pulled over and cut the engine.

When we reached the building, we found a wire fence encircling the whole property. The gate was in full view of the factory's door, so we crept along the fence until we got to a more concealed area.

I turned to Kagan and asked, "Do you want me to burn the wires, or would you prefer the honor?"

He chuckled and signaled he'd do it, then put his hand on the fence, letting his magic spread over it, and sizzling ripples began melting the wire. They made a big enough hole in the middle for us to pass through. First through was Kagan, followed by Brendan. When I touched the fence on my way through, a vision swam before my eyes: I saw the suspect, inside the two-story factory building. He was on the first floor accompanied by a demon-powered vampire, and he held some papers with scribbled descriptions about rituals. I spotted hieroglyphs on the papers, then the vision blurred. Suddenly my head felt extremely light, like I was about to faint.

"Alex, are you all right?" Brendan asked, concerned. "Get in here!" He pulled me in. I clung to his magic and it invigorated me, giving me fresh energy, enough to get through the fence.

"What did you see?" Kagan asked, not standing on ceremony once I was on the other side of the fence.

"So impatient," I remarked. I wanted to regain my composure before setting my mind on what I'd seen in the vision.

"This is serious, Alex. Did you see anything important?" Brendan scolded me like a petulant child.

"Okay, okay. Just chill out." I described the vision I had received upon touching the wire. It made sense that my superpower had kicked in: We were close to the full moon and I was deeply invested in this case.

The fae listened carefully, then noted grimly, "Hieroglyphs, huh? They're dealing with dark Egyptian magic. We'll have to search the factory thoroughly for evidence once we deal with our guy and the vampire."

Brendan nodded and we all headed for the factory walls and began climbing them. The uneven walls were easy for us to scale. We peeked through the shattered windows and saw our suspect, a wrapped package clutched in his hand.

"What's he doing?" I whispered to Kagan. He shushed me.

"Probably waiting for someone," Brendan said.

"Vampires?" I suggested. "Shouldn't we intervene? I have the feeling that whatever he's holding is pretty valuable."

"We wait until his connection shows up. Now be quiet," Kagan snapped. "In the meantime, call Carlos mentally and ask if he can join us. We'll need his help."

I connected with the shifter, and he said, the supernatural had gone to a grocery store, then to a building, supposedly to his apartment. He hadn't sensed any supernatural activity and was eager to join us when I filled him on the current events of the chase of the skinny boy. We negotiated; I'd teleport to the front of the Hellfire Cub and pick up him from there.

In about ten minutes Carlos and I were back on the factory walls with Brendan and Kagan, pressed against the windowpanes of the run-down building, watching.

With a sudden cracking sound, a yellow-green light appeared inside the hall, and a vampire appeared before the suspect. As they greeted each other, Kagan hissed, "Attack! Now!" and jumped through the window, shattering glass like a friggin' Rambo. This guy was out of his mind! But so were Brendan and Carlos: they followed him. Didn't people use the old-fashioned way anymore? I cursed my male colleagues and jumped as well, hoping it wouldn't destroy my boots and clothes. I was still annoyed by the loss of my jeans to the fangs of the three-headed snake. By the time I landed on the dirty factory floor, Kagan and the shifters were already charging at the vampire and our suspect, shooting at them with silver bullets. But the air around our suspects gleamed and a shimmering barrier surrounded them. The bullets ricocheted back at my colleagues. Kagan's magic came out, wrapping itself around the barrier bubble like a treacherous snake. With one sudden push his magic broke it into millions of tiny fluttering particles.

The human shouted and the vampire pushed him aside, stepping in front of us, his crimson eyes gleaming menacingly. As a vampire, he was calculating and sensible: they were pretty high in the monster hierarchy. But then I had fought only against common, bloodthirsty vampires, if we didn't count the horde of demon-infested vampires from last night.

My colleagues fired more silver bullets, but the monster dived to the side and they all missed him. He directed his gaze at the wall behind us, and it began crumbling over us. Fuck! We ran, trying to avoid the heavy stones and bricks that showered down on us, and Kagan summoned the wind element and a swirling gust took them away through the broken windows. A large brick had hit me, but otherwise I was okay. My clothes were dirty and slightly torn up, but I still had hopes I could save them.

The shifters transformed into animals, their eyes glinting with fury and revenge. With inhuman speed they pounced on the vampire, knocking him down. Carlos the tiger bit him hard on his neck while Brendan transformed back into his human form. Just when he was about to fire, a vampire kicked him in the arm and the gun flew from his hand. Brendan swung at the vampire who reeled backwards and took a step towards his gun, lying on the floor, but before Kagan or the werewolf could fire a silver bullet into the vampire's chest, we heard a sudden crack, the air shimmered in pale, silver-blue light, a multitude of glyphs vibrated, and before I could count to three the guy had disappeared. In his place, instead, were ten more vampires.

What the hell?

"Great, more fun coming our way," I mumbled and reached deep inside, summoning my magic. I needed all of it, and right away.

Chapter 16

The newly arrived vampires dashed at us, but this time we knew how to fight them. Carlos and Brendan had already taken down three, but half a dozen vampires were kicking and hitting the shifters and trying to bite them: the demonic vampires put up a good fight. We needed to get rid of them now. A sense of foreboding gnawed at me and I began to feel anxious. I dodged a blow from a nearby vampire and stood up quickly. He again swung his arms at me, but I kicked him hard in the face, then flung my enchanted silver knife straight into his heart. The bastard screeched in pain and collapsed, then began glowing with a greenish light. Then he disintegrated into dust in the air.

Kagan fought off three vampires, and each shifter tackled two. I was about to throw my knife again when something hit me hard in the back. My head reeled and I saw stars before my eyes. The pain passed throughout my body, but it washed away pretty quickly. My powers of healing were increasing. I turned in the direction of the attack. A ghoulish vampire sneered at me.

"Did it hurt, doll?" he asked, showing his pointy teeth, saliva dripping from them. Ew, disgusting. He charged at me, but this time I went for his heart. Before the knife bit into his flesh he caught my hand and the knife, stopping its motion. His brawny fingers gripped at the handle, his mouth so close to me that I could feel his breath: it smelled of dead bodies and corpses, mixed with blood. I clenched my jaw and kicked him in the ribs with all my force. He doubled over but his fingers didn't release the knife.

"First of all, nobody messes with me. And second" — I tightened my grip on the silver knife and, exerting all my strength, forced the blade into his chest, — "never, ever call me 'doll' again." With those words, I pushed the knife deeper, into his heart. The greenish light enveloped him like a giant bubble and I stepped back.

My colleagues were doing relatively well: Kagan had taken one vampire down, but two were still on his heels. He would be fine. The shifters had more trouble dealing with the vampires than the fae, though. I summoned all my magic, calling on the element of air. It came to me, its unruly nature palpable on my fingertips. Fire was powerful and highly destructive, but air was a completely different thing: It could take any form and direction you shaped it into. I directed a blast of air toward the vampires near Carlos and Brendan, trapping them inside the swirl of wind.

It felt so good to connect with my growing magic that I did something I wasn't intending — it just came naturally to me. The sensation of silver, burning silver, filled my whole mind, and seething rage exploded inside me. I hurled a huge wind blast at the vampires as well as the two near Kagan. The blast swept them away like a tornado, and they all exploded into greenish light in the air. Dust scattered all around us.

I was very proud of myself until I saw the shifters — their skin was as white as chalk, and they looked on the brink of death. They were barely standing upright. Even the fae seemed dazed and shaken. I immediately felt guilty, even though I knew the shifters wouldn't have been seriously harmed in such a short time.

"W-what happened?" I stuttered, looking at my hands in disbelief.

"Why are you asking us? You're the one who summoned that blast, Alex, and it wasn't a good one," Kagan said, surprise evident in his voice.

Brendan added, "What the fuck was that, Alex? Since when do you summon silver out of thin air?" He was still staggering, but his face looked a shade better.

"Sorry, Brendan, I didn't mean to hurt you or —"

"That could have killed us, Alex! Have you forgotten that we're shifters? What possessed you to blast a huge explosion of silver right under our noses?"

"I have to agree with Brendan on this issue. That was dangerous, Alex. It even made *me* feel sick. Next time, better warn us," Kagan said.

"Okay — sorry, guys, really. I didn't intend to, it just happened sort of... naturally," I apologized.

But I heard Brendan cursing under his breath and saying, "I feel like I don't even know you anymore."

I hurried to add, "I won't do anything like that again, I promise."

Brendan reluctantly accepted my apologies, and he and Carlos began to regain their powers. In a few more minutes they would be fine. I looked around the vast hall and a slight tingle went up and down my spine, stirring some inexplicable desire in my blood and veins.

Go upstairs, honey, the voice whispered to me, and I decided to trust it.

I headed to the far side of the hall and went up the staircase. The second floor looked almost identical to the first, except for an old cupboard, a messy bed, and a table with the remnants of a meal. Kagan followed me.

"It looks like the lion's den," I said.

Kagan examined the furniture. I went to the cupboard and cautiously opened it. Something swished and a sense of dread washed over me. I ducked, shouting at the top of my lungs, "Watch out!"

An arrow struck the wall behind me.

"Excellent reflexes, mate," the fae commented, plucking the arrow from the wall. "This could have easily gone through your head. Poisoned, too."

As he held it in his hands, I saw the glistening moisture on its edge

He stared into my eyes as if calculating who would have wanted to kill me. "And a lethal poison at that."

"What's up there, guys? What did we miss?" Brendan and Carlos came over to us, still a bit dizzy, but definitely much better. At least they had stopped staggering and their skin color looked almost normal.

I replied, "A booby-trap. Let's hope it's the only one." I peeked into the cupboard and saw scattered papers with notes scribbled on them.

"What do they say?" Kagan asked, glancing at the writings.

"Mm, it's mostly ingredients: black cow's milk, a two-tailed lizard, Egyptian weasel, ibis," I read aloud, careful not to touch anything.

"It seems like someone is preparing for some sort of a ritual," the fae remarked.

"Oh guys, you should see this," Carlos exclaimed, and we all turned our heads toward him. He held some ancient-looking scrolls, using a cloth to protect the delicate material. The scrolls reminded me of some of the books in Awen's vast library. "It's in Egyptian hieroglyphs, and I don't like the feel of it at all."

"Ancient Egyptian, like from the time of Osiris and Isis?" I asked.

Carlos nodded.

"Can you read it?" Brendan asked, coming over.

"I can give it a try. We studied Egyptian hieroglyphs at the shifter academy in Rio de Janeiro."

Carlos frowned and read a few lines, then translated them. It was all basically ingredients, just like the ones I had read in the papers scattered around. Carlos skipped a few more lines, his lips silently moving as he read. He brought his gaze back to us, paused, and exclaimed, "Holy shit! This describes a sacrificial ritual!"

"What?" Brendan and I said at the same time. The words 'sacrificial ritual' screamed trouble — big time trouble — and my heart began pounding against my chest wildly as if it wanted to come out.

"Yes." He pointed at some hieroglyphs in the book, none of which made any sense to me. I had greater success in understanding men than Egyptian hieroglyphs. "It says that the deaths of three innocents are required for the ritual. Their blood has to be mixed with black cow's milk, a two-tailed lizard, Egyptian weasel, black dog's blood, and ibis. Myrrh and frankincense for burning. The ritual occurs at the full moon, at its zenith. A long list of incantations follows, names of Egyptian gods and the like. Also, some verses have to be chanted seven times."

"Great," Brendan said sarcastically. "Does it say why? What's the purpose of the ritual?"

Carlos read further in the scroll. By the way wrinkles had formed on his handsome face, he was putting a lot of effort into it.

"I don't see any explanation as to why, but I bet good money it's for some dark, nasty purpose... Wait. Oh boy. This is bad — really, really bad." He turned to us, shock written all over his face. I felt my heartbeat quicken.

"One of the victims has to be a goddess. And her beating heart has to be sacrificed, too, along with her blood."

Chapter 17

"Wait, what?" I choked at his words, taken aback by the new information. "What kind of sick mind would want a goddess's heart? That's twisted!"

"You're absolutely right," Kagan said. "But don't forget, we are dealing with a sick, perverted supernatural. And perverted not in the sexual context, but *magically* perverted — which is much, much worse." He turned to Brendan. "I'm going to inform the Council about these events right away. They need to know. I also need to warn the Court of Heaven. The goddesses are obviously in danger. Brendan, see if you can find any of the human's fingerprints on the papers and furniture. We have to find him. They ought to be here."

Brendan pursed his lips nervously and I sensed anger and dark clouds forming around his aura. He didn't like the fae bossing him around at all. But he had no choice: Kagan was in charge of our investigation, and Brendan knew that very well.

Despite his anger, Brendan nodded. After pulling on a pair of latex gloves, he scooped up the sheets of paper we had found to check them for fingerprints, while Carlos checked the table and the empty plastic bags. Kagan, in the meantime, stepped aside and closed his eyes. I instinctively felt his elemental powers tingling and tickling my skin — all the four elements exploded in me and I felt strangely invigorated and agitated. He'd connected with the Magic Council a few days ago, but I hadn't felt it then like I did now. Maybe because of the moon, which was so intertwined with my magic and its activity. I knew that, if I wanted to, I could eavesdrop on his mental conversation with the Council: I was that powerful now. I saw no need to, though; he was simply relaying the latest development on our case.

"So, basically we have less than four days to stop the sacrificial slaughter of a goddess," I said, looking back at Brendan and Carlos. The werewolf had found and taken some fingerprints, and the faces of both shifters were grim. For the first time we realized the true nature of the culprit we were after: He wasn't simply killing innocent humans, but wanted to kill gods and goddesses also.

I asked the shifters, "Do you think the other victims needed for this ritual are the two murder cases we've been working on? Can he use blood that has already been spilled, or does he need the victims to be freshly killed right before or during the ritual?"

"That's a good question. Does it say in the scrolls?" Kagan had finished his mental talk with the Council. Carlos studied the hieroglyphs for a few more minutes, and I noticed tiny droplets of sweat forming on his neck and forehead. It must have been hard work.

"It doesn't specify either way," Carlos concluded.

"So that leaves the possibility that our two murder cases could be part of this ritual, which should be taking place in four days," I mused aloud. If that was true, the pieces of the puzzle were starting to fit together.

"That would explain why the culprit carved the Holy Order of Shadows' symbol on the victims' bodies: First to point us in the wrong direction and create strife between the two courts, and second to take some of their blood for the performance of the ritual later," Kagan said.

The information left a bad taste in my mouth. This stuff was making me feel sick to my stomach. An uneasy silence fell over the room.

Kagan broke it by adding, "The Magic Council thanks us for warning them. The Morrigan's going to talk to the other gods and goddesses, and they'll call us in when they have a plan."

We spent another half an hour looking for more evidence, but we didn't find anything else of interest. Kagan took the scroll and the sheets of paper, placing them in evidence bags. As he was sliding the paper into the bags, I spotted an occult symbol on one of the sheets: the triquetra symbol, but inverted. I was sure I had seen it somewhere else before, I just couldn't put my finger on where or when. It must have been in our shop. Or maybe it was the logo of some coven? I couldn't remember.

Turning to Brendan, I asked, "Hey, do you see this symbol?" and showed him the little sign on the paper. "Have you seen it somewhere, maybe at the Temple of Isis coven?"

"There were no meetings today, Alex, I told you that already," he snapped irritably.

"Oh right. I forgot. Then maybe at Desmond's occult shop?"

The werewolf studied the sign intently for a few seconds more before deciding, "No, I don't recognize it; why?"

"I think I've recently seen it..." Memories from the past few weeks swirled in my mind like a raging whirlpool ready to suck me in. A multitude of fragmented experiences danced before my eyes. Suddenly the image of the two witches at the lecture in Desmond's shop surfaced. One of the ladies who told us about Desmond's coven wore the same symbol on a pendant around her neck.

I told my colleagues about it, and they listened carefully without saying anything. Kagan only gave me a slight nod, and then transported us back to Manhattan and gave the fingerprints we had found in the run-down factory to the Magic Council. In just a few hours they had identified them, not long after we all reached Kagan's apartment, which he suggested we use as a working office while he met with the Council representative. The fingerprints all belonged to one man, Paul Robbins, age twenty-three, a resident of Cleveland, Ohio — a long way from New York. The man had no criminal record, not even a parking fine. His file photo matched the guy we had chased, though.

"Maybe he's possessed?" Carlos suggested. The fae's apartment was splendid — right in the heart of Manhattan, and the interior made us feel at home.

"That bartender at the Hellfire Club said his name was Jimmy," Carlos continued musing. "So he must be concealing his identity."

"It's hard to determine anything at this stage. Robbins could have been tricked by a sorcerer — he might have promised him special powers or threatened him in some way. Either way, a lot of humans — and supernaturals, for that matter — are being deceived by dark forces," Brendan said.

"Possessed or not, Paul or Jimmy, I want this man caught and behind iron bars. And the Magic Council and both Courts want him as well," Kagan growled. "If nothing else, he's been helping and serving an evil mastermind, and he has to take the consequences for it." Kagan's temper had been at its peak ever since he'd returned from his meeting with the Council representative. I had never seen him so fierce. I could only guess at what they had talked about, but it was clear it hadn't been a pleasant conversation.

"I keep thinking about the Egyptian hieroglyphs we found," I said. "The coven in my own town — the Temple of Isis — also has an

Egyptian connection, as well as a connection with that inverted triequetra; and Naomi and I both felt a dark energy in the aura of the coven's leader, Desmond. Not to mention that he had an issue of *Forbes* with Kagan on the cover. That can't all be just silly coincidences."

"What are you getting at?" Kagan asked.

"I think that boy, Paul — or Jimmy, whatever — is a member of that coven and, following that line of thought Desmond might be behind all this."

Brendan laughed derisively. "Alex, of all the stupid things I have heard, this takes the cake."

"Oh really?" I bared my teeth.

"Yes. The guy you despise so much, Desmond, is a perfectly decent fellow. True, there were dark overtones in his aura, but that doesn't mean anything. Besides, my shifter sense confirmed that he was telling the truth. Carlos, you were with me too — please tell Miss Shaw that Desmond told us the truth."

Carlos confirmed Brendan's statement, and I was puzzled: Could my hunch and inner voice be wrong?

What did you get me into? I scolded the inner voice.

I never said he's a murderer, only that he's odd and to be suspicious of his coven. There's a big difference, the voice replied in an arch tone.

Oh, shut up, I replied irritably.

"I know you want to put the blame on him because he's your competitor and steals your customers, but I seriously doubt Desmond has committed any murders," Brendan continued.

"He doesn't steal our customers," I retorted.

Oh, please, the voice began, but I told it to shut up again.

"You two — stop it. Alex raised some valid points, so we'll investigate the coven during their next meeting," Kagan ruled, and the matter was settled.

The next morning I told Naomi of the day's events, especially about the Egyptian scroll and the sinister ritual that had to be performed.

She was speechless for a few seconds, gaping at me.

"Wow, and I thought it was tough dealing with arrogant teenagers and spoiled middle-aged ladies!" Naomi exclaimed.

We spent that day making inquiries about the abandoned factory, but it didn't help us. The factory had been built in the late nineteenth century by some prominent industrialist as a steel enterprise and, after the Second World War, went bankrupt. The owners weren't supernaturals and had nothing to do with the dark powers of the universe, as far as we could tell. We looked again at both of the coroner's reports and reviewed the surveillance footage, but found nothing of interest. The question on the second murder was why the culprit had hidden the body in a dumpster. We also went yet again through the notes Carlos had kept about the two murders and through

Christina's diary, but they weren't of any help, either.

The next day, we visited the Hellfire Club, this time to question the club's owner — the leprechaun we'd met on our first visit. The Magic Council had seen to it that he and his employees would cooperate with us. We questioned the leprechaun about our suspect, Paul Robbins, and the sorcerer known as the Rune Keeper, but he didn't know anything about them.

"Seriously, how do you bigwigs at the Magic Council expect me to remember all my customers? This is insanity. The Rune Keeper? Jeez, there are as many nicknames as there are stars in the night sky. And I wouldn't bother remembering some small fish like that guy Robbins, anyway."

"He probably came in with the sorcerer, the Rune Keeper."

"I don't care if he came here with Kai or even Lucifer himself! I can't remember, I already told you," the leprechaun said irritably.

Kagan drew very near to him and leaned so that his face was only inches from the leprechaun's. "Listen, chap, world peace is at stake: there have been two gruesome ritualistic murders and the courts of Heaven and Hell are currently not on speaking terms. We need to solve those bloody murders and we believe the person known as the Rune Keeper knew the first victim. He might actually be the culprit — he is the key to the mystery. Besides, this Paul Robbins is a mere human — how did he get through your stellar security?" Kagan asked, his voice hard as steel. He'd already asked the bartender but he didn't know, either. Said he had some patron.

The leprechaun kept his nerve this time. "Yes, I am aware that there are occasionally humans in my club, but they always come with a patron who compensates me for their nonmagical nature with a small donation." He smirked and I developed a strong dislike for him. "I don't judge anybody. Human or not, all are equal to me."

"Wow, that's very generous of you," I said derisively.

The leprechaun pretended he hadn't heard me, and continued. "I offer my customers a nice nonjudgmental place, a friendly atmosphere for socializing. You'd do better to ask my bartenders about the guy you're searching for." The leprechaun gave me a dirty look, and called the bartender, who, as it turned out, was the one we were already familiar with — the panther shifter. Fate was on our side.

"What's up, boss?" the bartender asked, coming over. Then he saw us, and instinctively bared his fangs. His eyes gleamed the yellow-greenish color that I was so familiar with from Brendan. "You! Again? What do you guys want now? The first time you came and caused chaos, I bottled it up, but you came again and caused a new scene. Should I be worried now too? Any more chasing after people or blasting them?"

Kagan flashed his badge and said, "We work for the Magic Council. We're currently investigating two supernatural murders that have occurred in NYC in the past few days. We need you to tell us about the lad you pointed out to us the last time we spoke, or about his patron, the Rune Keeper. A goddess' life is in danger, and the magical order on earth is at stake." Kagan paused, waiting for his words to work their effect on the bewildered panther shifter. Then he went on. "Do you know anything that might benefit us in our investigation? I'm not playing around. Whoever the killer is, he's planning a magical revolution."

The panther shifter looked at his boss, startled. The leprechaun nodded.

"Umm, I d-don't know. The dude you're asking me about, I know him only by the name 'Jimmy.' Once or twice in his chats to other customers in the club, I heard him mention the Rune Keeper. But I don't think I've seen *that* guy here — not that I'm aware of."

"Wasn't that his patron, though? How did he get in without him?"

The bartender shrugged. "Not my job. The bouncers take care of that. Once the customers are here, I just serve 'em." He considered a moment. "I suppose his patron could have brought him in and then left him here."

"Okay..." Kagan hesitated, then asked, "Your name was...?"

"Norwik, sir," he hastily replied.

"Okay, Norwik, if you remember anything about this guy or his mysterious patron, please connect with me. Mentally." Kagan smiled and gave him a firm pat on the shoulder.

We left the club. On the street, I noted, "So, the Rune Keeper might not have been in this club."

"I dunno. Seems to me this case is pretty much a dead end," Brendan complained grumpily. "Whenever we learn something new and think we're making progress, this sorcerer is mentioned and we're back at square one. You can't deny it; we're stuck. It feels like the culprit has cast a spell on our investigation or something."

"Hmm. That's not an entirely impossible idea..." Kagan said thoughtfully, then exclaimed, "You've given me an excellent idea! But I have to go, I've got an appointment. You three, go look into that Wiccan coven Alex is so anxious about and report your findings to me. See you tomorrow outside my apartment, nine o'clock." With those words he transported himself and disappeared from our sight.

When we teleported to Desmond's occult shop, his gathering had just started. A long and rather tedious lecture followed, with lots of theory and little to no practice. Desmond beamed when he saw me and the shifters. He asked about Naomi and I gave him an evasive reply. I didn't like the thought that our potential murderer had a thing for my best friend.

During the lecture I took a chance and searched for the symbol I had found on the scrolls in the factory — the inverted triquetra — but in vain. After the lecture was over, I went to Desmond again and asked him about his coven members.

"We have a diverse group of people in the Temple of Isis," he said. "Is there anyone of particular interest to you?"

"I was dating a guy not so long ago — I'm wondering if he might be a member." I smiled and hoped he wouldn't get suspicious.

"What's his name?"

I showed him the suspect's photograph, which I had saved on my phone. Desmond shook his head and said, "Sorry, can't remember seeing this particular guy. But our coven gets hundreds of visitors, so it's still possible. Your friends already asked about him, though. Is that a mutual friend of yours?"

I didn't answer, just smiled and thanked him, and went to find Brendan.

"Why didn't you tell me you had already asked Desmond about Paul?" I snapped at him.

"Why bother? You've got a bee in your bonnet about this guy Desmond, and no matter what I say, you're convinced he's our man." He shrugged and returned to his conversation with an attractive witch. When the gathering ended about half an hour later, I gave the shifters enough fairy dust to teleport them to their hotel in Tribeca, then I went home on foot.

After the long, tedious day full of tension, suspicion, and uncertainty, it felt so good to be at home and see my best friend.

She asked me about the ritual that we had to prevent and I conceded that we all were worried: there was only one day left for us to catch the culprit. Neither we nor the Magic Council could allow a goddess to be slaughtered by a maniac.

As soon as I woke up the next morning, that was the first thing I thought of. We had spent the last two days following up on our leads, poring over witness statements, and staking out the Hellfire Club. The full moon would be tomorrow and we didn't have much time left. But we spent the entire day reading over statements, reviewing our notes, trying to get a hint of where else to look, and came up with nothing.

The following day I met Kagan and the shifters at the arranged time and place, in front of his apartment on the Lower East Side. Everyone was ready and silent, and there was no bickering between us. The awareness of the grim ritual to be performed tonight kept us all sober and focused.

The fae teleported us to the Veil using his own magic. After the run-down factory, I was struck again by the beauty of the Veil's grand modern glass building. The ogre at the entrance asked for our badges. When we showed them, he gave Kagan an ingratiating smile, his eyes full of respect, but he awarded us only with a condescending look. It obviously paid to belong to one of the magic dynasties. Shame I'd been born to one of the lower classes.

Only a few supernaturals occupied the magically charged grand hall of the Veil this time. I immediately noticed the Morrigan. She greeted Kagan amiably and gave the rest of us a cool but polite welcome. On either side of her sat two other women — definitely goddesses as well, judging by the feel of their magic. The lady on the left had flaxen hair and ocean-blue eyes, and very pale skin. The Morrigan's other companion had hazelnut hair and purple eyes — a strange combination. That wasn't her natural eye color, I figured, but an enchantment. The magic of both goddesses tasted like ripe delicious fruit on a hot summer day: potent, pleasant, full of surprises, but also dangerous. Even though their magic felt good, it could still turn nasty if it needed to. Gods were sometimes cruel, too, if they had to protect something or someone they cared about.

"I am pleased you were all able to come today," the Morrigan began. "Kagan relayed some information to us about a sacrificial ritual that is to be performed tomorrow night, I believe?"

Kagan nodded.

"That is very worrisome. Do you have any clue who the mastermind behind this madness is?"

I exchanged quick looks with the fae and the shifters. Kagan cleared his throat and said, "We're still working on that. However, we think the culprit has someone powerful in the Court of Hell, but don't know yet who."

"Ha! I knew it!" The Morrigan's eyes narrowed and two small dangerous flames flashed in them for a split second. "My good old eternal enemy is involved in this. He had to be."

I cleared my throat before saying, "Actually, we are not certain about Kai. In fact, we suspect the culprit's agent is betraying Kai and the Court of Hell as well, in a sense."

The Morrigan frowned. "But why? For what purpose? It could lead to a..." Realization dawned on her face and she added hurriedly, "a magical revolution? Is that what they're after? They *want* a magical apocalypse? That's monstrous!"

"We're not sure. It's only a guess. But people like this often want to break the established world order and create their own order out of the chaos." I had never been good with criminal and pathological psychology, and I hoped I'd explained it properly.

The Morrigan exchanged glances with her companions, then turned to us. "We need to stop this, this mastermind or whoever it is. Kagan, do you need any additional help? I can send the White Phantom Queen your way."

I tried my best not to gape. The White Phantom Queen was a mythical goddess who had the power to numb people and magical creatures by simply singing ancient lullabies to them. Then she slew them.

"No, it's okay. We don't want to scare the culprit. We don't want him to suspect anything, otherwise he may retreat," the fae replied.

"Sounds right," the Morrigan agreed.

"That's why we didn't inform the Court of Hell, and why we're asking you not to say a word to Kai. He would go mad and probably scare his secret double agent if he knew. We need them to think that we haven't caught wind of their plans. In the meantime, we have informed the Council and your Court — your goddesses are prepared, and when the culprit strikes again, we will catch him."

The Morrigan studied Kagan's face for several long seconds, which seemed like an eternity to me. I have heard the cliché that what seems like ages for humans is only seconds for gods. It was probably true.

"Your plan seems reasonable, but has one major flaw."

"And that is?" Kagan asked.

"What if the targeted goddess doesn't belong to my ranks? What if she is just a girl who doesn't even know she is a supernatural or a goddess? Then what will you do?"

Kagan's expression didn't change; in fact, he didn't even blink. He said, "The chances of such a turn of events are quite slim, as you know. I give you my word as a fae that I will do my best to keep such a thing from ever happening." The fae was trying hard to sound nonchalant and please her, I sensed, but the Morrigan wasn't a fool.

"But what if it does happen after all, my dear?" she asked. She was enjoying this, slightly mocking his overconfidence.

Kagan turned to the shifters and me and said, "Would you excuse us for a bit?"

Without asking any questions, we left the grand hall and sat in the corridor near the gates to wait for him. Curiously, the two goddess friends of the Morrigan left too, though they exited through another inner door. The fae and the leader of the Court of Heaven spent some fifteen minutes or so in the grand hall, then Kagan finally left the hall and rejoined us. He looked both anxious and pleased at the same time.

"So how did it go? Did you succeed in convincing her?" Brendan asked.

"For now, yes. But she's so stubborn I fear she may inform Kai and his court at any moment now, because she wants to save some goddess."

"Uh, excuse me?" I cut in. "'Some goddess'? Hello, a supernatural — who, on top of that, belongs to the Court of Heaven — is in danger and you don't give a damn?"

He turned to me, his eyes unusually calm and cold, resembling a winter sea.

"Of course I give a damn! But I also want to catch the culprit, without letting Kai throw his demons into the effort. That would do more harm than good. There are larger things at stake than one goddess' life, like peace and the magic order on earth. But rest assured, Alex, I'll do my best to see that, whoever she might be, she doesn't get hurt."

I studied his face for a few long seconds. For the first time I was seeing his true colors: Kagan was powerful and ruthless, and, even though he believed he was a protector of the human and supernatural worlds, he wouldn't give a second thought to letting a goddess die for "the greater good."

"You are heartless, Kagan," I said simply.

"What? I said I — "

Brendan interjected, "Hey, you two stop it. No one is getting killed — we won't allow such a thing to happen. We'd do better to investigate and prevent the coming murder than stay here and argue over bullshit."

Kagan nodded. "That's what I thought I said. Let's…"

I couldn't hear the end of his sentence because my vision blurred and I suddenly found myself in our occult shop, the Steaming Cauldron. Vampires inside the shop advanced menacingly on Naomi and ransacked the displays of potions, artifacts, and magic objects. Items were shattered and tossed on the floor, the mess giving me a headache. Naomi's skin was as pale as chalk. I immediately felt the vampires' magic — they were the same type we'd fought four nights ago. I saw

Naomi reach for her transport charm, but a vampire swung at her and hit her hard in the ribs. I had to intervene. With horror I saw Naomi's transport charm fall on the floor, spilling over.

Please, help me, came my best friend's inner cry.

Chapter 18

I shouted and stomped my feet on the floor. Brendan took me by the elbow, shaking me lightly.

"Alex, what's the matter? Have you lost your mind? Why are you screaming?"

I blinked at him, coming back to myself. "My friend's being attacked by vampires in our shop! We have to help." I was about to teleport myself, but hesitated: I needed backup and had to know whether my colleagues were coming with me or not. I looked at them expectantly, but no one moved or said anything. *Oh, fucking great!*

"Please, are you coming?" I said, without even trying to hide the desperation in my voice. I had to get to Naomi ASAP and help her.

"Alex, are you sure your vision was true?" Kagan asked. He looked genuinely concerned.

"Absolutely," I snapped at him. I couldn't believe the fae doubted my judgment. "There's no time for talk! Naomi could be hurt or injured. She is not a fighter like me, she's a hedge witch." The thought of my friend's life being in peril was unbearable and I was about to teleport, with or without them, when Kagan glanced at the shifters and reluctantly said, "Okay. Let's go."

I nodded and reached for the invisible thread in my center and felt the magic intensify around us. The air started vibrating and a yellow cloud appeared before us. We stepped inside and the void took us, bringing us to our shop, and just in time: Two vampires had cornered Naomi near the cash register and were trying to overpower her. To her credit, she kicked and screamed, grappling with them. She even kicked one of the vampires hard in his crotch. She reached for a potion and flung it straight into the face of the nearest vampire. He screamed in pain and the bloodlust in his eyes intensified.

With a sinking heart I saw all the mess this vampire gang had created: the scattered magical objects, potions, and artifacts that lay on the floor. No one could hurt my friends without taking the consequences for it. I hurled my silver crescent knife, the one that had belonged to my mother, into the vampire that was closest to Naomi. The silver blade hit him straight in the back, just behind his heart. He screamed in agony and the greenish color enveloped him. I called my knife back. In moments the vampire disappeared, the only traces of him some debris on the spot where he'd stood.

I hurled my knife at the other vampire closest to Naomi. My co-investigators were all fighting the remaining vampires in our shop, five or six of them. A silvery cloud burst up before me and I spotted the guy we were chasing. "Hey you!" I yelled and called back the weapon. Though I shouted, I could barely hear myself above the noise — everyone was fighting, blasting magic, or shattering and breaking items in our small shop. The young guy grinned at me, something eerie and wicked in his expression — as if he knew something I didn't know, as if he were ahead of the game, *his* game. Not for long!

I was about to hurl my chakram at him — I didn't want to kill him with my special knife — when he made a motion with his hand and dark purple sizzling flames erupted in the space around me. What the hell?

A lightning bolt struck me and darkness fell over me.

***

When I came to, I found myself in a dingy basement, my hands bound with shackles looped over an old pipe above my head. A strange smell floated in the stale air. Someone was making a potion — a concoction of herbs with other peculiar items. I could also hear a quiet, monotonous humming, almost like chanting, and I suddenly realized the sacrificial ritual was in progress.

I tried to get myself out of the manacles, twisting my wrists against the metal. I immediately regretted it: A searing pain pierced my body and my mind throbbed. Shit! The cuffs must have been forged from iron. It wasn't that bad, though; I had my healing superpower, plus I could block my magic and prevent it from coming into contact with the iron. I wouldn't feel any pain then, though I'd also lose my elemental magic. However, the pain was unusually strong and the sickening feeling mounted in the pit of my stomach. There had to be something else making me sick.

I took a closer look at the dark chamber I was in. My eyes had adjusted to the dim light and now I saw, in the back end of the basement, a few male figures bending over a cauldron. They were humming something in a foreign language — not English or Latin, which I had learned at the Academy. Could it be Egyptian?

Once the shock eased and I acclimated to the pain, my sense of magic told me that all the walls around me had iron in them. The room had no windows, and even the ceiling and floor concealed iron. Fuck!

Someone chose this cellar especially for you and made it all in iron to hijack your magic, the voice in my head said.

Great! At least the fae had shown me how to cope with this. But this wasn't like a simple pair of handcuffs. Holy magic, I couldn't believe the amount of iron that was all around. If I blasted the space with wood, I could very easily destroy everything, me included.

For now, block your elemental magic and the iron won't hurt you, the voice said, then added, *Someone's coming. I believe it's your captor.*

Once the inner monologue had ceased, I could hear distant steps approaching me. I obeyed my inner voice's command and blocked my magic.

"Ah, she is finally awake," a sonorous male voice commented, loudly enough to wake the dead. As if things weren't bad enough already, now I had to deal with someone who talked too loud.

The steps grew nearer and I spotted a shadow looming over me. "Miss Shaw, welcome to my humble chamber," the man said. His face was still in the dark and I couldn't make it out, but the voice sounded familiar. To my chagrin, it wasn't Desmond's. Then a flickering light illuminated the space as the figure pulled the switch on a hanging light bulb and I raised my gaze to the figure hulking over me.

I gasped: It was the man with the piercings, the guy who had given the lecture about the Cult of Isis at Desmond's occult shop. It all began to make sense.

"You!" The word escaped my mouth spontaneously. The discovery of this man's involvement in the murders I had been working on had taken me completely by surprise. For the past few days I'd believed Desmond was the culprit. Well, that possibility still wasn't ruled out.

"Yes, it is me," he said proudly. "I'm glad I finally got you, Alex." His eyes glinted menacingly in the dim light and I spotted their maniac glow: This guy was clearly nuts. But then again, only an insane person would stir up a magical revolution, incite a war between gods and demons, and wreak havoc between supernaturals and humans.

The chanting of the men in the other corner of the basement grew louder, though it was still more of a humming than actual chanting.

"I have to thank you for taking the bait, my dear. Finding a goddess' heart is pretty difficult, but you proved to be very useful. Many, many thanks." He smiled again viciously.

A goddess' heart? What? I was a goddess? More things fell into place as the realization hit me: that was what my mother must have been — a goddess.

I cleared my throat and tried hard to gather my thoughts before I said, "I don't know why I am surprised. I knew something was fishy about Desmond, with his occult shop and that coven of his. I didn't think you were involved in this insanity, too, though. How did Desmond lure you in — or did he possess you?"

The guy laughed at me, the veil of his ordinary human aura suddenly tearing off. And then I felt it: his magic, powerful, sinister, and overwhelming. It scorched my skin, and I tasted something vile in the back of my throat, as if someone had poured a concoction of poison mixed with bile into my mouth. I felt filthy just by association. His magic burned deeper inside me and I choked.

"You're so ignorant, aren't you?" he croaked with delight. "Desmond has been quite a good disguise — his natural human energy is somewhat dark, but make no mistake: He is not of my caliber, nor does he belong to our order. I knew from the moment I met him that you'd suspect him and ignore everything else. The mind, be it human or supernatural, is an amazing thing, isn't it?"

This guy loved to hear himself talk. Too bad he couldn't see his own viciousness. I asked him, "So Desmond isn't involved in all this?"

"Nope. Disappointed, aren't you?" He mocked me. "That was all part of the grand plan. I know that a goddess, even a half-goddess like yourself, has powerful magic and can feel other supernaturals' power too. I had to go undercover and block my magic, and Desmond's dark energy came to my aid. I daresay I did pretty well, since you were oblivious to my true nature up till now." He chuckled, and the urge to punch him and wipe the smile off his stupid face overwhelmed me.

"Well, congratulations, you're a genius... uh, what was your name? Whatever, you can be proud of yourself — you had me fooled," I remarked, putting as much venom into my voice as I could.

"Which name? My human or magical one?" he snickered at me, then added, "Desmond knows me as Garrett, Garrett O'Brien. So nice to meet you, goddess."

The desire to vomit welled up again, but I suppressed it and tried to focus on getting out of here alive. Too much iron was around me to apply

Kagan's advice, unless I wanted the whole space to collapse around us. Besides, the amount of iron would cause me a hell of a lot of pain. My healing power was at its peak, true, but I didn't want to tempt fate. I had to find a way out of this and I needed help.

Please help me, I begged my inner voice mentally.

Just buy us time, Alex. Distract him, I'll handle it, the voice replied.

I said, "Your behavior is truly remarkable, Garrett, but why? What's the purpose? I still don't see what you gained by killing the bank manager, Mr. Stone. And what about the poor homeless guy?"

I didn't actually expect him to answer me, but I had to try. The chanting had grown louder, the sound of it malignant. My skin felt as if someone was piercing it with multiple small burning needles, and the pain in my stomach and head intensified.

Garrett stepped closer to me, now only a few inches from my face. His dark, rotten magic, stronger than before, washed over me, and I wished I had fainted. Never before had I tasted such obnoxious magic. Even the demon-powered vampires weren't as bad as Garrett's power. I felt a surge of energy inside me, echoes of suffering, terror, and unknown wicked crimes. His magic sounded like madness — the screams of insane asylum patients or the sinister cackling of an evil witch. I tried to jerk myself free, but the shackles bound me tight. He gripped my face and his vile power pounded inside my mind, my body convulsing. The pain was like hundreds of burning cigarettes pressed into my skin.

"And why would I want to tell you that, sweetheart?" he whispered in a tone of innocence.

It took a great deal of power to answer him. "Maybe," I coughed, "because it's the least you can do." I took a deep breath and continued, "After all, you're going to butcher me and sacrifice my heart. Without me, you won't be able to complete your ritual."

He seemed to consider my words and took a few steps backwards. Thank magic! I instantly felt a bit better. "I'll make a trade. I'll give you the information you want before I kill you, but you've got to give me something in return." He approached me again and I braced myself for the worst — his touch and his rotten, sick magic.

"What do you want?" I asked cautiously.

He regarded me and said, "A very small thing. I'd like to know your mother's name." He held my gaze and warning lights started flashing inside my head, sending the message: *This is trouble*. I tried to suppress the lights since they gave me a headache.

"Why?" I asked suspiciously.

"Because I might have known her."

Oh, no — no way. That was an absolutely taboo topic.

Buy us time, Alex! pleaded the voice in my head. The chanting in the chamber had grown even louder and flames of dark brown with a purplish cast were streaming out of the cauldron in which the potion was being prepared. The vapors looked more like shadows on the walls than anything else, dark and eerie, and they intensified the feeling of foreboding in the pit of my stomach.

Hurry up, I said to the voice in my mind.

"So, what is your decision? Are you going to tell me your mother's name?"

I swallowed hard. "Okay, but first you'll have to tell me why you killed those people. I know the bones of your plan but not the flesh of it. And why do you intend to kill me?"

He sighed. "Because *someone* has to do it, genius." He waved his hand in the air. "The true order must be restored."

I gaped at him. "What?"

He sighed and said with annoyance, "Don't you see? The world is terribly mixed up — good coexists with evil, and both energies often tolerate each other. The worst, though, is that everyone accepts this situation. Most aren't even aware of it. This is completely wrong. Evil is the true master and its demonic nature will soon rule over the world. As my master says, 'Let darkness prevail all over the worlds.'"

I shivered at the ardor and feverish excitement in his voice. This must be why his magic tasted so rotten. I've never subscribed to the theory of sin, but if sin existed and had a flavor, it would taste like this guy's magic. Garrett was so wrapped up in his maniacal zeal that he didn't notice the disgust written on my face.

So much the better. A little more time. It's more difficult than I thought, the voice in my head said.

Garrett continued, saying, "Kai, of course, is aware of this. He himself made a prophecy many centuries ago, even prior to the war between demons and gods. 'In eight thousand years,' he said, 'my kingdom will come on earth. There shall be no more gods, no fae, nor any other supernaturals that exist in the universe we now know — the true master will subdue them all. Our Lord shall reign over the world of the humans and over our own. No longer will we hide from humans, nor be ashamed of our magic nature; the humans will serve us, and fear us, for they have no magic in them and are of a lower nature.' " He was speaking fanatically, as if reciting some scriptures — demonic scriptures? — and his eyes gleamed with religious fervor.

So Kai was behind all this after all? I suppressed my snarky comment about him saying humans were 'of a lower nature,' and said, "So you are following Kai's explicit bidding then? These are all his orders?"

Garrett shook his head and smiled in his evil way. Even just the sight of his smile made my stomach churn.

"No, he would never break his word. Quite a few demons have tried in the past to persuade him to impose his rule and order. 'Why wait so many thousands of years when hell can shower upon earth right now?' they said. He wouldn't listen, though. His reply has always been, 'All in good time.' And that's why we had to intervene. That fool Kai sticks to the agreements he made with the Morrigan and the rest of the Court of Heaven. Who cares what gods want? Their powers and influence will vanish soon, anyway."

So Garrett was a rebel — a rebel against Kai, the chief of demons. Hmm, interesting. How would that end up for Garret and Kai? More importantly, how would it end up for me?

"Your master is someone else, then? Another demon? An incubus maybe?" I suggested, though this seemed rather unlikely.

A smug smile danced across his face. "No, Alex, no. Incubi are minor demons with inferior magic — how did you pass your Magica Academy exams? Cheating, huh? How wicked of you." He smirked at me. "I serve an *inferni*." He said it with great pride and something even stronger — awe.

Inferni? Oh, hell no! This was bad, bad, extremely bad! Inferni were the worst kind of demons, extremely potent and wicked, even by Kai's standards. That was why he had most of them locked up in a separate prison in Hell, known as the Inferno. Brendan had told me about it. It was much, much worse than any ordinary hell.

"And who is that?" I croaked fearfully.

Garrett smiled menacingly and commanded, "Tell me about your mother. I already answered your question."

"No, you haven't. I still don't know why you killed those two men."

"Oh, Alex — isn't it obvious? Don't you smell the answer in the air?" He snickered and I stared at him. The scent of the magical potion from the far corner was suddenly strong in my nose, and I remembered: Three people's deaths, and their blood had to be added into the mixture for the ritual to be completed.

"So you took their blood for this ritual?"

"Yes, that was the point. Daniel was one of my human minions. The occult shop Magica World is a cover. I was searching for ways to settle here in your hometown, so I could get closer to you, when I came upon Desmond. He wanted to open an occult shop and I sponsored him. I let him be in charge so I wouldn't attract attention. Through the coven I recruited more serious and ambitious people interested in the dark arts, and occult practitioners, the wannabe magicians." He chuckled. "Most of them are useless, of course. They have no magic, but they serve me dutifully and do whatever I bid them. Like my boy, Paul, whom you're already familiar with, right?" He pointed to one of the figures in the far corner near the cauldron. They had started dancing in trance, their eyes glowing in feverish fanaticism, singing in high-pitched voices. They were oblivious to us and the room they were in, completely out of this world.

I asked Garrett, "But how did he get into the Hellfire Club? Or how about his wielding magic back at my bookshop? How did he do it?"

The bastard gave a derisive laugh and said, "Are you really that stupid, Alex? Doesn't your best friend make potions and charms? You should know it. Anyway, I made one for my boy, too and all he had to do was sprinkle around the magical dust." He laughed out loud, then went on, "As to how he got into that club, I had a vampire escort him in. Now, to answer your question about the first victim, Daniel — he served me well, it's true. But he got too greedy for superpowers and magic. I had to get rid of him, and decided to sacrifice him. In any case, we needed the deaths and blood of three innocents, and he qualified as one. He should have felt honored. As for the homeless guy, he was randomly picked. The only thing we had to be careful about was hiding his body, so the news of his murder wouldn't come out before the meeting between gods and demons at the Veil. If Kai had learned about that murder, he wouldn't have been so mad at the Morrigan and the rest of the Court of Heaven, since the homeless man wasn't a worshipper. But we couldn't wait until after the meeting to kill him because the moon would be too far out of phase by then — the two innocents needed to be killed within a day — or, I should say, within a night — of the first quarter."

I processed all this information feverishly and finally asked him, "I don't see how Daniel was innocent."

Garrett waved his hand depreciatingly. "Oh, please. He never did anything truly wicked; I just brought him to the Hellfire Club a few times, that's all. He kept pressing me to initiate him into the dark arts so I gave him a book on sorcery. But he remained innocent and nonmagical."

"Unlike you," I remarked, thinking to myself that his definition of wicked had to be creative, considering his own crimes.

Garrett grinned and ran his hand down my neck. His evil magic surged through my skin and senses, suffocating me. I gasped for air, and the bastard laughed. Clearly he enjoyed this. He dropped his hand and I took a deep breath.

"As they say, you can't make an omelet without breaking eggs, you know that. Now," he ordered, "answer my question, Alex: Who's your mother?"

The lump at the back of my throat tightened and I swallowed hard.

How much more time do you need? Can I blast this guy yet? I asked my inner voice.

I'm nearly done. But pay attention to his story. There is something much bigger at play here. That inferni business is worrisome.

I had to agree with the voice.

A sudden slap across my face brought me back to the present situation. "Inferno, calling Alex," Garrett said, and chuckled.

I cursed. My momentary distraction was too noticeable. "I just feel sad for the poor people you slaughtered — they didn't deserve their miserable ends," I said to account for my distraction.

"You are all fools. Good blinds you and makes you weak," he bellowed. "Can't you see that humans don't deserve to live among us at all? Their numbers need to be greatly reduced, and those we leave alive will serve us. Now, answer me before I lose my patience — who is your mother?" He leaned in, only inches away from my face.

I instinctively recoiled, but I felt how my magic had built a shield between us: His magic didn't make me feel nauseated any longer. In fact, it didn't affect me at all.

We're almost done, my voice chimed in gleefully. *I need another minute or so.*

"I never knew my mother, unfortunately. I saw her perhaps once every two or three months. She never said what she was doing or where she lived. The only thing I know about her is her name: Andred." That was only her everyday name. No way would I tell the bastard her true name. For all I knew she was still alive somewhere. "Or at least that's what she told me. She always looked so young: not more than twenty-five, and sometimes I thought she must be immortal. I last saw her when I was seventeen years old. That's all I know about her."

He took a step backwards and mumbled, barely audible over the chanting of his minions at the back of the basement, "So I really found her. Andred's very own blood!" Then he turned to me and said, in a louder voice, "How old are you?"

"I'll be twenty-five in two months' time."

His face beamed. "I am so sorry you won't live to see your twenty-fifth birthday, but if it's any consolation for you, I knew your mother. Her name was indeed Andred, a warrior goddess. And isn't this a twist of fate — eight years ago I killed her; now I get to kill her daughter, too." He laughed and his white teeth shone.

My heart raced, the blood pounding in my ears. I didn't care about anything at that moment other than my need to wipe this fucking sorcerer — or whatever he was — off the face of earth.

"You bastard!" I yelled, ready to blast him with the biggest fireball I could summon.

Calm down, Alex. Don't lose your temper before he spills the beans. The Magic Council and both courts, even Kai, they all need to know what —

I shouted back at it. *I don't care! I want to kill this bastard! My mother probably suffered a more gruesome death than he will!*

You'll kill him when the time is right, but now, be sensible, child.

There was truth in what my inner voice said, even though I didn't want to admit it. I was overcome with revulsion for Garrett.

I made a tremendous effort to pull myself together and to sound calm when I said, "So I am indeed a half-goddess, then. Congratulations! First the mother, then the daughter." And I spat in his face.

As I expected, he recoiled. The smile fell away from his face. His eyes were again cold, piercing, and cruel. He stepped closer to me and punched me straight in the mouth with all his strength. Pain hit me, though not as strong as I would have expected from the blow. Apparently my inner voice had summoned all my magic, using it as a shield. Realization hit me: Was this magic part of my goddess power?

I tasted blood in my mouth — the punch had split my lip and blood was running down my chin. I had to figure out this half-goddess business, but I'd leave it for later. Right now I had to make it out of here alive.

"Bitch!" he yelled. "Fucking goddess scum! I've always hated gods, but you are the worst of them all!" He delivered another blow to my face and the flow of blood intensified, and a throbbing pain began pounding inside my head. However, I didn't feel any weaker.

"That should teach you some manners, bitch, before you meet your end," he chuckled, the maniac glow in his eyes back. "You're pretty hard-headed for someone who never learned to use her special magic. Poor creature: Having the powers of a goddess, but the old fool Awen hasn't even taught you how to use them. He even hid the fact that you were a goddess, am I right?"

"How do you know about Awen?" My tremor was back. It horrified me that Garrett knew about Awen. My mentor was everything to me: My mother, father, friend, and teacher. I couldn't allow anything bad to happen to him. True, he was very experienced and powerful, but this inferni business was extremely dangerous.

"Tut-tut, Alex. Do you think I'm stupid? I've been searching for you for quite a long time. Your mother made it very difficult to find you. She was protecting you from us — can you imagine it? I've been searching for you for years and finally I found the traces of a teenage girl who fit the description of Andred's daughter. That's why I had to work with that fool Desmond and fund his occult shop. It wasn't just for recruitment of obedient minions. This way I could spy on you and get a better look at your abilities and magic. I wanted to make sure you were indeed a goddess, Andred's very own blood. It was hard to judge by just observing you, although my instincts told me you were indeed a half-goddess. But I had to see you in action, in a fight. When you went to the Hellfire Club, I sent two of my dark wizards to test you. And you didn't disappoint me." He smiled and pressed hard on my cheekbone. Thank magic, my shield was protecting me.

"But will my death qualify? As you said, I am only a half-goddess."

"It's the blood that flows in your veins that's important, and since you have your mother's blood you're perfect for our purpose. I am sorry you won't see our glorious ritual, but know that, thanks to your heart, the gates of Inferno will open and all the noble, powerful inferni Kai has kept locked for over a millennium will be free." He beamed with delight. "The magic apocalypse is coming and no one, not even your boyfriend, is able to stop it."

Now! the voice said. *Blast him and this damn chamber with wood, just like Kagan showed you. You won't feel any pain, but you'll have to teleport yourself if you want to make it out alive,* the voice said.

At last! And just in time: Garrett snickered and drew a silver knife from a nook in the wall. The blade glistened ominously in the dim light as he raised it to slash me like a sacrificial lamb.

I summoned all the magic I'd been building up and blasted the entire space with wood. The room shattered, filling the air all around with bricks, smoke, and debris. The explosion threw Garrett to the floor, just a few yards away from me. He looked dizzy and confused.

"Not this time, asshole!" I shouted, just as a concrete brick hit his head and he slumped to the floor. The arcane chanting figures in the corner also collapsed. The explosion had caused the cuffs binding me to crack open, and my hands were free again. I teleported myself to the Steaming Cauldron before any of the crumbling ironclad walls had a chance to fall on me.

Chapter 19

When I arrived in our shop, it was pitch dark inside — the only light came from the full moon shining through the windowpanes. I smiled ruefully: that's why Garrett had waited as long as he had to slaughter me, to do the deed during the moon's zenith in accordance with the ancient Egyptian dark rituals. I was about to connect with Kagan mentally when a slight noise caught my attention, coming from the back of the shop. I strained my hearing, but the midnight silence was broken only by the rhythmic ticking of the wall clock near the front door. I reached inside me for my magic when I heard quick footsteps rustling behind my back, but before I could turn around, someone had struck me hard on the head. All the tension, tiredness, and fear of the last twenty-four hours took their toll on me: I crumpled to the floor, only to see Naomi's face above me. The last thing I remembered seeing before the darkness closed in was the guilty expression on my best friend's face.

When I came to, I was in my own room, in bed, with my clothes still on. I began gingerly testing my limbs, but the movement sent a piercing pain throbbing through my head. If it weren't for my blasting the iron underground space I was held captive in, I would have healed long ago.

"Ouch," I grumbled.

Naomi rushed over to me. "Alex, I am so sorry! I thought you were one of those nasty vampires that attacked me earlier, or a thief. I feel terrible for hitting you. How are you?"

I touched my head and felt the lump that had formed there. "Well, I've had better days. But never mind, the full moon is at its zenith now, so I'll heal in a few minutes or so." I had barely finished saying it when I felt tiny energy vibrations on the lump. The energy intensified, swirling like a vortex around my head, followed by an unusual sense of light-headiness. It lasted only a few moments; when I placed my hand on the injured spot, my head was normal once again, and I felt completely healthy. I grinned at Naomi and asked, "How long was I unconscious?"

"Just a few minutes. It's very handy, you having your super healing power." Relief was written across her face. "How did you get away from that guy and the vampires? We've been worried sick about you."

"Ugh. I've had a hell of an adventure in Garrett's dark chamber."

"Garrett?" Naomi asked, puzzled. "Who is that?"

"Do you remember the lecture about Isis and Egyptian mythology and religion, back at Desmond's shop last week? It was just before my consultant gig with the Magic Council started. Garrett was the presenter."

"*That* guy?" she shrieked in disbelief. "He was behind all this? And what about Desmond — was he also involved? You were probably right to be suspicious about him but I didn't listen to you."

I waved my hand dismissively. "No, relax. He isn't involved. Garrett said he'd just used Desmond for his evil plans. However, Garrett has a powerful ally — one of the inferni, but I have no idea who that might be."

"Oh!" It was all Naomi could say.

I felt suddenly exhausted. Even though I had healed myself and was perfectly healthy physically, I couldn't wash off the sick energy I'd had to endure in Garrett's lair, not to mention the fact that the purpose of his magical ritual was to use my own heart. I shivered and cleared my throat. "Naomi, I witnessed a sacrificial ritual and I'm still shaken up. Can I have one of your invigorating potions, please?"

"Oh, for magic's sake, Alex, you should have told me sooner, honey." She rushed out of the room and returned in a few minutes with a cup of hot tea.

"I put a revitalizing potion in ginger tea, with some soothing herbs also. This should wash off all the dark magic influences." She smiled and handed me the cup. I drank it thirstily — it tasted delicious. Soon enough, I did feel better and stood up.

"That guy Garrett's been spying on me, Noe. Coming here, the murders — everything was part of his plan."

"Poor thing — what you've been through! Did he torture you?"

"Worse. He told me about my mother." I swallowed and felt a thick lump at the back of my throat. Before I could control myself, hot tears poured down my cheeks. "He killed her. She was a warrior goddess, Noe — and that means I'm a half-goddess," I sobbed.

So much for keeping secrets! I didn't think it would be a problem that I'd told Naomi about it. Awen, on the other hand, had always known who I was, but had never told me. Why?

Naomi gawked at me, then she hugged me impulsively. "It's okay, Alex, you're home. Everything's going to be all right," she said comfortingly.

Through sobs I asked, "And what happened with Kagan and the shifters? Where are they?"

"They fought off the rest of the vampires and killed them. Then they went to search for your trail and Kagan called a meeting with the Magic Council regarding the case and your disappearance. Alex," she added a little cautiously, "maybe you shouldn't believe everything Garrett told you — he could have been playing mind games with you."

I shook my head vehemently. "He was totally nuts, that's for sure, but all the things he said... I don't know, but I didn't feel like he was lying. But then, I don't know what he was really doing. Anyway, I have to call Kagan and tell him about Garrett. Noe, he wanted to start a magic revolution, to perform some crazy Egyptian ritual and release the inferni from Inferno."

Naomi stroked my hair and stood up from the couch. "I'd better leave you alone then. If you need me, don't hesitate to come get me." She gave me a compassionate smile and exited my room. It's always good to know there's someone on your side who understands and supports you.

Once alone, I connected mentally with Kagan. Thank magic, he wasn't asleep yet. He said he was looking for clues as to where I might be, and sounded deeply concerned about my safety and well-being. *How strange,* I thought. *He said he would let a goddess die to catch the culprit.*

Don't forget it was him who taught you how to get past iron and summon wood, my inner voice chimed in.

I reassured Kagan and told him about my experience in Garrett's dark chamber.

"I thought we'd lost you," he admitted frankly once I finished with my story. *"The shifters and I tried to track you down, but someone had blocked your magic. The Council summoned me to NY to*

brief them when I told them about the new developments, so Brendan and Carlos kept searching for you."

"That was kind of them. Where are they?"

"I think in your hometown. Alex, do you know the place where Garrett held you captive?"

"I'm not sure, but I think it's in his coven's building, or in close proximity. Remember when you showed me how to summon wood to defeat iron? Well, I did that but the whole building had iron so I turned it all to wood, not just the basement. So whatever house I was in, it must be utterly destroyed."

"Perhaps the shifters are already there," Kagan said. He hesitated for a moment, then said, *"Alex, do you want me to drop by and see you? Personally, I mean. Of course, I'll report to the Council what you just told me about Garrett's plan of a magical revolution, the inferni, and the revolt against Kai. But I'd like to talk to you in person. Are you okay with that?"*

I laughed. *"Sure thing, Kagan. Come on over. We're partners and it'd be better to tell you everything from beginning to end, face to face. I may have forgotten a detail or two. I'm not used to mental communications. This is Brendan's thing."*

"You do pretty well," he admitted. *"You never cease to amaze me."* I sensed hesitation in his voice.

"Yeah, that's the other thing I'd like to discuss with you." I still hadn't told him what the sorcerer claimed about my lineage. Naomi's reaction was that he'd lied to me. Maybe he had, or maybe he hadn't. In my gut I believed he'd told me the truth; he was about to kill me, so he had no reason to lie. And me being a half-goddess would explain my peculiar magic, especially around the full moon.

"Okay, I'll teleport in just a minute," he said. *"I'll connect with Brendan and Carlos first and tell them you're safe and sound at your place, so they needn't worry about you."*

A short while later, a sizzling white-yellow radiance appeared in my room for a split second. The next moment, Kagan stood before me, his tight shirt highlighting his biceps, his jeans molded to his legs. I felt a thrill of excitement at the sight of him.

"Kagan," I said, and went over to him. I had mixed feelings about him, and in that moment I didn't really know what I felt.

"I just talked to Carlos and Brendan." He spoke hurriedly and looked agitated. "They're at the ruins of a building not far away from your shop. They found four human bodies in what was the basement, and half a dozen or so in the remains of the occult shop they went to a few days ago. Everyone's dead."

"Magica World?" I gasped — had Garrett intended to slaughter me in the shop's basement? Right below customers' feet? I shivered. But it had been pretty late in the evening, so at least there had been no customers in the shop.

"I guess. Anyway, the shifters said they couldn't find Garrett's body, or any supernaturals. All the victims are human."

"That's impossible!" I cried. Had he really managed to escape somehow? But, for magic's sake, *how*?

"It's quite possible," Kagan said. "Given the fact that he's into the dark arts, not to mention teamed up with an inferni..." He hesitated, then asked, "He didn't mention his inferni mentor's name, did he?"

I shook my head. "No, not a word. It really bothers me that he got away. Can I look at the ruins?"

"Sure. I'll transport the two of us over there. We can talk later. Carlos and Brendan are still there, gathering evidence and searching for clues. A few people are standing around and the police also showed up, but the shifters are doing fine. Thank goodness it's night; otherwise the whole town would be there. I bet this is the most interesting thing that's happened in your town for a while. "

"Don't be too sure about that; plenty of interesting things go on in Ivy Hills," I teased.

"I'm sure." He smiled at me and added, "Are you ready?"

I nodded, and Kagan connected with his magic, summoning it. The familiar yellow light sparkled in the air around us, and the magic portal appeared and grabbed us. I was used to the routine by now.

When we stepped out of the portal, we found ourselves in a dark, ruined place, debris and dust all around us. It didn't look like the basement I'd been locked up in not so long ago. Two police officers were roaming around the remains using flashlights, and paramedics tended to the dead bodies, which were being put in body bags. Brendan noticed me and waved his hand.

"Alex, are you all right?" He rushed over, genuine concern evident on his face.

"Yes, I'm fine, thanks for asking."

"I was worried about you. Kagan told us what happened and... well, I just wanted to say, you were very brave, and handled it well." Brendan never liked expressing his feelings, but now I sensed a lot of emotions bubbling behind his otherwise iron façade — unusual for him.

"I'm fine. What worries me is that the bastard got away and is still on the loose." I got emotional and involuntarily raised my voice.

"I wouldn't worry if I were you," Carlos chimed in. "Kai is notorious for his hatred of traitors: Once he catches wind of Garrett — was that his name? — and his betrayal, he'll no doubt not only kill him, but torture him as well."

"That may be true in theory, but the fact that this guy is cooperating with an inferni is a big red flag. Besides, this inferni is most likely to be part of Kai's inner circle. Kai probably doesn't even suspect that one of his trusted servants is plotting against him," Kagan noted.

"Poor Kai," I said sarcastically. The memory of his magic came back to me like a flood, and I shuddered. He was a powerful, wicked creature, but at least he played by the rules and wouldn't stir up a magical revolution. That was a small comfort.

"Kai will undoubtedly investigate his minions, if only because the traitor tried to start a war between the two Courts and kill one of the Council's investigators," Brendan said.

"Independent consultant," I corrected him.

"Whatever. It's outrageous. I reported our latest findings to the Council and they said it's time for a meeting between the two Courts and us." Kagan's voice was stern and unusually cold.

"Just one more thing to look forward to," I grumbled. I wasn't in high spirits tonight, not after my encounter with Garrett.

The shifters glanced at me, and I turned to the fae, pulling him aside.

"Um, I wanted to talk to you in private."

He agreed. "Okay, but where? It's past midnight and I don't want you to come across any more monsters tonight." He forced a smile.

"That won't happen — not tonight, anyway."

"How do you know that?" he teased, but I was in no mood for that.

"Let's walk together for a while. You can see me to my house." I tugged at his muscular arm, and the action set off butterflies in my stomach. Kagan nodded and turned to the shifters.

"Okay, guys, let's call it a day — or should I say a night. As soon as the Magic Council confirms with me regarding our next meeting, I'll let you know."

We parted ways with Brendan and Carlos and strolled along the street. The cool fall air cleared my thoughts and soothed my temper. A late night stroll always helped me balance my emotions and mental state. The full moon shone above us and illuminated the space all around, so we didn't have to use any magic. We walked in silence for the first few minutes, aware of each other's presence, until I broke the silence.

"Garrett said he knew my mother."

"Did he?" Kagan didn't stop walking, nor did he look at me.

"Yes. He said she was a goddess, and that he killed her himself. That means I am a half-goddess." I stopped and turned to face the fae. "So, it turns out, I was that goddess you wanted to let die." I put as much contempt into my voice as I could muster. Kagan tried to hug me, sliding his hands around my arms, but I stopped him. "Don't! No need to apologize to me, Kagan. I understand where you come from and your values. Let me finish my story before you say anything."

He nodded and I went on. "Garrett also said he'd been searching for me ever since he killed my mother. That's why he connected with Desmond and loaned him the money to open his occult shop: in order to spy on me, and recruit minions. Garrett confirmed that my mother's name was Andred, and claimed she was a warrior goddess." I paused then added, "Your comments?"

Kagan stared at me for a long moment; then he closed his eyes.

I lost my patience and cried, "Oh, come on! Won't you tell me anything? Naomi thinks he may have lied to me." I hesitated for a second, then asked in a lower voice, "He didn't, did he?"

Kagan opened his eyes and sighed. "I think he told you the truth, Alex. I also think you misunderstood me back at the meeting with the Morrigan: I never had any intention of letting you or any goddess die. I just thought Kai was somehow involved in all of this, and didn't want to invite him in to play an even bigger part." He watched my reaction very carefully. "This doesn't come as a big surprise to me, truth be told. I never really believed you were merely an elemental mage." A faint smile flickered across his face.

I wanted to believe him. But could I?

Yes. I still can't read some things about him, but I guarantee he's telling the truth.

So he wasn't an asshole, after all? He actually cared about me? I felt my smile breaking out against my will. It took an effort of will to remember the last thing he'd said so I could reply sensibly. "You're right—I never was just an elemental mage. And what about the Magic Council and the two Courts—did they know I was a half-goddess, too? Andred's daughter?"

"Not really. Though the Morrigan figured out the nature of your magic pretty quickly. Right after the vampire ambush, when I spoke with her about the case, she asked about the goddess in the investigation — about you. Did the Morrigan say anything about my mother?"

He shook his head. "No, not a word. Anyway, I am happy that you're safe and sound. And I'm especially glad you used the trick I showed you with the wood element."

He grinned and ran his hand over my waist. I slipped out of his grasp and strolled along the street. I was only a few hundred yards from my house, and I just wanted to go home. I intended to take a well-deserved rest. I'd spend at least two days doing nothing but sleeping, eating spaghetti and pizza, and binge-watching my favorite shows. I'd had enough of betrayals, vampires, goddesses and gods, the Magic Council, and all the rest — I needed some fucking sleep, for magic's sake! No emotions and definitely no romance with the arrogant fae. No way!

"Come here. Alex, wait!" He walked after me and I increased my pace. Just before my door, he caught up with me, seized my arms, and pulled me toward him. I pretended I didn't want his embrace, but his masculine scent drew me in, and his potent magic sounded in that moment like strong ocean waves. It made me dizzy and I gave in to his desire. His lips sought mine and he dug hungrily into my mouth. Kissing him felt like nothing I had ever experienced. It was like the Fourth of July in my mouth, magic sizzling across and on my tongue, invigorating and titillating me.

"Whoa, that was... intense," I said once I'd pushed him away from me. I needed a break, and took advantage of the moment to take a deep breath.

He leaned in to kiss me yet again, but I stopped him. "It's pretty late, Kagan. Don't be pushy on our first date." The words were barely out of my mouth when I realized what I'd just said. Where did such thoughts come from?

"So, this is our first date?" he beamed with delight.

"No, of course it's not a date — that was a slip of the tongue, Mr. Fae. Don't make a big deal out of a simple mistake."

But he wasn't listening to my explanations. The silly smile was still pasted on his face.

"Your subconscious mind said it quite right, Miss Goddess." He placed a light kiss on my cheek. "I'm very much looking forward to our first real date, Alex. I'll make sure to take you to a lovely restaurant."

So he wanted to treat me? I guess I could go on a date with him after all. Maybe.

"But not any old restaurant — I want someplace nice, like Temptation," I said.

"Done. I'll make reservations. Is tomorrow at eight convenient for you?"

"Perfect," I replied, and slipped inside before he could steal another kiss.

Epilogue

I had hoped to spend the next few days sleeping, eating Italian food, and binge-watching my favorite TV shows, but I could tell as soon as I woke that it wouldn't work out that way. I had to get some answers. The first day after the fight in the basement passed in a frenzy and before I realized, it was eight o'clock and time for my date with the fae. But that morning I had a talk with Awen — the one I'd been longing for all my life. My mentor was surprised when I asked him about my mother.

"She was a goddess, wasn't she? And I myself am a goddess, a half-goddess," I said.

He exclaimed, "Christ, Alex! Who told you all this?" Awen was horrified. I described my encounter with Garrett, crazed and drunk on dark magic, and his attempt to slaughter me as a sacrificial lamb in order to release inferni from Inferno. Awen's face became a shade darker with every new bit of information I told him. By the end his face looked like a storm-brewing sky, his brow furrowed.

Once I'd finished with my story he asked quietly, "Did you kill the bastard?"

I sighed. "Unfortunately, no. He got away. And the real problem is that he has an ally, a demon — worse yet, an inferni. And I have no friggin' idea who that might be. The only thing I know for certain is that it isn't Kai."

Awen cursed — the first time I'd ever heard him do it — and paced around his living room. Finally he came over to me and said, in a deadly serious tone, "I knew this day would come; I only wish it had been later. Well, the beans have already been spilled." He sighed and went on, "Everything he told you is true. Your mother got in the way of some nasty demons who wanted to free the inferni from their special hell, and as a result, the sorcerer you know as Garrett killed her. He wanted to take your life as well. He searched for you tirelessly for years, but I have been protecting you, even since before your mother died. I never told you who you were since I'd promised your mother I wouldn't tell you your true nature until you turned twenty-five. On your twenty-fifth birthday we can have a long talk, but you'll have to wait until then. You see, my child, I had only your best interests at heart. That was the real reason I advised you not to announce your superpowers and abilities to strangers and to keep a low profile. I feared you'd attract unnecessary attention, and that monster was after you. Alex, do you forgive me?"

"There's nothing I need to forgive you for," I exclaimed and hugged him. He'd been protecting me my whole life without my knowledge. "If anything, I'm the one who should be asking you for forgiveness — I've been pushing you to tell me about myself instead of trusting your judgment." My eyes filled with tears and I sobbed. My mother's image surfaced before me and I remembered her beauty, her youth, and most of all her dazzling smile. She had the loveliest smile I've ever seen. Hot tears streamed down my cheeks.

"Andred would be proud if she could see you right now — her very own little daughter! You resemble her in so many ways," Awen said with unusual gentleness in his voice. He looked at me with affection and love, and I felt closer to him that I ever had.

"But tell me, why didn't she want me to know I was a half-goddess until I turn twenty-five?" I persisted. That bit troubled me somehow.

He extracted himself from my embrace, sat down on the living room sofa, and frowned. "That's a very good question." He regarded me for a few moments and finally said, "Your powers are intensifying, right? You have started to hear your inner voice more and more — you're communicating with it, aren't you?"

I nodded and he went on. "I thought so, which is why I advised you to listen to it. This voice is part of your goddess nature, as well as one of your more, let's say, unusual gifts, like your healing ability, and the fact that you can teleport and read an object's past. When you turn twenty-five, though, your goddess powers will increase significantly, and I doubt the moon phases will influence your magic anymore."

I gaped at him. So that meant my inner voice was... my inner goddess?

"You have inherited a piece of the goddess' soul, and that inner voice is your link with the goddess inside of you, yes. It is a gift from your mother. Since your father was a mage — a powerful elemental, but still merely a mage — you're a half-goddess and your powers are, as a result, less powerful than Andred's. That's why they have appeared only at certain times, usually connected to the moon phases. However, as I said, after you turn twenty-five, they will increase drastically, though I cannot predict to what extent. You also need training. I can provide you with some, but I think the Magic Council has more qualified supernaturals than myself, especially at the Court of Heaven."

"I see," I muttered. "And what should I do from now on, Awen? Will the Morrigan want me to join her court? Am I on her side, their side?"

"That's difficult to guess, child, but I'm sure she'll want to talk to you in private. After all, Andred, your mother, was one of her most loyal servants." He smiled at me ever so lovingly. "I should imagine she is very well-disposed towards you. You can probably benefit a lot from your mother's good name."

I pondered over his words, then remembered something. "And what about my father? Is he... alive? Does he care about me?"

Awen laid his hand on my knee and said, "I'm sorry, Alex, he died a long time ago, when you were still a baby. He was a brave and noble man, though. He loved your mother deeply, and she loved him just as much. He lost his life in a tragic accident and your mother never quite recovered from it. It was you who kept her sane and on the right track."

"Until that monster Garrett killed her," I spat, venom burning in my insides. How I wanted that asshole dead! Because of him, I'd forever lost my mother and would never have the opportunity to know her. He'd ruined my childhood and young adult years. One thing I was sure of: I wouldn't stop hunting him until he was dead.

Awen squeezed my hand. "What's done is done, but I'm sure she's helping you somehow," he reassured me.

Just then I received a message from Kagan. The Council and both Courts wanted to see us, the investigators, and express their gratitude to us for successfully solving the murder cases. Before I left, Awen said, "Everything's going to be all right, Alex. But you have to kill him. He won't rest until he kills you."

I felt a chill go up my spine. I knew Awen had the second sight: Did he have a premonition of danger?

"So get some rest and prepare for when he comes back, as he surely will."

I turned my eyes toward my mentor and stared at him for a few long moments. So many questions swarmed inside my mind — I wanted to ask him about his warning, and about Garrett — but I didn't have the heart for it. Not now, anyway. It wasn't the right time. I needed to get some rest instead — he was absolutely right about that.

***

I met Kagan and the shifters shortly before noon at the fae's apartment. He teleported us to the Veil where representatives from the Courts of Heaven and Hell were waiting for us. This time, though, there was no strife between them. Even Kai was in a good mood — as much as was possible for him, anyway. The conversation was short and simple: they thanked us, then Kai asked me about Garrett and I told him everything I knew.

By the end of my story, Kai was furious, his eyes glinting menacingly, and his magic was thundering and roaring around us like restless ocean waves. After I finished, both the Morrigan and Kai thanked us and we were dismissed. I stood to follow my colleagues, but the Morrigan's voice made me stop in my tracks.

"Alex, could you please stay with us for a while?"

I hesitated and flashed a glance at Kagan. He nodded, then drew nearer to me and whispered in my ear, "Go! She probably wants to tell you something important. I'll send you a text later about our date tonight; you haven't forgotten, have you?" He winked playfully at me, then left the grand hall. Once they were all gone, the Morrigan turned to me.

"So how are you, Alex?"

"What kind of stupid question is that?" Kai snapped.

"You ought to be more polite toward me and my court, Kai. Mind your tongue," she said, her tone as sharp as a razor.

Kai waved a hand dismissively. "Yes, yes, I'm very grateful and all that, and it's all my fault — I know. I'll make sure the traitors are severely punished. I'll show them who's boss." Anger flickered in his eyes like two small volcanic explosions, and I shivered. If he got his hands on Garrett and his master, he'd probably throw them into the most gruesome hell possible. Or even create one, if it didn't already exist.

The Morrigan glanced at me. "I apologize, Alex, for my colleague's outburst and behavior, but such is his nature. Anyway, I wanted to talk to you and learn what you intend to do from here on out. As a half-goddess, you can't really join my ranks, but given the fact that you thwarted the killer, and considering who your mother was, I'm inclined to raise the issue before the rest of my court. We might make an exception for you.

"Another possible option is for you to work for the Magic Council. I have talked to Galvyn, their president, and he said they can hire you as a full-time investigator. Kagan spoke very highly about your detective skills." She smiled and her benign energy invigorated me. Both offers sounded fantastic, and I didn't know right off the bat which one to choose.

"I'll need some time to consider the offers. They're both very attractive," I replied.

"Of course, dear, take your time. How about you give me your answer in a week's time? Just email me your response." She handed me her card, which had an email address printed below her name.

As I was leaving, my phone buzzed and I saw Kagan's text. He informed me he'd come to my place at eight p.m. sharp and requested that I be dressed nicely: no jeans, no boots, and no blood on my clothes. I had to laugh at that: I couldn't remember the last time I wore a dress.

I teleported home, and finally got my well-deserved break: I ordered a pizza and sat down to watch one of my favorite shows. Naomi was working at the Steaming Cauldron, so I had the whole afternoon to myself. She sent me a few text messages throughout the day to tell me how busy the shop was, bringing in more customers — and more money — than we had since Magica World had opened. Maybe that was why we had so many clients today: We didn't have any more competitors, now that I'd destroyed the last one's store. I smiled. Fate has a sense of humor, as well.

Thank magic, Naomi was able to replace the broken potions from the vampire attack with new ones. In addition she brought out some new artifacts and objects we recently received. She also ordered more goods to have in our inventory.

And yet, poor Desmond. He'd lost his shop, his partner and sponsor, and pretty much his business. I was relieved when Brendan informed me he wasn't among the victims found after I'd blasted the basement, and I hoped Desmond was safe and sound, wherever he was.

While I was watching my show, I used my relaxed state of mind to contemplate the revelation that I was a half-goddess. Thinking back to the incident with the incubus at the Hellfire Club the first time we had gone there, I suddenly realized why I had blasted him — the goddess inside me didn't like demonic nature close to herself at all.

Shortly before Kagan arrived, I started looking through my wardrobe for something to wear. I came across a nice red dress and tried it on. I couldn't remember buying it. It fit me perfectly, highlighting my breasts and waist. Holy magic, I looked exquisite! I found a pair of high heels I hadn't worn for ages, but they matched the color of the dress perfectly, so my outfit was all ready.

Kagan arrived right on time. Clad in slacks and a blazer, perfectly shaved, and deadly powerful, he looked gorgeous. His magic rolled over mine and I longed to kiss him and feel the strength of his masculine embrace.

He whistled and exclaimed, "Wow! You look stunning, Alex." He hugged me and gave me a light peck on the cheek. "This is for you." He handed me a splendid bouquet of red roses and I blushed. I thanked him hastily and went to the kitchen to find a vase.

"Are you ready?" he asked when I returned.

I nodded and said, "So, where are we going, Mr. Fae? Temptation or some other posh New York restaurant?"

He grinned. "No, not at all. We're heading to Dal Riata." His grin deepened, but I was puzzled.

"Dal Riata? What's that?" I had barely said the words when a memory flashed through my mind: I'd heard the name before. Wasn't it an Irish pub, or club or something? Maybe in Dublin?

"It's the meeting place for Seelie and Unseelie fae — a neutral zone. I'm sure you'll love it. The food is delicious and the ambience is lovely." He stretched out his hand, and I hesitated before taking it. Frankly, I preferred my home setting to Ireland, but if he promised I would like it...

His magic intensified and the familiar portal appeared before us, sparkling in a white-yellowish light. We stepped inside and the spell took us. We landed in a dark dingy alley and I turned to the fae. "What the hell? Couldn't you just teleport us straight to that Dal Riata place?"

He shook his head. "This is a compulsory ritual for every non-fae when they first enter one of our cities. Wait a second, Alex." He laid his hand on the red, dusty bricks in front of us. Suddenly they began wiggling and shifting, and soon a cleared path appeared before us. He stepped inside and motioned for me to follow him.

I found myself in a place that seemed frozen by time. Flaming torches lit the whole space. Early medieval castles and ancient-looking houses lined both sides of the road. As a passing group of leprechauns greeted us, I spotted the fairy star embroidered on the castles' flags.

"Whoa, whoa, whoa! What is this? A whole new town inside the city of Dublin?"

"It's actually one of the few remaining authentic fae streets in the whole world. It's called Áedán mac Gabráin, after one of the greatest Gaelic kings. There are only three other fae streets like this — one is in Wales, another in Edinburgh, and the third in Canada."

"Canada? Well, that's a surprise."

He nodded and pointed to a small door on the lower level of one of the castles we were approaching. "And here's our very own fae club — Dal Riata."

I raised my eyebrows and chuckled. "You can't mean it."

But Kagan said, "It's the best place for fae. And not only us: quite a few supernaturals hang out here too." With those words he strode toward the small, insignificant-looking door and opened it, stepping aside for me to go first.

"This is all very impressive, Kagan, but let me warn you: I'm not going to sleep with you. Not tonight, anyway."

"So maybe another time?" He winked at me.

I shot him a dirty look and he hastily added, "Then a kiss at least?" A mischievous smile tugged at the corners of his lips and he leaned toward me. His action gave me goosebumps, and I involuntarily shivered.

"We'll see about that, Mr. Fae. Largely depends on the food in here." I walked into the venue and he followed me.

The place was a very unusual one, decorated in colors of dark yellow, brown, dark green, and the like. Celtic music played at a comfortable level. Upon entering, the customers' fairy-dust magic engulfed me, making me feel lightheaded, as if I'd smoked opium. Kagan headed for a secluded table in the far corner. As we made our way across the room, I spotted two vampires as well, though they didn't look typical. A few witches, wizards, and even shifters drank and talked, either at the bar or the tables scattered around. It was hard to explain why, but I did like this place: it felt like home. As soon as we sat down, a waitress appeared, bringing a menu list. She herself was a fae, if a low-level one; one of her eyes was green, the other hazel, and her hair was flaxen with some pink strands. She greeted Kagan with a beaming smile.

"Hello, Mr. Griffith, how are you? Would you like your usual, the shepherd's pie?"

"Yes, Helen. Can you please bring a candle to the table, as well?"

She nodded curtly and turned to me. It was clear that she envied me. Small wonder: being on a date with the hot, super-wealthy member of one of the magic dynasties, the almighty Kagan Griffith — it was nothing to sneeze at. And it certainly wasn't my typical off-work evening. Ever since the werewolf had dumped me, I'd been feeling like a bit of an underdog.

"And for you, ma'am?" the waitress prompted me.

"Um, I'll need a moment to decide, but for now, one Magic Nights smoothie." I was leafing through the pages, but nothing caught my eye.

"I'll bring that right out."

She left us and the fae said, "You ought to try McIvy's pizza — you'll love it."

"Mm, sounds promising." I searched for the name on the menu.

"So, how did it go with the chiefs back at the Veil?" he asked.

I took a moment to gather my thoughts. "Well, not bad. Actually quite good; the Morrigan offered me a job at the Council, and also said she's going to call a meeting where she'll raise the issue of me joining her court."

Kagan studied my face for a few long moments before asking, "And what have you decided? Will you take the offer?"

I sighed. "I haven't made up my mind. I'm going to think it over and give her my answer in a week. She gave me her email address to let her know. I'm pretty exhausted and can't think straight right now."

"I thought you might be. I'm happy to say I've got the perfect present for you." He reached into his jacket and pulled out an envelope and handed it to me. Inside were two airplane tickets and a hotel reservation. I looked at him questioningly. "A holiday in Bali is just what you need," he said. "You'll get recharged and refreshed. They have interesting spiritual and local customs over there, the food is delicious, and the weather is divine. You'll be reborn."

I looked at the ticket. The idea of Bali was very tempting, and yet… "Who is the second ticket for?" I asked suspiciously. Something told me he intended to accompany me.

"Well… in the best-case scenario, I'd be your companion, but you can take whomever you like."

"Even a guy?" I teased him.

He frowned. "Well, I was thinking of a friend — a girlfriend, that is."

"I don't think Naomi can come with me. Someone's got to take care of our shop."

"Find another employee. By the way, have you heard from that guy you were so suspicious of? Desmond?"

"No, but Brendan told me he wasn't in the shop when it exploded. It makes me wonder where he is now."

"He's probably traveling back from the paranormal conference he visited in Dallas."

"What?" I exclaimed.

Kagan shrugged. "I was a bit suspicious of him as well, so I checked him out. He was at that conference yesterday, and should arrive in your town at any moment."

"That's good to know," I remarked. The waitress returned, bringing my smoothie and Kagan's pint of beer, and a candle, which she lit. I ordered the McIvy's pizza.

"A very good choice. You won't regret it." Kagan smiled at me. "So, what have you decided about your trip to Bali?" he persisted.

"I'll talk to Naomi; maybe another friend of ours can fill in temporarily, or we can find another occult enthusiast. We'll have to come up with something quickly."

Kagan gently laid his hand over mine. Not taking his eyes off mine, he said, "I want you to have a real nice rest. You know this isn't over. Garrett — or whatever his real name is — and his inferni master won't stop here. They'll strike again."

My mentor had used almost the same words! It freaked me out a little.

"Yes, I know that." I pulled back my hand and took the smoothie. It tasted of yogurt, honey, raspberries, and ice cream — a pretty good combination — and I felt a light sizzling across my tongue. I put the drink on the table and looked back at the fae.

"I don't quite get it, Kagan. What's your angle here?"

"What do you mean? My family has sworn to protect both worlds and keep the peace not only between humans and supernaturals, but between gods and demons too."

"And you have no ulterior motives at play? I mean, apart from trying to get into bed with me."

A faint smile flickered across his face. "No, not at all."

"Here you are, Mr. Griffith." The waitress appeared as if out of nowhere and served him a big plate of what looked like mashed potatoes, vegetables, and minced beef. She flashed him a smile, but left without even a glance at me. I got it: I didn't matter here. A few moments later, she reappeared with my pizza. I took a bite of it and wasn't disappointed — the food was very good indeed.

"Delicious, as always," Kagan exclaimed and devoured his mouthful greedily. "One of my favorite meals, ever since I was a small kid." Between bites he said, "There's nothing you should be wary of about me wanting to help you get some rest. You're a valuable investigator, fought well, and thwarted Garrett's plan. You deserve a holiday more than anyone." The music in the bar grew livelier, as if to confirm his statement. I regarded him, and had to admit it felt nice here, in this place. The vacation he was offering me seemed like a gift from God, and besides, he'd helped a lot during the investigation. So what was bothering me?

Something else is at play here, the voice inside my head chimed in. I hadn't heard it all day. Maybe it had also needed a recharge.

What's that? I asked.

You'll learn when the time comes. For now, relax: Your boyfriend's right. The voice chuckled inside my head.

I snapped back, *He is not my boyfriend!*

Whatever, love.

I gave up arguing with it. Kagan got up from his chair and beckoned me to join him on the dance floor. I followed him and for the first time in a long while, I felt happy. Tonight, I was going to have some fun.

Thanks For Reading

Did you enjoy reading Bound by Sorcery? Indie authors survive by the strength of their reviews. If you enjoyed Bound by Sorcery, please leave a review and let me and other readers know!

To leave a review, visit:

Amazon: http://amazon.com

Goodreads: https://www.goodreads.com/book/show/36098948-bound-by-sorcery

Chapter 1

I hit the trimmed grass having closely avoided Kagan's fairy dust flare. He had shot it straight at me like a missile. It wasn't anything deadly; he was just using his fae magic. I bet he was drawing magic from the earth. The fae usually drew power from the elements around them, like the sun, the moon, the wind, etc.

We were sparring in the fae's meticulously maintained garden at his castle in Ireland, where we'd been practicing and training for the past five weeks. Ever since we returned from our short vacation in Bali, our first as a couple, he insisted I hone my untamed magic to prepare for my next fight with Garrett, who was sure to come back and attack me again.

About a month ago, while working as an independent consultant for the Magic Council on two ritualistic murders in New York City, my ex, a werewolf, asked me to join the investigation. We discovered a conspiracy masterminded by a dark supernatural being, Garrett, and his secret inferni master against the chief of the demons, Kai. They were planning a magical revolution, which would inevitably lead to a supernatural apocalypse. Oh, and I, having known all my life that I was merely an elemental mage, learned that I was a half-goddess. Exciting times, even discounting Garrett's obsession with killing me.

We didn't succeed in identifying his magic — he was very good at concealing it — but we suspected he might be a sorcerer. The day after Kagan and I returned from our exotic trip, I received an anonymous post card in my mailbox, bearing the text, "Are you missing me?" A strange, almost rotten magic filled the air around me when I touched it. I instinctively dropped the card, and a second later it exploded in sizzling flames. Not powerful enough to kill me; Garrett just wanted to remind me of himself and the fact that he hadn't given up on finishing me off.

Kai, the head of the Court of Hell, had taken measures to prevent any further conspiracies: He severely punished the only known inferni in his Court thinking he must have been Garrett's accomplice, and sentenced him to a long stint in a torture facility. Of course, he could have simply thrown him in Inferno, among the other inferni, if he was feeling lenient, but clearly that day he had not. It was no secret that Kai's special asylum was way worse than Inferno and Hell combined — tortures beyond compare. Its only drawback was that one couldn't stay there forever — that was why Kai would send the offenders into either Hell or Inferno after that, depending on the severity of their crime.

I'd also heard Kai had put a new, super-resilient — according to him — protective charm on Inferno, one guaranteed to block any Egyptian rituals. Kagan told me that Kai had conjured the spell together with a lich. Due to the threat of a magical apocalypse, the Morrigan wouldn't get off Kai's back, and thus he had combined powers with the lich.

Inferno was the most powerful type of hell, where the inferni had been locked for centuries. Garrett and his secret inferni ally were scheming to unlock precisely this type of Hell.

I was hoping the inferni Kai had punished was Garrett's accomplice and not someone else, and also that Garrett wouldn't dare to strike on his own. Why was I doubtful? Kagan had told me rumor had it there were quite a few more inferni in Kai's inner circle, inferni whom he trusted. One of them had betrayed him and was Garrett's mysterious ally, but had he gotten the right guy? So much for my dreams for peace.

"What is it? Scared of facing my fairy dust?" Kagan's voice brought me back to the present. A satisfied smirk twitched at the corner of his lip, and it enraged me.

Kagan had been cornering me for the past quarter of an hour, trying to blast me. I had so far avoided his attacks, but it was starting to annoy me. I was half an elemental mage and half a goddess; I could do much better.

During my confrontation with Garrett, I'd begged my inner voice — the link to the goddess in me — for help. It summoned all my hidden magic and turned the concrete basement in which I was held captive to a wooden enclosure. A few days later, when the danger had passed, I asked the voice for an explanation. It told me it had handled the situation the best it could since I'd begged for its help. I wasn't trained, and therefore summoning all my hidden power would have resulted either in me demolishing the place or fainting on the bare floor.

When I told Kagan about it, he worked out a nice plan to train me so that I could control the other half in me — the goddess and its magic. For now, though, I couldn't properly use my hidden magic. It'd have been much easier if my own mother — a pure-blooded goddess — could train me, but her presence in my life had been fleeting. Besides, she was long dead, killed by that same Garrett and his inferni ally. Yeah — karma is a bitch.

"Why should I be scared of your magic?" I teased him, anticipating his next blast of fairy dust.

As a fae, Kagan had the gift of being able to manipulate and bend his opponent's emotions, mind and will. He'd confessed this to me in Bali. But unlike supervillains, he used it for good deeds only, and very rarely. Aside from that, he belonged to one of the magic dynasties, and his family had sworn to keep the peace between humans and supernaturals on earth. I'd met him during the investigation of the ritualistic murders in New York City.

"You *are* scared. Otherwise why would you avoid my fairy magic?" he asked, his eyes gleaming with amusement. I noticed something else flicker in them. He was reaching for his magic.

Before he could blast me again, though, I forestalled him and hurled a sizeable fireball right at his chest. He was faster than I'd hoped, and ducked out of the way, then stood up quickly and blasted me again with his fairy dust.

This time I wasn't fast enough. Before I could hit the grass or jump out of the way, his sparkling golden fairy dust hit my body. A strange sensation engulfed me. I was in the fae's sway. The fairy dust blurred my vision, but I didn't feel any pain, nor was there any blood or gore. Instead, I heard his magic inside my mind, hissing tenderly but persistently, almost whispering to me to surrender.

Never! Magic is as alive as any person. It has its own language and fingerprint. Mine wanted to fight back, and I wasn't about to repress it.

I pushed Kagan's magic back by remembering a protective spell. I wouldn't accept defeat. Not now, anyway, when I knew I was much more powerful than just an ordinary elemental mage.

When the two collided, the air around me vibrated in yellow-purple sizzling light that eventually faded.

I swept away the tiny droplets of sweat forming on my forehead and neck. The weather was warm for the end of November. The sun had already started to rise. We'd begun our training session in the dark. I was clad in sports leggings and a long-sleeve shirt, the fae — in a gray t-shirt and sports pants. Apparently the cold breeze didn't disturb him.

"Not a quitter! I like that. But I want you to summon your goddess power — I know you can do so much better. Garrett won't be as gentle," he said, his face suddenly stern, bearing no trace of the amusement of a few moments ago. He was right, and I knew it.

"I am doing my best." I steeled myself and gritted my teeth in firm resolution. I couldn't help but feel slightly frustrated — I had a long way to go to reach the level of control I wanted over my powers. "But that magic just doesn't come out." I had the sinking feeling my goddess power kicked in only when I was in dire situations. For anything else, I had a hard time convincing my subconscious mind to let it out, like right now.

"Try harder, Alex," he said, harshness discernible in his voice. "You've got to win over a cruel inferni — the inferni who wants nothing more than to finish you off. On the spot."

Okay, I muttered to myself, gritting my teeth. The mere mention of the bastard responsible for my mother's death sent my anger into overdrive. I focused and summoned another fireball in my hand, letting the magic build inside me for a bit longer than usual. I felt my power tug at me right in the center of my chest. I liked to imagine that I had something like a well of magic inside me that I could tap into. In the meantime, Kagan didn't stand idly waiting for me, but shot another ball of fairy dust in my direction. I avoided it by ducking low down, my head and body one with the grass. This whole sparring session was beginning to get on my nerves. The whole purpose of it was that I would learn to seize control and dominate him, not vice versa.

"Being humble, huh?" he called, and I regretted that I had allowed him to listen to my meandering thoughts. The golden rule was that nobody should sneak and listen to one's internal musings without permission. Clearly, Kagan was challenging me on purpose to irritate me even more so that I might lose balance and clarity of mind.

"Come on, Alex, connect with your raw goddess power," Kagan said, irritation obvious in his voice.

I narrowed my eyes, focusing on him. I needed a good view of this arrogant fae to blast him off his feet. He stood with his arms folded over his chest, his eyes gleaming with stubborn will. I didn't wait a second longer. I gathered all the magic I'd summoned inside of me and hurled it to the fae. He dodged it with the grace of a gazelle.

"How the hell?" I grunted, throwing up my hands in frustration.

He chuckled. "Faes have excellent agility. Forgotten your lectures at the Magica Academy, have you?"

I cursed him silently. "I want to see you lying on the grass, on your back. Helpless."

"Umm, I like the sound of that scenario," he said, a mischievous grin pulling up the corner of his lips. I immediately regretted saying it.

He was about to hurl another lot of fairy dust at me. Distraction was just another way to test me and make me more resilient to mental manipulation.

Suddenly, the pendant in the form of a chakram on my chest — a gift from Anumati, a Hindu goddess of the moon whom I'd met in Bali — glowed in a strange greenish light. This was a warning. The goddess had told me to touch it whenever I wanted to channel my goddess power, so I touched the pendant with my left hand.

The space around me began vibrating in a pale-yellow light. I connected with the magic inside me and a new wave of energy fluttered in my veins, invigorating me. It felt so good that I wanted it to last forever — as if I were drunk on magic.

The fae shot his fairy dust at me, an ominous swirl of shimmering magic. This time, though, I stopped it midair without using my elemental air power. I held his fairy dust for a moment in the air, then pushed it back at him. He fought back, resisting my push, but his magic was now no match for my own. Finally his own fairy dust hit him in the chest, and he dropped to his knees.

Back to where it came from, I thought and smiled. This is what happens when you want to blast someone and overpower them. The fae pulled himself together pretty fast. He jumped up from his knees, a triumphant smile dancing on his lips.

"You did it, Alex." He strode toward me, admiration clear on his face. And I'd thought he would be disappointed that I blasted him with his own magic, not with mine. He wrapped his arms around me and squeezed me tight. His touch always gave me butterflies. "I am so proud of you. How did you do it?"

I gave a shrug. "It wasn't anything special. I just touched Anumati's gift." My hand wandered back to the necklace.

His smile faded. "You did? And I thought you had connected with your own goddess magic." He let go of me and paced around furrowing his eyebrows.

"Why should it matter? Anumati must have known I needed a push and extra magic to release my goddess power; that's why she gave this gift to me. Besides, you were the one who suggested we go to Pura Besakih," I said. Pura Besakih, the temple where I met the Hindu goddess, was a large complex consisting of several places of worship. Its magical history spoke of a massive volcanic eruption that destroyed a large part of the city nearby. But the temple, protected by the gods, was untouched.

"Yes, I did, and I am glad she gave you this necklace, but I want you to control and summon your own goddess magic, not rely on an external object. What if Garrett figures it out and takes it away from you or he blocks the item's magic? You need to be confident in your own power."

I frowned. He raised valid points. "Maybe if that ever happens my special magic will awaken. Meeting Garrett surely classifies as a life-or-death situation." My lips curled up in an apologetic smile as I realized how lame my excuse sounded.

Kagan looked at me thoughtfully for a moment.

"The Council entrusted your training to me. I promised Awen that I'd train you properly. I feel responsible. And... you're not even trying."

I knew about the Council, but had no idea my mentor, Awen, had spoken to the fae. The Council naturally wanted me to be in full control of my magic — I was working for them, after all. Prior to the Bali vacation I wrote to the Morrigan, but it turned out the gods in her Court didn't want a half-goddess like me in their ranks. So I accepted the Council's offer, which came with a very good salary. However, someone had to train me, and Kagan had offered his services. The Council agreed, as did I. Better him than anyone else.

But... why wouldn't my mentor train me himself? Like in the good old days?

"Awen asked you to train me?"

Kagan waved is hand dismissively. "He thought it'd be better for you; I wouldn't go easy on you." He arched his eyebrow up. "And that's why I'm pushing you harder. I know you can improve your abilities and control."

I sighed. "I am trying my best. I've tried so many times during these five weeks, you have no idea."

Kagan was shaking his head. "No, I don't think you are. I think you can do better."

"Sweetheart, please don't be so hard on me and on yourself. We're in no immediate danger, and you know my goddess magic doesn't come out of me unless there is an emergency."

"Then you just need a little push. Give me the necklace." He held his hand waiting for me to give it to him.

My eyes widened at the boldness of his idea. I swallowed hard, but refused.

"No," I said firmly, looking him in the eye.

"C'mon, babe, give it here." His smile grew radiant. It almost dazzled me. As it often happened when he turned on his charm, his smile made me go weak at the knees and weakened my resolve. Not fair. He knew I couldn't resist his smile.

No doubt, fighting was easier with the pendant, but I decided to trust the fae's judgment.

I was aware that I had to improve and at the very least try to release my magic without external help. Reluctantly, I gave him the pendant. He gifted me with another dizzying smile, then turned his head toward the castle and set his sight on the stone statue of a dragon sitting at the center of the huge garden.

"Hell, no! Have you lost your mind?" I practically shrieked, realizing what he intended to do. "I haven't bargained on you bringing to life your freaking giant dragon. No way am I fighting that! And without Anumati's necklace!"

The jerk just smiled. "You said you needed a challenge. I think this is close to what you need in order to unleash your magic. Life-or-death situation, as you said."

He was right, and I hated him for that.

The fae had closed his eyes and was now concentrating. The air around us swished, a light-blush swirl splitting out of it. It circled around the stone dragon statue, shimmering in a purple-red light. The fae transferred a last, stronger surge of magic to the dragon, and in the next moment the animal woke up to life, its nostrils flaring with its breathing. Low, guttural sounds emitted from his throat, and small circles of fire puffed out of its nose. His tail thrashed on the grass, drawing my eye. I blinked and held my breath. Did I really have to fight this *thing*?

Kagan's lips broke into a loving smile and he looked at his dragon — who was his family guardian — before clearly ordering him, "Go after her. She is your challenger."

Shit! The dragon's sleepy eyes focused on me first with a blank stare, then they awakened, pinning me intently as angry flames flickered in their depths.

"No, no. Don't listen to him. He is lying." I took a step backwards trying my best not to run away even though my heart had started to thud, pounding in my ears like drums. Dogs don't like it when people start running away, and my intuition told me that maybe dragons' psychology worked the same way.

"It is pointless, Alex. He won't change his focus unless he hears the magical words from me." Kagan grinned and sat down on the grass, crossing his legs. "I feel we're about to watch a really good fight," he commented.

I cursed him mentally and focused my attention on the approaching dragon. His eyes had become bloodthirsty, the flames puffing out of his nostrils bigger; he was looking at me like a rabid dog. I gulped. If the fae's strategy had any point, it'd be proven in the next few minutes.

I gathered all my courage and charged at the beast with a big fireball. It gently caressed his huge body and dissolved into thin air. All I'd managed to do was enrage the dragon. The creature stopped in his tracks, fixing his penetrating cold blue eyes on me. Reddish angry flames blazed around the pupils, his stare deadly. He was figuring out what type of supernatural I was. The flashes of fire from his nostrils grew more intense, and he began beating his wings heavily in the air. He took flight, his eyes boring into mine till I had to close them.

I prayed to my inner voice, I begged it for help. It tentatively answered my plea.

So, you're not able to handle a big, bad dragon, the voice chuckled inside my mind, taunting me as it always did when I was in trouble.

It is the fae's fault, I replied, not daring to open my eyes. Fate only knew how close to me that dragon was by now. I could already feel the hot steam from his heavy breathing flow over my skin, tingling and burning me.

Then why did you give the necklace away?

Oh, will you stop teasing me and help me out here? I need you. I need my goddess magic.

Okay, honey, I'll save your ass one more time. With these words, a new kind of magic surged within me, tugging at me, and I felt its familiar taste as I did the night I fought Garrett.

I opened my eyes. The dragon was only a few feet away from me in midair. His eyes, gleaming with malice, locked with mine, and he opened his large mouth.

Right before he could spit fire at me, I did something I didn't expect. The voice told me to sing a song, saying the words in my mind, and so I obeyed. My voice carried out in the air, clear and tender. I didn't know the lyrics. It was a totally unfamiliar song to me, the words strange and beyond my comprehension.

The dragon stopped, blinked with his bloodthirsty eyes, steam coming out of his enlarged nostrils, his mouth open and ready to bite. I kept singing, the tune strangely relaxing, pricking on my skin, its ancient melody clinging to the air around me. The dragon's large red eyes slowly lost their bloodthirstiness — they became blank again. The beast stopped flipping his wings and crashed down to the grass next to me, his eyes averted.

Still singing, I walked to him and touched his massive body. A stream of bluish magic infused into its skin at the point of contact. His breathing gradually steadied and slowed, and soon enough he closed his eyes; he'd fallen asleep.

What did you do? No — more importantly, what was that? I mean, how is it possible to pacify one of the most ancient and magically potent creatures with a song? I asked my inner voice.

There are so many things you don't know. Gods and dragons are intrinsically linked in the chronicles of creation. We gods have the power to command dragons; they are vehicles through which we channel our magic.

Wow — good to know. I turned to the fae. He was looking at me in bewilderment, his mouth open. "How did I do here, Mr. Griffith?" I took my hand off the dragon.

"It seems pushing you did you some good," he remarked, finally finding his voice.

"Probably, and yet, I'll ask you not to push the envelope too often in the future. May I have my necklace back, now? Please."

I held my hand out. He chuckled and placed the necklace in my palm, his thumb gently stroking my hand as he did so. "As you wish, Princess. Very good job, by the way." He wrapped his hands around my waist. "See, you *can* unleash your magic. Just needed a small challenge. Who knew you could boss around my guardian angel?"

I cracked a smile. "Yeah — I am full of surprises. Now, if you'll excuse me, I have to prepare for work." I pecked Kagan on the lips and took out my best friend's transportation charm. During or close to full moon my magic was sufficient to teleport me anywhere. Since the moon was waning, I'd have to use the charm.

I sprinkled the fairy dust and the familiar silver cloud appeared. I stepped inside it.

***

The magic portal spat me in my own apartment in the small town of Ivy Hills, Connecticut. The coziness and warmth of my home came from the reassuring magic of my best friend Naomi — a hedge-witch. Although her power lingered and was infused in every crevice of our house, it didn't shake off the remaining rush of adrenaline from the battle.

My thoughts churned, and I wished I had at least hugged Kagan goodbye. I missed his energy already. With difficulty, I pushed this thought to the back of my mind. Now wasn't the right time for sentimentality. It was past eight-thirty, and I needed to be in the Council's headquarters by nine.

I showered and dressed in a long-sleeved shirt, my leather jacket and a pair of old jeans. These were my go-to clothes because my assignments sometimes ended up destroying them.

When I was ready, I smiled in approval at the reflection from the wardrobe mirror. A tough, badass-ish looking woman was staring back at me. Were my mother alive, she would have been proud of her little baby. Hot tears rolled down my cheeks and I hastily wiped them away.

The thoughts of my mother reminded me to take out the second most valuable weapon I had — after Anumati's necklace — from my drawer: my own mother's silver encrusted knife that my mentor had gifted to me a little over a month ago. The knife was enchanted and extremely powerful. It had helped me enervate quite a few vampires and demons in the past. I grabbed two more enchanted knives, and was ready for work. I patted my pockets to find my badge was in my jacket.

What drew my attention, however, was the necklace on my chest. Each time I used it, it changed its form. The bronze pendant was now engraved with some intricate symbols. Its ability to transform made the necklace as alive as a person. The image I discerned now reminded me of a wheel, though I couldn't be sure.

My eyes glazed over and my hand moved up to touch the necklace. I welcomed the pale yellowish glow as memories assaulted my mind. I remembered how Anumati had gifted me this precious little gem. We were in the sanctum sanctorum of the main building inside the temple complex of Pura Besakih when Kagan called her.

She first appeared as a black buck, but she took human form when she saw us. To me, she was gorgeous. With her long, raven hair, white skin and lavish Indian clothing, she looked like a Bollywood actress or a heroine from 1001 Nights.

Kagan introduced us, and I seized the opportunity to ask her about my mother and the reason why my magic was connected to the moon. Her reply was evasive and advised me to talk to Cerridwen, the Celtic goddess of wisdom and knowledge. She further explained that every five thousand years the headquarters of the Court of Heaven changed, but now the governing body was in charge of the Celtic gods and she couldn't answer without their consent. She gave me this magical necklace with the instruction to touch it when I was in trouble or wanted to activate my goddess magic and then disappeared. I tried not to use it recklessly, without good reason, just like this morning, during the training session with the fae.

Later, when I relayed my encounter with the goddess to Awen, he confirmed the ruling gods changed as she'd said, and also told me that the Egyptian Era had immediately preceded the current Celtic Era.

I blinked back to the present and went down to our joint kitchen to grab a quick breakfast before work.

I and my best friend and business partner, Naomi, lived here, above our occult shop, the Steaming Cauldron. Since I'd been training with the fae, Naomi had been forced to cover both her shift and mine, with the help of an assistant. At least, we could now afford one. About a month ago, our financial situation was dire, as a competitor shop had appeared in our small town, but we got back on our feet and our customers began to come back to us. It helped that the competitor shop's owner turned out to be the bad guy I was assigned by the Magic Council to stop. He was killing humans for his nefarious purposes. So now we were back in the black.

I stepped into the kitchen to find Naomi talking amiably to someone on her cell phone. My skin prickled. It was her new boyfriend, Desmond Cohen — the guy who, together with Garrett, had run the competitor's shop that almost brought us to ruin.

Up until I faced Garrett, I had suspected Desmond was the culprit, but Desmond hadn't been involved. In fact, he wasn't even a supernatural, just an ordinary, innocent guy interested in the occult. He was devastated when I destroyed his business and his partner went missing. In my defense, Garrett had imprisoned me in the shop's basement at the time.

Of course, we didn't tell Desmond I ruined his shop and killed Garrett's minion members in their Wiccan club — the existence of our world was top secret. We told him a fierce storm that night destroyed his coven and shop. Garrett had gone missing and we didn't know anything about him, which actually was the truth.

We told Desmond all this in our kitchen over a cup of tea. Naomi used one of her potions to make him believe our story and stop him from questioning us any further. A hedge-witch, Naomi's magic lay in inventing and preparing all sorts of potions and herbal mixes. Thank magic for her potion, otherwise Desmond would have never believed us. That night the weather had been clement — not a single cloud, let alone a storm to destroy his shop and kill his Wiccan coven brethren.

After the tragic events Desmond moved to a nearby town and started to work in another occult shop. He and Naomi, however, kept in touch and began to forge a relationship. It was particularly strange to me, since Naomi had told me Desmond's feel of dark energy put her off, but after I destroyed his shop and business she apparently changed her mind. I hoped she hadn't started dating him out of pity — she had a strict rule that she must be attracted to anyone she dated.

"Yes, I know, babe," Naomi said quietly on her cell phone and fixed her eyes on me. I smiled at her and went to the cereal cupboard. I put some of it in a bowl, mixed it with yogurt, and sat down opposite her.

"Okay, when can we meet?" She stood up and went through to the shop. It was closed until nine a.m. She didn't want me to eavesdrop on her conversation with her lover. I tried not to let that bother me; after all, we are all entitled to privacy. How would I like it if she was privy to all my private conversations?

With two spoonsful of my breakfast to go, she reappeared in visibly high spirits.

"So, how did it go with the fae? Did you set his sexy ass on fire?" She chuckled, and I flashed her a dirty look.

"No, I didn't. But I fought his guardian dragon. Or rather pacified him," I replied.

Naomi gaped and her eyes sprang open in shock. "You don't say! I want all the details!"

I smirked and told her what happened. "He wanted me to use my goddess magic. He asked for Anumati's necklace, and I gave it to him." I touched it as if to assure myself it was still on my chest. "And then he summoned to life his guardian dragon."

Naomi almost choked at my last words. "His... what?"

I explained about the dragon statue in the fae's garden and our subsequent fight. She listened carefully, and at the end exclaimed, "Wow — good that you could subdue the dragon using your own magic. You never cease to amaze me, Miss Shaw. You can now mind-control dragons through music magic. Ha!" She playfully nudged me with her elbow. "And clever of Kagan to think of that challenge."

I beamed. "Yeah, I have a smart boyfriend, haven't I?"

She chuckled. "He certainly brings out the best in you."

I smiled and stood up. It was nearly nine a.m. and punctuality was very important when you worked for the Magic Council. I waved to my best friend, then took her teleportation charm and sprinkled it around me. A glittering silver cloud appeared, and I stepped inside it. I felt the familiar tug at my center, and the void took me.

Buy Infernal Curse on Amazon!

Sing-up for my newsletter!

If you want to be notified when my next novel is released and get free stories and occasional other goodies, please sign up at my mailing list at:
http://www.antaraman.com/bbsf
Your email address will never be shared and you can unsubscribe at any time.
Also, you'll receive 2 free fantasy books!

Also By Antara Mann

Have you read them all?

Infernal Curse (The Half-Goddess Chronicles Book 2)

All hell is about to break loose and only goddess magic can stop it.

Alexandra Shaw is days from coming into her full goddess powers but things are not going to plan. There's a surge of demonic and vampire attacks in all major cities of the U.S. What's worse, powerful mages are disappearing, and the Courts of Heaven and Hell struggle to keep it all hushed up.
As a Magic Council Investigator, Alex's caseload is piling up fast. With the powerful fae Kagan Griffith at her side, she's got a chance of tracking down the missing mages. But saving them is only one of her worries. An old enemy is stalking Alex from the shadows, ready to attack. A month ago he wanted her beating heart. Now he wants her magic.

But as Alex quickly learns, there are far more terrifying things than death itself...

With an ancient curse threatening to wipe out her life and those of all her loved ones, will Alex be able to cheat her destiny again?

Buy it: Amazon

Cursed Magic (The Half-Goddess Chronicles Book 3)

Goddess Alexandra Shaw thinks her troubles are over when she comes into her powers, but a moment later she is hit by a terrible curse.

Her mentor's quick intervention staves off the spread of the dark magic, but this is only a temporary fix, and there's no knowing when she will succumb to its toxic poison. Only a truly gifted shaman from Yorubaland can fully lift the curse. But in order for Alex to succeed, she'd have to team up with chief demon Kai, and learn to manipulate and control his dark, demonic energy.

While Alex and her boyfriend Kagan search for a cure, a new and deadly type of evil returns to Earth with devastating consequences.

Will Alex be able to fight off the attacks of mystical shamans, ancient monsters, and the Yoruba gods, and once again stop her archenemy, the inferni, from launching a magical revolution?

Cursed Magic is a fast-paced urban fantasy adventure featuring a kick-ass heroine, a fae hero, and lots of magic.

Buy it: Amazon

Alice in Sinland: A Story of Murder, Greed… Violence, Adultery and Treasure

Alice has a wish…

Alice Roseburg is an expatriate New Yorker, now a young attorney living in London. Her career is on the fast-track until she begins having lucid and haunting dreams after representing the wealthy buyer of a castle in Scotland, a property with a dark and demonic history. A mysterious man has begun shadowing her, demanding, "What do you want?"

Some wishes need to be spoken aloud. "I want to be a star."

Alice quits her career, cashes out her savings, and moves to New York City to follow her dreams on Broadway. But she soon discovers that finding her place in the limelight is far trickier than she ever imagined.

"What do you want?" the dark one asks.

Her rapid rise to stardom attracts the attention of Aaron Chasin, a pop-music producer, wrapped in questionable promises and sinister ambition.

"What do you want?" the Devil demands.

"More," Alice says, "more."

But when the limelight fades, the debt remains...

Buy it: Amazon

Aaron in Sinland

Aaron Chasin is a 30-something failed British indie musician. He wants to be a respected and successful A&R rep — to discover and promote new musical talents and turn them into superstars. Only his personal demons stand in his way: alcoholism, anger, and a long-forgotten childhood trauma. Aaron must face his fears or his happiness, health, and well-being are at stake. Things change drastically for him when he meets the enigmatic tantric guru Shankar Govinda, who initiates Aaron into a new and exciting world of occult spirituality.

But is it the answer to his prayers or a whole new nightmare?

Buy it: Amazon

The Witch's Kiss Bundle (Episodes 1&2)

He's a Genie, trapped in a magic lamp. She is an ugly old witch. They will fight the dark forces… together.

A terrible curse hangs over the mighty Ezemalda. Her faithful servant, the Genie Majestic is bound by a contract with the evil sorcerer – the Dark Prince. With a cunning plan they manage to free themselves and open a workshop for good magic only.

When a beautiful desperate mortal asks for their help, they know they must do all they can to free her from her predicament. After selling her soul to the Dark Prince, Countess Sybil van Dyk seeks to reverse her enchantment at the magic workshop of the Genie and the witch. As they work to set the countess free, the Genie and Ezemalda embark on a new adventure in their battle with the Dark Side, not suspecting what signing a contract with the Dark Prince on new moon portends.

Buy it: Amazon

The Witch's Kiss Episode 3

NEVER BEFORE HAS PASSION BEEN MORE DANGEROUS.

Furious that once again the Genie and the witch Ezemalda escaped his clutches, the Dark Prince enlists the help of Lilith, the dark queen of sexual magic in his quest for revenge. Tricking them with a drink, Lilith bewitches Ezemalda and the Genie with obsessive sexual dreams. The Dark Queen's plan backfires when Ezemalda comes up with an antidote, but she will not be stopped and implants a dangerous idea in all the kingdom's subjects. With everyone around them now convinced that the Genie commits terrible acts against women, even rapes them, he and Ezemalda have to find a new way to stand against the dark forces and clear their names.

Buy it: Amazon

The Wishing Coin

What would you do if you possessed a magical coin that could fulfill all your darkest wishes?

This heartwarming and witty modern fairy tale follows an ambitious young woman who finds an easy way to fulfill all her selfish desires.

TV reporter Julia Preston is having a bad day. First, a promised promotion is given instead to ambitious newcomer Bailey – then Julia finds out Bailey is also dating her ex. Walking home, seething with anger, Julia encounters a street vendor selling wishing coins. Skeptical, she's not interested until he offers an old tarnished coin with some geometrical figures that intrigue her. It soon becomes clear that she has come into possession of a miraculous weapon to use against those who have wronged her. When Julia's wishes begin to come true she believes her life has taken a turn for the amazing. But a dark secret behind her TV success is revealed and Julia's conscience is put on a trial.

Would you be happy if all your wishes come true? Would you be still you?

Buy it: Amazon

Back To The Viper - A Time Travel Experiment

If you could redo the worst mistake of your life, would you? At what cost?

Botching the biggest performance of her career ten years ago has left lead singer Ashley Greendale as an unfulfilled barista at a local coffee shop. Just as she was beginning to believe that superstardom was far from her grasp, her eccentric scientist friend, Harry, offers her a once-in-a-lifetime opportunity that she wouldn't dare pass up - to travel back in time and redo her career-ending performance.

Taking her band with her known as The Jackal, Ashley and her music group rocks on to repair their missteps from the past. But fame and fortune come with a price - now they must decide if they're willing to pay. Are they willing to live out their dreams and lose everything they've ever known?

Buy it: Amazon

About The Author

Antara Mann started writing at the age of seven. Nowadays, when she's not reading and writing, you can find her practicing yoga, as she has developed a keen interest in self-improvement, spirituality, and becoming a better human being. She enjoys writing fantasy and paranormal suspense stories and believes in unity in diversity. In her opinion, the best books and stories are crossovers between genres.

Say Hello!

Antara talks about writing, literature and her yogic journey on her blog http://www.antaraman.com/. Subscribe to her newsletter to be the first to hear about new releases, giveaways and pre-release specials here: http://antaraman.com/list.

You can alternatively follow her on Twitter, get in touch on Facebook or send her an email at antaraman9@gmail.com